W9-AUI-199

Also by
Christine Warren

Stone Cold Lover
Heart of Stone
Hungry Like a Wolf
Drive Me Wild
On the Prowl
Not Your Ordinary Faerie Tale
Black Magic Woman
Prince Charming Doesn't Live Here
Born to be Wild
Big Bad Wolf
You're So Vein
One Bite with a Stranger
Walk on the Wild Side
Howl at the Moon
The Demon You Know
She's No Faerie Princess
Wolf at the Door

Anthologies

The Huntress
No Rest for the Witches

Hard as a Rock

Christine Warren

St. Martin's Paperbacks

HARD AS A ROCK

Copyright © 2015 by Christine Warren.

All rights reserved.

For information address St. Martin's Press, 175 Fifth Avenue, New York, NY 10010.

ISBN: 978-1-250-01267-8

Printed in the United States of America

St. Martin's Paperbacks edition / April 2015

St. Martin's Paperbacks are published by St. Martin's Press, 175 Fifth Avenue, New York, NY 10010.

10 9 8 7 6 5 4 3 2 1

For Ally, for waiting patiently until she was of legal age. But seriously, would you stop making me feel so old? Sheesh.

Chapter One

"Wynn? What is it? What's going on? Did you find him?"

"Um, in a manner of speaking."

"Huh? What's that supposed to mean?"

Wynn Powe stared down into the wide, shallow crater that marred the otherwise serene landscaping of
the old Van Oswalt estate and pursed her lips. "I found
what's left of him. I think. The pieces are pretty small."

"Oh, my God! Pieces?" Ella gasped into the cell, her
distress obvious and right in line with the feelings Wynn
currently battled. "How bad is it?"

"Are you familiar with the term *smithereens*?"

Ella groaned. "What happened?"

Wynn crouched at the edge of the hole and reached
down to sift through the debris. Soil and grit and small
chunks of limestone and granite tumbled across her fingertips. "At a guess? Some pretty serious explosives, but
I just got here myself. My plane was delayed last night,
and I didn't land until after two this morning. But I'm
surprised I didn't see anything on the news when I woke

up. A bomb going off in Lake Forest should have gotten more than a little bit of media attention."

Heck, given the average income of the residents of the affluent suburb north of Chicago, a bomb going off in their neighborhood should have merited a SWAT team, the activation of a National Guard unit, and a televised statement by the president. Wynn had eaten breakfast in front of the TV and booted up her laptop before she headed out this way. She should have seen headlines.

"You seriously think the statue blew up?"

"El, I'm looking at a scene straight out of 1945 Dresden. Check it out." Wynn switched her smartphone to the camera function and snapped a picture of the scene before her, then sent it to Ella. "Apparently, the fact that the Order didn't get to blow up Spar last month only made them more determined. This guy did it right."

"Crap. I wonder when it happened. I mean, when you're operating on rumors and chasing a stone statue through multiple owners across multiple continents, it's easy for details to slip through the cracks, but nothing I saw indicated he had been damaged. Of course, the last record I have was for his installation at that location about five years ago. Still, I would have thought I'd have heard if anyone knew about the damage. I don't suppose it could have happened recently?"

"I don't know. The crater's not still smoking or anything, but how would we tell? Maybe if my plane hadn't been delayed, or if I had left on Monday like I should have—"

"No." Ella cut her off swiftly and decisively. "No second-guessing. It's not your fault, Wynn. Put the blame where it belongs. On the *nocturnis*."

Yeah, that shouldn't be hard. Blame a secret organization of evil magic users intent on resurrecting seven of the most powerful demons ever spawned and thereby ending the world as she knew it? Wynn could get on board with that.

"This is really not good." Ella's tension and worry came across loud and clear, despite the geographic distance separating Vancouver and Chicago. "I have to tell Kees, then we need to call Fil and Spar. If we're really going into the next stage of this fight already down a Guardian, we're going to have to do some serious rethinking of our strategy."

Wynn ended the call and pocketed her cell phone with a grimace. For her, Ella's words only drew attention to the fact that as far as Wynn could see, they didn't even have a strategy. What they had was a problem of epic—not to say biblical—proportions: An army of evil minions appeared determined to set the Seven—at least one of whom was already at least half awake—loose on humanity, and five decidedly un-super-heroes were all that stood against those assembled forces of Darkness. If the situation had been the plot of a summer blockbuster movie, Wynn would have dismissed it as totally unrealistic and just assumed the good guys would wind up with nothing but bloody stumps to perch their white hats on.

Okay, so maybe that was a little harsh. Wynn supposed that two of their band of brave Bedlamites actually did count as heroes. She, Ella, and Felicity—aka Fil—might be nothing more than puny humans, but Kees and Spar were bona fide Guardians. If those guys didn't qualify as heroes, then the definition needed some serious editing.

As a race, the Guardians had come into being to protect humanity from the Seven demons—an evil so powerful that when joined together, they could rip the very
fabric of reality into pieces and condemn the world to
an eternity of suffering. The Guardians, seven warriors
who took the shape of stone gargoyles when resting in
the times between battles, had been summoned to earth
by a group of human magic users known as the Guild
of Wardens specifically to fight against the Seven. When
defeated, the demons had been bound in separate prisons so they could never achieve their goal of conquest.
In Wynn's book, that made the Guardians heroes.

Unfortunately, it would take all seven Guardians to
face the threat that loomed over them today, and so far
Wynn had only noticed two of them being conscious and
ready for action. Everyone had been counting on the dust
at her feet to make number three. So what the hell were
they supposed to do now?

Wynn stepped back from the blast site and winced.
She'd sprained her ankle a couple of weeks ago wrangling
with the *nocturnis*—the shorthand name for members
of the Order of Eternal Darkness—in another city, and
the joint still gave her a twinge when she moved wrong.
With a grim expression, she shifted her weight and took
a belated look around her.

The driver's door of her battered white Toyota hung
drunkenly open, and the buzz of the alarm told her that
she hadn't even bothered to take the keys out of the ignition when she'd caught sight of the scene of destruction. She'd rounded the curve of the drive, seen the hole
in the ground surrounded by stony rubble, and her stomach had done an Olympic-caliber dive straight into the

soles of her sandals. She had slammed on her brakes, thrown the shift into park, and flown straight to the debris field.

As if rushing could have turned back the clock. She'd obviously been too late, which was not the way she wanted to go into this battle. Half a step behind wasn't going to cut it when it came to stopping the Order from succeeding with their plans. In fact, it had cost a life back in Montreal. One of Fil's friends became another victim sacrificed to the Seven, and Fil herself had nearly ended up the same way. It had been a close call, and something told Wynn there would be more of those before this thing ended.

She had never considered herself to have any particular precognitive abilities. She was a witch, not a psychic. She couldn't see into the future, no matter how much she might want to, a fact attested to by her generally really weak divination skills. Her powers ran more along the lines of powering charms, hex removal, and herbology, hence her small business making soaps, lotions, ointments, and teas, which supported her pretty nicely. Ask her to whip up a remedy for itchy, dry skin and Wynn was your girl; ask her what would happen if you took a certain path into the future, and all she could tell you was that time would pass. Not exactly useful stuff.

Power, the kind of power that passed down through her mother's family, had its own agenda in Wynn's experience. Possessing it made her a witch, but she didn't get to choose what form it took. The power did what it wanted, and she could either accept that and learn what it wanted to accomplish, or she could fight it and try to make it do her bidding, which usually just ended in frustration and a lot of nasty side effects for everyone and everything in the vicinity.

It had taken her a while to stumble onto that realization, and even longer to come to terms with it. When she had been a little girl, Wynn was certain down to her bones that she had been born to be a Warden. Seven generations of her family before her had served in the Guild—all men, of course—but anyone with eyes could see that the same magic that flowed in their veins flowed in hers. She had just as much power as her younger brother, but magic had never been enough for the crusty old men in charge. All they cared about was that she didn't have a dick, never mind that her metaphorical balls put their actual ones to shame. The Guild viewed female Wardens in the same light as demonic minions and the Ebola virus—such things might exist in the world, but virtue and good hygiene would probably be enough to keep them at bay.

Misogynistic bastards.

So Bran got to be the Warden in their generation, and Wynn got to be a witch, just like her mother and her aunts and her female cousins. Not that she disliked being a witch, but there were days when she still felt so restless, as if something more hovered just out of her reach. Only knowing her luck, reaching for it would land herf ace-first in a pool of quicksand.

Dusting her hands off against the legs of her jeans, Wynn took another look around at the Van Oswalt estate. Built in the late 1800s as a retreat by one of Chicago's many tycoons, the house rose from its park-like setting north of the city in Victorian splendor, a mix of brick and sandstone and intricate decorative work in both wood and stone. Even though she had read that the last of the family to live there had left the place nearly ten years ago, the Van Oswalts had never relinquished their hold on the property. Maybe they were sentimental millionaires, but it seemed a shame to Wynn to let such a beautiful old building sit there all closed up and empty.

No one could call her an expert in real estate, but she couldn't imagine that someone wouldn't snap the property up in a minute if they were to put in on the market. Not only did it feature the gorgeous old mansion, but its multiple acres and location on a bluff overlooking Lake Michigan made the land itself worth its weight in gold. She thought she remembered something about beach access, and imagined there would be stairs down the face of the cliff and a dock and boathouse nestled below. After all, that was how the other half lived, wasn't it?

At least the Van Oswalts appeared to be paying someone to maintain the grounds. Though she imagined they had run a little less wild while the family had been in residence, a little more French country garden and a little less English cottage garden, nevertheless the lawn had been mown, the hedges roughly trimmed, and the windows properly shuttered, not broken or covered in ugly plywood.

Heaving a sigh, half disappointment with her morning and half envy of stupid rich people, Wynn walked back to her car and pushed the door closed with a thud. No sense in letting the batteries run dead and leaving herself stranded out in the middle of nowhere. As far as she could tell, the homes in this particular enclave right on the lake had to sit on multiacre parcels. Any tow truck driver worth his salt would charge her a year's salary to jump her ancient battery, let alone haul her butt out of here and back to the city if the jump failed. Talk about the last thing she needed.

No, wait. The *very* last thing she needed was that figure in the navy-blue uniform that appeared to be striding her way from the top of the driveway. She should have realized an enclave of the super-rich like this one would have private security roaming around to keep the riffraff away. Glancing down at her faded jeans, loose-fitting top, stretched-out tank, and simple sandals, she wondered if she counted as the riff or the raff.

"Miss, you're currently trespassing on private property." The man raised his voice to be heard over the crunch of gravel as he approached.

Even from a good fifty yards away, Wynn could make out the solid, stocky build of a onetime high school football star and the baton, radio, and gun strapped to his belt. He was certainly equipped to mean business, even if his tone of voice hadn't already clued her in.

"Just because the home behind you is currently unoccupied doesn't give you to right to be here. I'm going to have to ask you to identify yourself and wait with me while I summon the local authorities."

Wynn huffed, taken aback. "Seriously?"

The look on the guard's face, now that he'd drawn close enough for her to make out his expression, answered her question for her. If this guy had a sense of humor, she doubted anyone had ever gotten up the nerve to mention it to him.

"You don't need to call the police," she reasoned, reaching behind her for the car door handle. "I'll leave right now. I just drove by to take a look at the place. I didn't even try to go up to the house."

The security guard tensed and drew his brows together to glare at her. "Miss, you need to step away from your vehicle. I can't let you leave until I've consulted with the Hierophant."

"With who?" Wynn blinked, the reference catching her off guard. She'd heard of the Hierophant in Montreal, and the name had boded nothing good at the time. It took a minute for her brain to catch up, and that was all the opportunity the guard needed.

He launched himself at her, hands outstretched, as if Wynn had suddenly found herself in the middle of a zombie movie—the freaky modern kind where the zombies moved fast instead of shambling forward at an easily outrunnable pace, the way the gods and George A. Romero had intended. She didn't care if he was after her brains or any other part of her body, Wynn intended to keep them all.

Instinct took over, and she let herself drop, landing ass-first in the dirt an instant before the guard's hands would have closed around her throat. She heard a grunt and a thud as his momentum drove him into the side of her car, but she didn't wait to watch the impact. Immediately upon hitting the ground, she rolled to her side and pushed up on her knees to scramble as fast as she could away from her attacker. As soon as she cleared his immediate space, she lurched to her feet and took off running. Her ankle screamed a protest, but she ignored it. If the choice was hurt or die, she was going with hurt, and going as fast as she possibly could.

Her brain raced along even faster, processing several

pieces of information simultaneously. First, it issued a
mental slap upside itself in the form of reminding her
that by taking off in the direction *opposite* her car,
Wynn had just removed herself from her best means of
escape. That left her with two choices; to run into the
empty house—assuming she could even get inside a
structure that appeared to have been well secured against
trespassers—or to head for the road, where an unfamiliar
woman being chased by a security guard employed by
anyone who might actually see her was more likely to
elicit help for the guard than for her. So, essentially,
she was screwed.

Second, her brain provided additional support to that
primary conclusion by finishing its delayed parsing of
the security guard's short speech. The phrase "consult
with the Hierophant" indicated at the man who had attacked her wasn't likely to be a run-of-the-mill rental cop
who just wanted her taken away by the local police and
charged with criminal trespass. She doubted this boiled
down to the desire to teach her a lesson about respect
for her financial betters. No, unless she missed her
guess—and given the mess she'd just witnessed in Montreal, it really counted as more of a certainty than a wild
guess—that phrasing indicated a pursuer who was employed by a group slightly more sinister than the residents of Lake Forest.

Like, say, the Order of Eternal Darkness.

In other words, her brain supplied, she was now in
deep shit.

It got deeper when she heard a muttered curse that
couldn't have come from more than a couple of feet behind her. A hand reached out and grabbed for her, catch-

ing the back of her shirt and hauling hard enough that she stumbled and nearly lost her balance.

"Oh no, you little bitch," the guard panted as he attempted to drag her closer. "I got you now."

Fear spiked, adrenaline pumping so hard Wynn could barely hear over the roaring of her own blood pounding in her ears. She reached up and grabbed the two sides of her blouse, ripping them apart like She-Hulk. Buttons popped and flew, one of them catching her in the cheek just below her right eye, but she ignored the sting. The two halves of the shirt parted, and she tore herself from the tattered remains to take off running for a second time.

The guard cursed, loud and vile, but she didn't pause to see what he did with his hands full of poly-cotton blend. She headed down the drive for the road, her mind racing frantically through her options. Getting to her car still seemed like the surest way to get out of here, but turning around and heading directly for it would amount to serving herself up to her pursuer on a bed of purple kale. If she wanted to make it safely, she'd need to double back around *and* set herself up with a considerable lead over the guard.

Ignoring the pain of the small pieces of dirt and stone that had worked their way into her sandals and the throbbing of her sprained ankle, Wynn made her move and leapt off the gravel for the line of trees that bordered the drive. The wooded area might be small, but it was dense, and any cover at all made it that much harder for her to be seen and subsequently captured.

Oh, and, you know, killed.

It took a moment for her eyes to adjust to the dimmer

lighting under the canopy of leaves, and she just barely missed getting a face full of pine needles. Darting around tree trunks and slapping aside branches, her pace slowed, but so did her attacker's. She could hear him lumbering after her, hear him swearing in frustration as the terrain also interfered with his speed.

Wynn gritted her teeth in satisfaction and focused on the glimpses of bright sunlight that penetrated the trees at the edge of the copse. She needed to judge the best point to leave the cover of vegetation, where the distance between her and the car was shortest and she would have the highest chance of reaching it before the guard reached her.

Her breath rasped in and out of her chest, and she knew she'd have to find her way out soon. Her ankle was screaming like a blonde in a horror flick, and she could feel the stitch developing in her side, so she knew she didn't have much more running left in her. That lifelong disdain of jogging as a form of exercise was really coming back to bite her in the ass, wasn't it?

Huffing a little, she once more wished that being a witch was a lot more like *Harry Potter* made it out to be and a lot less like being a good cook. This whole situation would be vastly improved if all she had to do was dig her magic wand out of her bag, point it at the security guard chasing her, and shout, "Stupefy!" Too bad it didn't really work like that. She'd have better luck picking up a hunk of stone from the ground and chucking it at the guy's head. Back when she'd played junior high softball, she'd had a pretty decent arm.

Wynn grunted and stumbled a couple of steps as the cover of trees gave way. She stepped out into the bright sunlight and blinked against the sudden glare, momentarily blinded. Shit. She needed to get to her car, like now.

Sandals digging into the crushed stone, she swiveled in the direction she thought she needed to go and poured on one last burst of speed. She could hear the snap of branches as her pursuer pushed his way out of the woods and knew she had only seconds to get into her vehicle, lock the doors, and take off like a bat out of a belfry. Already, she was thinking of how tight a turn she'd need to make to head back to the main road, but she shouldn't have worried. She never made it that far.

One minute her legs pumped, carrying her over the even field of the driveway; the next, the world dropped out from under her, and Wynn took flight. For all of the distance between her face and the crater left behind by the demolished Guardian statue. The two items met with an abrupt impact, Wynn's cheek and temple getting the butt end of that encounter.

In the adrenaline-fueled race to escape her attacker and the sudden alteration in light levels, she had completely missed seeing the ditch in front of her, and now it looked like she might as well have served herself up to the Order on a silver platter. Or maybe that should be bloody altar-stone? Whatever.

Wynn rolled to her back, unable to suppress the groan that welled from her throat. She'd hit the ground hard. The side of her face, her knees, and the heels of her hands felt like raw hamburger where she'd hit the disturbed bed of soil, gravel, and stone debris. Not to mention the state of her already injured ankle, which currently throbbed like a bass drum and felt as if it was beginning to swell up again, at least judging from the way the straps of her sandal now seemed to be taking on the role of accidental tourniquets.

The crunch of a man's shoe on the drive tore her focus off her discomfort and forced it back onto the more urgent matters. Like attempting to not get herself offed like the secondary female lead in a low-budget slasher film. She wanted to be the battered but victorious survivor girl, damn it.

Wynn managed to roll onto her hands and knees and was scrambling to get her feet back under her when the high-speed train slammed into her from behind. Back into the dirt and stone she went, only this time the weight on top of her also managed to force all the air out of her lungs. She struggled to remember how to breathe even as a hand fisted in her hair and dragged her head up out of the crater bottom.

"You shouldn't have come poking around here," the security guard growled in her ear even as he used his free hand to press a shiny knife blade to the skin of her throat. "Do you work for the Guild? Did they send you? You Wardens are supposed to be dead, not hanging around here making trouble."

The Guild? Wynn started to shake her head, but the feel of a trickle of her own blood against her skin stopped her cold. She hesitated in confusion, trying to figure out the correct answer. If her attacker knew about the Guild, then he definitely had to be connected to the *nocturnis,* but if he couldn't tell for himself whether she was a Warden, then he couldn't be an actual member of the Order; their own magic had no trouble identifying the energy of a Warden's power. Was this guy not a full-fledged *nocturnis* but some kind of hired lackey instead?

"Are there more of you?" He jerked harder on her hair, and she bit back a yelp. "There's a reward out on your heads, you know. The Order is searching, but why should the big boys get all the cash, right? You got friends I should know about?"

Sickness roiled in her stomach. Was that why she hadn't heard from Bran in nearly a year? Had someone like this gotten ahold of her brother and used a knife to silence him as well?

Instinct curled her fingers around the wrist beneath her chin, and her nails dug into flesh, but the guard didn't even flinch. He was way stronger than she was. From the looks of it, he really was about to slit her throat. Goddess, her mother would never recover. She was already burdened by the weight of Bran's disappearance. Losing Wynn, too, might just knock her the rest of the way down.

Boy, could she use a Guardian of her own right about now.

The Order's minion shook her, using his grip in her hair to rattle her from side to side. Her eyes teared at the sharp pain, and she clenched her teeth to keep from crying out. Only a low hiss escaped her. She wouldn't give the bastard more satisfaction than that.

"Tell me, bitch," he snarled. "Either way, you're gonna die, but if you give me what I want, I'll at least make it quick."

The pain and rage-fueled tears rolled down her cheek and dripped onto a chunk of ragged granite, punctuating the only response Wynn could muster. "Fuck. You."

The blade was sharp enough that she didn't feel the initial prick, but it didn't matter. The earth beside her opened up and the knife slid from her attacker's suddenly nerveless hand, thudding to the ground about the same time she did. His grip on her hand disappeared the instant that something else emerged in a blast of stone and magic.

Wynn's cavalry had arrived, in the form of one very large and very angry Guardian, a Guardian that was supposed to be nothing but the teeny-tiny pieces still scattered around her.

Huh. How about that?

Chapter Two

Knox emerged into the human world aware of two things—that the woman beneath him must be protected, and that the man clutched in his large, claw-tipped hands needed to die. It was just a matter of how and how soon. He would personally prefer bloody and right now, but something urged him to caution.

Quickly he glanced around him and evaluated the scene. At his feet, the human woman half lay, half crouched in a field of rubble. To his battle-ready senses, she reeked of magic, a rich and earthy variety that spoke of witchcraft rather than the Guild. She had straight, even features marred with dirt and abrasions, and masses of tumbled hair the color of dark ale. He also noticed several nicks and a seeping line of blood at her throat. Someone had held a knife to her pale, fragile skin, and the thought made Knox's lip curl up to expose the length of his fanged incisors.

In his hands, the male human trembled. "You're supposed to be dead! The Order blew you up! They bragged to us about it. I saw pictures. The statue was broken into a million pieces."

Knox frowned and searched his awareness. He knew he had just moments ago been summoned into existence. Before now, there had been only nothingness, but with his appearance on the mortal plane came all the knowledge he needed to join his brother Guardians in carrying out his duty to protect humanity from the threat of the Seven. He knew exactly who and what he was, knew the history and skills of his kind, and knew that if this man was associated with the Order of Eternal Darkness, then the demonic forces he served had written their minion's death warrant.

However, Knox also knew that the villain in his grasp did not lie. All around them lay the scattered remnants of a fallen brother. A Guardian had been destroyed here, so Knox had come to take his place. He didn't know the details of why or how, but he knew his duty.

"Your masters are not nearly so powerful as you think, human," he advised, shifting his grip so that he held the man aloft with one hand fisted in his clothing while the fingers of the other curled around the evildoer's throat. "They cannot rid themselves of the Guardians. Where one of us falls, another shall rise. We will not surrender, and your masters cannot protect you from our wrath."

"Wait!"

The sharp cry froze Knox instantly. He looked away from the servant of the Order and glared at the human witch. Why did she seek to stop him? The man had attempted to slay her, had succeeded in causing her injury, in making her bleed. Why would she not desire revenge? It was, after all, a uniquely human emotion.

He hesitated. Perhaps she wished to take a more active role in the man's punishment. "You wish to dispose of him yourself?"

"Dispose of him?" The human's voice squeaked unattractively. "No, I don't want to dispose of him! I want you to let him go. You can't just kill a guy in Lake Forest, for the Lady's sake. You'll be on the wanted list before he goes cold. The police will be all over you."

The small woman glared at him fiercely, her brown eyes regarding him not with the wonder or reverence his inherited memory told him to expect, but with something that looked an awful lot more like . . . irritation? Did she not realize who he was?

"Do not concern yourself, human," he instructed her, ignoring the way the man in his grasp squirmed and choked. "This creature is a servant of the Darkness and does not deserve your compassion. You see, I am a Guar—"

"Yeah, yeah, I know, you're a Guardian." She waved her hand at him, her tone dismissive.

Dismissive?

"Sworn to protect humanity from the ultimate evil of the Seven demons of the Darkness," she continued, her tone sounding suspiciously bored as she recited his reason for existence. "Trust me, I can see what you are, but that still doesn't mean you get to kill the security guard. You'll get both of us arrested if you try. So do me a favor and put him down before he slips into a coma, okay? He's already looking a little bit blue around the edges."

Startled, Knox looked at his captive and saw that the human woman was right. His huge, bat-like wings rustled in irritation. The male had ceased struggling, and the edges of his lips had paled and begun to turn a strange bluish-gray color. His eyes began to roll back in his head even as Knox released his hold and let the human drop to the ground, where he lay motionless.

"Thanks. Now, be a good Guardian and shift into something I can fit in my car, would you? We need to get the hell out of here before one of the neighbors decides to walk his poodle down the driveway and gets a look at us. Explaining why we're here could be put down to curiosity and some innocent trespassing. Explaining why I look like I went twelve rounds with the champ, and a security guard is lying unconscious at our feet, would probably be a hell of a lot trickier."

The witch spoke while she climbed, stiff and wincing, to her feet. She stumbled a little as she attempted to catch her balance, and he looked down to discover that one of her feet looked bruised and swollen under the hem of her heavy blue trousers. Clearly, she had sustained more injuries than the obvious cuts to her neck. When she turned her head and wiped her hands against her thighs to brush off the dirt, he also caught glimpses of numerous scrapes and abrasions.

She appeared in need of medical care, and Knox found himself fascinated by the way she seemed to ignore her own physical condition in favor of talking. A lot. Or giving orders, really. To him.

A Guardian.

He shook his head and flexed his shoulders, settling his huge wings into careful folds against his back. "You say that you know what I am, but you do not seem to fully grasp the situation, human. I am a Guardian; this man is a servant of the *nocturnis*. Therefore, it is my duty to dispose of him, ensuring your safety. Then I must locate my Warden and discover what new threat the Seven have concocted that requires my presence in this realm."

The woman snorted—actually *snorted*—at him and rolled her eyes. "Trust me, bat man, of the three of us here right now, I'd bet fifty bucks I am the least confused about who's who and what's what." She pointed at each of them, emphasizing her identifications with a jabbing finger. "He's the bad guy, you're the good guy, and I'm the chick with the information about why the chances of you having an actual Warden are currently running slim-to-none."

Knox sifted through her speech and pulled out the disturbing nugget of information. "What do you mean by that, witch? Where is my Warden? How could I have been summoned if, as you say, he does not exist? What has happened to him?"

On the ground, the security guard groaned and shifted restlessly. The witch made an impatient noise of her own and reached out to grab Knox's hand. While he watched, nonplussed, she began attempting to tug him away from the semiconscious cult member.

"Seriously, I promise to explain everything to you, but right now we have to go," she urged as she attempted to limp toward the small vehicle parked several yards away. "We really need to not be here when that guy wakes up. Can you just give me the benefit of the doubt and trust me for, like, five minutes? We have to go. Now."

He could hear the insistence in her voice. This female puzzled him. While she was the first human he had encountered—actually, the first anything he had encountered—she did not behave as he expected.

Something inside him whispered that she should be either awed or frightened by him, especially in his natural form. Most humans, he gathered, would find his bat-like wings, long, razor-sharp claws, and harsh features intimidating.

Clearly, this female was not like most humans in his inherited memories. The differences intrigued him, and he found himself wanting to accompany her for more than the information she had promised him. He wanted to learn more about her, as well as the reason he was here and what had become of the Warden who should have greeted him upon his arrival.

"Very well," he conceded, allowing her to lead him to her vehicle. "I will accompany you away from this place, but I will expect a full explanation from you of the significance of your words, female. A very good explanation."

"Yippee. I'm so looking forward to it," she muttered, though her tone sounded quite contrary to her words. She stopped beside the automobile and opened the door. "Now, how about that shifting thing, hm? Because I don't think all of this—" She gestured at his nearly seven-foot form. "—is going to fit in my Corolla."

Much as it irritated him that the small female continued to give him orders, he found her attitude, her defiance, and her confidence inexplicably intriguing. Knox eyed the interior of the small car and was forced to agree that in this case, the witch's orders made sense.

Calling on his inherent magic, he pictured a shape less conspicuous in the mortal realm. An instant later he stood before his companion in his new body and found himself surprisingly comfortable in the denim and cotton garments that came with it. Perhaps this confining human shape had its advantages.

He nodded in satisfaction and looked to the woman. "Will this do?"

Will this do me? *Now, that is the question.*

Wynn took in the Guardian's human form and hoped her eyes were not literally bulging out of her head, because they sure as heck felt like they were. It felt as if the usually obedient organs couldn't take in enough of the new view in their natural state and wanted to reach out and touch the gorgeous specimen of man that now stood before her.

Because . . . wow.

Somehow, the immortal warrior had condensed his huge, bestial form into just over six feet of white-hot sex appeal. Gone were with enormous bat wings, the animalistic facial features, the pointed ears, fangs, claws, and bulging, rock-hard muscles. In their place she took in chiseled bone structure, intense dark eyes, and slightly less bulging rock-hard muscles. Only the smooth-shaven head seemed pretty much the same.

The Guardian looked like the kind of man women drooled over and men tread carefully around. His size could get him a job bouncing at any club in Chicago, and he had the sort of sharp gaze and situational awareness that spoke of a highly trained military professional. In a way, she supposed that's what he was, but in this form she almost expected to see him wearing fatigues and carrying an assault rifle. And why did that image really kind of turn her on?

Tearing her attention away from his thick, jean-clad

legs—and lingering only briefly on the impressive pecs displayed under his snug black T-shirt—Wynn cleared her throat and focused on his face. His brutally masculine face.

"Uh, yeah," she managed to squeak out. "Yeah, tha-that's fine. So . . . let's get going, huh?"

Feeling the heat rise in her cheeks, she slipped into the car and fumbled with the ring of keys still dangling from the ignition. The Guardian folded his long frame into the passenger seat while she tried very hard not to look at him. Unfortunately, the confines of the car put them so close together that her peripheral vision picked up the way he bent and twisted as he tried to make himself comfortable in the small space. It would never work. Used mostly for herself, running errands and dropping off deliveries of her herbal bath products, Wynn's car rarely carried passengers. As a result, the front seat had been set forward to create more cargo space in the back. The huge Guardian just wasn't going to fit, not without a few adjustments.

"Here." Wynn gritted her teeth and leaned over to grip the lever beneath the seat cushion. "If you slide all the way back, you'll have a bit more legroom. And the thingy on the right side will let you recline the back if you need to."

Above her, she heard the Guardian draw in a deep breath and felt him tense, which just made her tense up as well. And that was about when she realized what she'd just done. To reach the adjuster lever, she had basically draped herself over the man's lap and stuck her arm down between his legs. She felt the heat of his body radiating through the thick fabric of his jeans and warming the skin of her stomach. Her upper stomach. Right up against the undersides of her breasts.

This time it was her turn to gasp. Throwing herself back into her own seat, Wynn jerked her arms back and slapped both hands onto the steering wheel. The plastic coating felt cool, which made a nice contrast to the nuclear-level heat she was generating in response to the Guardian's warmth. Hers currently radiated off her cheeks and made her wish for one of those nice, lacy fans, à la Scarlett O'Hara. Goddess above, she'd met this guy ten minutes ago, and now she'd nearly sexually assaulted him in her own car. Admittedly, she hadn't intended to do it—although a sick voice in her head made yummy noises at the thought—but still. Talk about inappropriate. No wonder he was looking at her funny.

"Sorry." She cleared her throat and concentrated unnecessarily hard on grasping the ignition key between her trembling fingers and turning on the engine. "Anyway, um, that's how the seat works, so feel free to slide back. Or whatever. We should go."

Outside the car, the security guard on the ground began to stir as if beginning to wake.

"I believe you are right. It is time we were away," he said as she shifted into drive and yanked the wheel to turn the car toward the road. "The sooner we leave here, the sooner you can begin to explain yourself, witch."

Wynn pulled out onto the road and broke every speed limit in the neighborhood in an effort to get them back to the highway as quickly as possible. Her eyes remained glued to the road, but she frowned at his chosen form of address. "Hey, watch it with that, all right? There's no need to be rude."

"Rude?" He sounded puzzled. "In what way do you find my manners lacking?"

She chanced a sidelong glower. "You called me 'witch.'"

He stared at her, looking baffled. "I do not understand. You are a witch."

"And just how the heck do you know that?"

"I can sense it. You might not be a Warden—the magic around you is quite different—but you possess certain powers all the same. Therefore, I am confused as to the reason you would object to being called the thing that you are."

Wynn felt her mouth tighten and she made a sound of annoyance. "It's just not something you go around calling people, okay? *Witch* has some not-so-nice connotations for most people these days. Most humans."

"Then what do you call yourself?"

She opened her mouth, then snapped it shut. "What I call myself isn't relevant. A person can call themselves names and still be insulted if someone else uses the same words. Anyway, I have a name. It's Wynn. Try using that."

"Wynn." The Guardian repeated the word, seeming to roll the flavor of it around in his mouth. "Very well. You may call me Knox."

The short, terse syllable somehow suited him. Wynn blew out a breath as she finally merged onto 41. She supposed she would have to call him something other than "Guardian."

"Well, at least your memory wasn't damaged by whatever explosive they used to blow you to smithereens," she muttered. "How did you manage to survive that anyway? I saw about a bazillion little pieces of gargoyle in that crater back there. I didn't think damage done to your sleeping form was something you guys could recover from."

"It is not. You saw the remains of one of my fallen brothers. The Guardian who previously slept in that place was destroyed. I came to take his place."

Surprised, Wynn flicked a glance his way. "You did? But how? I thought only the Wardens could summon one of you guys. I mean, I know things have been crazy lately with the Guild all but wiped out, and Ella and Fil managing to wake up the other guys, but summoning is supposed to be way more complicated than just awakening. How did you get here without a summoning?"

"What do you speak of?" he demanded, turning in his seat to pin her with a dark scowl. "Who are these others you mention? Do you imply that there are others of my kind already woken in this time? What exactly is going on that would require more than one of my brothers to do battle?"

He barked the questions at her, one after the other, his tone full of anger, impatience, and confusion. He obviously did not enjoying feeling in the dark.

Wynn sighed. "Right. So I promised to explain, didn't I? How about I tell you what's been going on around here, and then you can tell me how you managed to show up just in the nick of time when there hasn't been a Warden spotted within a hundred miles of Chicago in more than eight months? Sound fair?"

"It sounds necessary," Knox growled, and Wynn couldn't help but agree.

The problem was how to summarize the spotty information she'd learned from what Ella Harrow, the first woman to encounter a waking Guardian, had managed to piece together. Of course, Wynn also might want to deal at some point with the shock of finding herself pulled into the middle of the whole mess.

A detached part of her mind rationalized that she likely had a mild case of shock. The attack on her by the security guard, the chase through the trees, and the injuries she'd sustained during their struggle had sent adrenaline pouring into her system. Now that it had mostly burned off, she could feel the faint tremor in her fingers and knew she could attribute her mild chill to the same source.

Shock, however, didn't fully explain how she felt about sitting next to a real live Guardian, or where the hell she thought she was taking him. Her system had been operating up until this point on a kind of autopilot, reflexively beginning the journey south from Lake Forest to her own home in Dunning inside the city. She hadn't considered actually bringing Knox into her home, but now she had no idea what else to do.

Sure, the recent events in Montreal might have pulled her into the convoluted drama of the Order of Eternal Darkness and their latest attempts to free their demonic masters, thus bringing about the end of the world; but somehow Wynn had viewed herself as hanging around on the periphery of the mess. Ella and Fil had Guardians of their own, ones they had woken—inadvertently, maybe, but still—and bonded with, so their part in the coming battles seemed clear. But even when Wynn had agreed to follow up on Ella's lead about a possible Guardian statue in Chicago, she really hadn't seen herself as more than a bit player.

What the hell had she been thinking? It was hard to remain on the edges of a situation when your family had been involved with the central characters for the last seven generations. For centuries, male members of the Llewellyn clan—her mother's family—had been called to the Guild as Wardens. Her own uncle and brother served as just the latest in a long line of defenders against the servants of the Darkness. Sure, Wynn was a woman, and therefore not invited to join the Guild herself, but had she really believed she could avoid the whole situation just because no one had issued her a membership card? When the Darkness rose, everyone with power got involved, because the alternative ended with the enslavement and extinction of the human race.

Goddess, she could be an idiot at times.

"Okay," she began, blowing out a deep breath and flexing her fingers around the steering wheel. "Most of this is secondhand knowledge, but here's what I know, or what Ella's been able to figure out so far."

"Ella? Who is this Ella?"

"Ella Harrow. She's a friend of a friend up in Canada," Wynn explained. "She was the first."

As succinctly as she could, she told Knox everything that had happened, beginning with Kees's awakening in Vancouver. She summarized the things Ella and her Guardian had discovered, including their meeting with Warden Alan Parsons, their encounter with the *nocturnis* and the minor demons, and the devastating news of the destruction of the Guild of Wardens' headquarters in Paris.

That was the bit that made Knox growl low in his throat. "Did any survive? What about those who did not work from headquarters? The ones stationed elsewhere in the world?"

"I'm getting to that."

She told him about the disappearances of Wardens, of Alan's murder, of Jeffrey Onslow in Ottawa going underground for his own protection before Fil and Spar could locate him. She only neglected to mention her own brother's disappearance. After all, Bran had no part in the events in Canada. The cast of characters in this drama already required a glossary and tables for cross-referencing to keep them straight. She saw no need to complicate matters.

"Fil? Spar?" He snapped out the prompts, clearly impatient to hear the whole tale.

"Fil is really Felicity Shaltis. Spar is the Guardian she woke. They're actually how I got involved in all this."

Wynn explained how Fil had contacted a professor they both knew at McGill University looking for a way to remove the demon mark a member of the *nocturnis* had left on her hand. When Wynn had finally sought out the stranger, she had found the other woman severely ill from the taint of the mark. After severing the bond between Fil and the demon, Wynn had gone on to help the newly minted Warden and her Guardian locate and stop an attempt by a cell of the Order in Montreal to feed human souls to the member of the Seven the cult had managed to summon.

Knox hissed out a curse. "You mean there is already

a member of the Seven loose upon this plane? But I cannot feel it. Are you certain it has truly crossed over?"

That was the usual way that the Guardians woke. They could sense when any of the Seven grew strong enough to affect the human world, and the disturbance would act like an alarm clock, prompting a Warden into waking the nearest of them to deal with the threat. These days, with the Guild scattered and the threat of the Order's attempts to free their masters from their prisons, things seemed to be working a bit differently. Kees, Spar, and now Knox appearing without a Warden to call them forth gave testimony to that.

"We think so," Wynn answered reluctantly. "The good news is that we think it wasn't ready, so it's still pretty weak, and it's remained in hiding as far as we can tell. If the Order managed to free it, they haven't managed to nurse it back to health. At least not yet. So far, the issues we're seeing have come from the *nocturnis* trying to feed it, but that's bad enough. And if they manage to repeat the ritual or whatever they used to break it out of jail, we'll really be in trouble. One of the Seven is enough of a threat. If they unite more of them on this plane, the world as we know it is toast."

Knox grunted in agreement. "Then you know all of this because your encounter with this Felicity forced your involvement." His gaze turned on her, dark and unsettling. "It is unfortunate to involve those outside of the Guild and the Guardians ourselves in this struggle. Such was never meant to happen. Still, you seem to possess a remarkable grasp of the workings of our world for one who is new to us."

Wynn squirmed a little and focused on the road as she maneuvered through the traffic into the city. "Well, I'm not entirely new to it. My mom's family has produced Wardens before."

"When?"

"The first one was in the late seventeenth century. Back in Wales. My whole-bunch-of-greats-grandfather. Gruffydd ap Llewellyn."

His brow arched, but he didn't really look surprised. "It is no wonder you have magic then, if your family has birthed Wardens before."

"At least one per generation," she admitted. "The Guild always wanted the boys, of course, but the women in my family are nothing to sneeze at. Both sides are lousy with witches. I'm just one of many."

"Did you know of the trouble with the Guild before you encountered the *nocturnis* in Montreal?"

She felt him watching her and kept her expression carefully neutral. For some reason, she didn't want to tell him about Bran. It still hurt to think about, let alone talk about, her baby brother.

"No," she said. "We've been removed from the inner workings for a long time. As far as I know, there's never been a Guardian in Chicago before, so contact with the Guild headquarters was minimal, from what I've heard. Plus, the Guild doesn't exactly share well with outsiders. At least, they didn't before this. Now, though, they might be willing to loosen up a little, especially since it looks like they'll have to reconstruct themselves from the ground up. With Ella and Fil now active Wardens, at least something is already different."

"You speak as if you believe the Guild has never allowed a female Warden," Knox observed. His voice held no insult, just mild curiosity and a hint of skepticism. "Are you not aware of the history of the Guardian? Females were instrumental in the continuation of my kind."

Wynn rolled her eyes. She couldn't help herself; it was like a reflex. "Oh, I know the stories. How when the first Guardians lost interest in protecting humanity, it was seven female Wardens who brought them back and persuaded them to care about mortals again. That was a long time ago, though. Since then, the Guild has been a little less enthusiastic about welcoming anyone with ovaries into the fold. I don't know if they were afraid of losing more Guardians to mate bonds, or if they just turned into a bunch of curmudgeonly chauvinists, but I can tell you that before their building was destroyed in Paris, I was aware of three active female members of the Guild. Those aren't exactly numbers that sing of gender equality."

Whatever Knox intended to say got cut off by the tolling bells of her cell phone's ringtone. She tapped the screen to answer without bothering to glance at the caller ID. "Hello?"

"Wynn, honey, hello."

Her mother's voice came over the line. Not exactly who Wynn had been expecting, but at the moment, she welcomed the distraction.

"Hey, Mom. What's up?"

"I need you to come over right away."

As if the words weren't enough to freak her out, something in her mother's voice made Wynn's stomach clench like an internal fist. "Mom? What is it? What's wrong? Are you okay? Are you hurt?"

"No. No, honey, I'm fine." Mona Powe gave a sigh that trembled over the connection. "I didn't mean to scare you, but I need you to come over. The police are here. About Bran."

Wynn's heart raced, and she felt the familiar sickening rush of mingled hope and dread that struck anytime someone hinted at news of her brother. "Did they find him? Is he okay?"

"They didn't find him, but they have something of his. Along with a bunch of questions. Can you come now? Where are you?"

Wynn glanced around and pinpointed her location. She'd pulled off 41 onto 94 a few miles ago and was already cruising through Chicago. "I'm in the car right now. I was out. I can be there in ten minutes."

"Okay, good. Be safe, *bach*. I'll see you soon."

The term of endearment did nothing to ease Wynn's anxiety. She ended the call with a frown. Whenever her mother slipped into Welsh, it was a sign that her emotions were close to overwhelming her. Calling Wynn "little one" meant that whatever the police wanted to discuss, it had brought all of Mona's fear, worry, and hope rushing back to the surface. They'd all been through this so many times already. How much more could the family take?

"Change of plans," she told Knox. "I need to go to my mother's house for something, and I need for you to stay quiet and pretend to be human for me. Can you do that?"

The Guardian looked at her. "Do you believe now is the time for family reunions? I would think that the more pressing matter is to finish our discussion and make contact with those of my brothers who have already awakened."

"Yeah, we'll get to that," she said as she navigated the city streets toward her mother's house. "But this is kind of an emergency."

"And the rise of the Order with the possible release of a world-destroying demon is not?"

Wynn made a sound of frustration. "Fine. If you want, you can sit in the car and save the world from here. Be my guest."

She turned onto her mother's block and immediately spied the conspicuously unmarked police sedan parked at the end of the narrow drive. Luckily, there was a spot open at the curb, and she pounced on it.

Switching off the ignition, she reached down to release her seat belt. Her hand was already on the door handle when she dropped her phone in the center console. "Ella's in my contacts. Feel free to give her a call. Then you and Kees and Spar can go out and conquer the forces of evil. I've got to go see my mom."

If she slammed the door before sprinting toward the back porch, could anyone really blame her? As days went, this one already pretty much sucked, and it was only one fifteen. She couldn't wait to see what happened next.

And yes, that was sarcasm.

Chapter Three

Knox had no intention of leaving the witch's side. Not only had her every reaction since his appearance intrigued him, but he also found himself disturbed by the way her voice had changed after she had listened and spoken into the small communications device. She sounded upset, distressed, and some part of him urged him to rid her of the source of her anxiety. Grabbing the phone she had left behind, he exited the car and followed her toward the house.

His mind still whirled as he tried to process the information she'd given him. If the Guild of Wardens had been nearly destroyed and any of its surviving members had gone underground for their own protection, it became even more critical to protect the woman who just might have unintentionally summoned him into existence. His knowledge of his kind told him such a thing should not be possible, but he could conjure no other explanation of his presence in the mortal realm. Wynn appeared to possess extraordinary powers for a human, and if the Order truly had created the chaos she claimed, he could not afford to let her out of his sight—never mind the beast inside him that snarled and snapped at the very thought of parting from her.

He entered the house only two steps behind her, while the keys dangling from the inside knob on a red string still jingled cheerfully. Her lack of hesitation in letting herself in without alerting those inside spoke of her familiarity and comfort in the home. He surmised that her relationship with her family must be close, and the greeting she exchanged with a slightly older human female confirmed his impression.

As soon as Wynn crossed the threshold, the woman rose from her seat at a square, wooden table and opened her arms. The witch stepped into her embrace and returned it with obvious emotion. The earthy magic that surrounded his female stretched and blended with a similar, equally strong energy emanating from the other. This must be his female's mother.

The Powe matriarch had to have seen more than fifty human years, but she appeared as if no more than a dozen years separated her from her daughter. Not that her face bore no lines, but hers bracketed her eyes and mouth in a way that indicated a woman who smiled easily and often, and her skin glowed with a luminous quality that made her look younger than her years. Her features closely resembled Wynn's, with the same straight, feminine lines. The warm brown of her eyes mirrored that of her daughter's, and while her hair had a slightly redder tinge to the brown, it only emphasized the similarities. Both were beautiful women, but only the younger caused his senses to lock on every time they caught a trace of her.

"*Cariad,* I'm so glad you're here." The mother spoke with her cheek still pressed to her child's, but her eyes flicked toward the door and widened when they locked on Knox. A look of surprise turned to one of shock as she pulled back and glanced between the newcomers.

"Wynn, who is this?" the older woman asked. "He looks like . . . but he can't be—"

She broke off, and Wynn shook her head. "Not now, Mom. I'm sorry, but Knox was with me when you called. I didn't want to take the time to drop him off somewhere."

"Drop him off? Wynn, y—your *friend* is not the sort of . . . person that can just be dropped off like a taxi fare." She shot her daughter a censuring look and stepped toward Knox, clasping her hands together and inclining her head in a regal acknowledgment. "*Gwarchodwr,* welcome to our home. I am Mona Powe, and I am at your service."

Knox returned the formal greeting with a nod. Somehow he had not expected to be recognized as a Guardian by a human before he had so much as opened his mouth in her presence, especially not when he wore a human skin. It seemed that extraordinary women really did run in the Powe family.

"My thanks," he relied. "I am Knox. Forgive my intrusion, but your daughter said you had urgent need of her."

"Wynn Powe?"

Two more figures rose from seats around the table.

These two were male, both of average height and apparently bracketing their fourth decade, one older, one younger. Each wore a jacket and tie along with a stern expression and hard eyes. They each ran an assessing glance over him before focusing on his human.

Wynn turned from her mother to face them. Knox could see the wariness in her gaze and the tension in her stiff posture.

"That's me," she said, her chin notching up as she spoke. "My mother said you have news about my brother."

Her brother? Knox frowned. Why should the police be bringing Wynn's family news of her brother? Was he involved in some activity contrary to human law?

The older of the two men held out a hand and rested the other on the back of the table's remaining unclaimed chair. "I'm Detective Jim Pulaski, and this is my partner, Detective Jansen. Why don't you sit down, Miss Powe? Then we can fill you in on why we contacted your mother."

Wynn crossed her arms over her chest. "Thanks. I'm fine standing."

Detective Jansen flashed her a smile, the expression causing Knox's spine to stiffen. "You want to join us for a cup of coffee? Your mom makes a good pot."

"No. Thank you." She glanced at Mona. "Mom, what's going on?"

"Sit, Wynn." Mona instructed, returning to her own place at the table. "I can make you tea if you want, but you should let the detectives talk."

Knox watched as irritation and worry warred in Wynn's expression. The battle continued to rage when she finally gave in and sat. Knox felt the unexpected urge to go to her and stand at her back like a protector, but his position by the door afforded him a better view of all parties at the table. He leaned one hip against the counter beside him and watched the detectives take their seats. Jansen sat with his back to the room, but Knox could see the faces of the other three humans. He also saw the way the two women joined hands atop the table.

"Miss Powe," Pulaski began, "we understand your mother and your uncle filed a missing persons report on Bran Powe on March 7 of this year and included a statement from you because you were out of town at the time. Is that correct?"

"Of course it is. If you've got information on my brother, I'm sure you've read his file."

The police officer looked up from his notes, but he didn't appear to react to Wynn's clear impatience. "And at that time you reported that you hadn't heard from him in almost a week, which you stated was 'very unusual.' "

So Wynn's brother had disappeared. Knox found that interesting. A man from a family of Wardens had gone missing at the same time as the Guild came under concentrated attack from the Order. Had his female sought to keep this information from him because her brother was involved? Perhaps her feelings about the Guild's chauvinism came from having a sibling accepted into their ranks when she had been denied.

Knox could see his witch's temper flare before she reined it in. It made her aura pulse with little bursts of energy the color of spring leaves.

"It was unusual. Bran and I are close. Even though there are almost four years between us, we were always like best friends. We usually talk every day, even when one of us is out of town. Several times a day isn't unusual. Not talking for more than a day or two is."

"After taking your report, officers spoke to several members of your family, along with a number of Mr. Powe's known friends and associates at the University of Chicago, where your brother was a full-time graduate student and teaching assistant. They also inspected Mr. Powe's residence, but could find no signs of foul play."

Wynn's mouth tightened. "We know all this, Detective, though it's reassuring to hear you've brushed up on your facts before coming out here to upset my mother. Now, do you have anything new to tell us, or is this some kind of routine cold-case follow-up?"

The two police officers exchanged glances. Knox saw Jansen's shoulder's shift as if he was reaching into a pocket, then the man pushed a folded piece of paper across the table toward Wynn.

"This is new to us," the younger officer said. "We'd like to know if it's new to you, too."

Wynn picked up the note, unfolded it, and read aloud. " 'Call Wynnie-the-Pooh. Out of salt. Important. Dig on Coleman, Garvey/CG Towers. Uncle Griffin. Paris. Bank for box.' " She glanced up, her expression guarded. After only an hour in her company, Knox could read her that well at least. "It's a to-do list. Bran made them compulsively, like multiple times a day. He always said if he didn't write it down, it never happened."

"So that's his handwriting?" Pulaski asked.

"Of course." She examined the note again. "There's no date on it. Is this recent? Where did you find this?"

"We don't think it's recent. It showed up at the station on Friday in an envelope, along with a notebook and a stack of newspaper clippings. No return address, though. Did someone in your family send it? Were you trying to make us look into your brother's disappearance again?"

"What?" The accusation drew a disbelieving snort of laughter from Wynn and a startled look from her mother. "What do you mean, 'again'? Because our family has assumed that the police have been trying to find Bran all along. Are you telling us that's not true?"

"Are you?" Mona echoed, his distress clearly building. "Have you not been looking for my baby boy?"

"Miss Powe, Mrs. Powe, your son's case has been open since the missing persons report was filed, but I'm sure you realize that without any evidence of a threat to Bran's safety, there's not all that much we can do. He's a grown man. He's allowed to disappear if that's what he wants to do."

"So then what you're saying is that the real reason you came here was to tell us that you think we sent you one of Bran's old lists because we're trying to get you to waste police resources on a case you're not really interested in. Is that it?"

Wynn's eyes flashed with anger, and Knox found himself fascinated by the way temper flushed her cheeks a rosy pink. He felt heat move in his own veins and scowled. Was the human causing him this strange sensation? He had found himself beginning to admire her, it was true, and he had noticed himself thinking of her in possessive terms, as "his witch," or "his female." She demonstrated a quick mind and a fierce loyalty to her family, qualities he respected. Perhaps such emotions had sparked his reaction. That at least made more sense than the way his senses lit up in her presence. That reaction he still preferred to ignore.

Detective Jansen leaned forward and stared intently at Wynn. "Is that what you did, Miss Powe? Did you send us those things?"

Wynn opened her mouth—almost bared her teeth—at the younger detective, but his partner gestured him to back off.

"We came here," Pulaski said, his tone calm and reasonable, "because this is new information for us, but I have to admit, it doesn't make much sense to us. We hoped you could help us understand if it sheds any light on what Bran was up to before he went missing. I kind of assumed that when he wrote 'Wynnie-the-Pooh,' he was talking about you."

His voice made it a question, and Wynn answered with a nod. "Yeah. He's called me that since we were kids, at first because everyone thought it was adorable, later because he knew it drove me crazy, and in the end it just became habit. A way to tease me, like a pet name. But as I said, I hadn't talked to him in the week before he vanished. What would make you think this list is from the same time that he was last seen?"

"We can't know for certain, but there are some things in the notebook it came with that made us think it might be from around that time."

Wynn shrugged. "I'm sorry, but I have no idea what

you think I can tell you about a list of reminders. I can take a look at the notebook, though, and see if there's anything in there I can help you figure out."

"Right now, let's just concentrate on the list," Jansen said, nodding at the paper. "Does any of the rest of that ring any bells for you? Did he talk about any of that the last time you spoke to him?"

"Not that I remember. I mean, this just looks like everyday stuff. Do you call your sister and tell her every time you run out of salt?"

"No, but I don't usually make a note that running out of salt is important, and underline it for emphasis."

Mona leaned forward and examined the list. "Wynn is right. This is all very ordinary, isn't it? 'Uncle Griffin' refers to my brother, I'm sure. Didn't you all speak with him when we filed the report?"

"We did." Jansen nodded. "He didn't have much more to say than the rest of you. He couldn't think of a reason why Bran would have disappeared, either. We'll show this to him, too, though, see if it stirs anything up."

Pulaski tapped a fingertip on the paper near the bottom of the list. "What about the rest of it? Like this part. Did Bran ever talk about going to Paris? Did he have a thing about visiting over there?"

If Knox had not been watching so closely, he would have missed the split second of pause in the breathing of both women. Neither stiffened, or gasped, or gave any outward sign that the city meant anything in particular to their family, but Knox knew that for the family of every Warden, the French city held a special significance.

"He had visited, once," Mona said, looking up to meet

the detective's gaze with perfect poise. "While he was an undergrad. I know he enjoyed it, but he hadn't said anything to me about planning a trip back. He likes to joke about being a starving academic, but it's not that far from the truth. I doubt he has the money to spare for such an expensive trip. He would have to make an effort to save, and I'm certain he would have mentioned that."

"Yeah, plus there's that rule Mom has," Wynn added. "No leaving the country without advance notice and a complete itinerary to hang on the fridge."

Mona smiled. "I'm a mother. I worry."

Pulaski's own mouth hitched up at one corner. "I hear that. I got kids of my own."

"What about the rest of it?" Jansen took over again, drawing their attention back to the list.

"'Bank for box,'" Wynn read again. She looked at Mona. "A safe-deposit box, maybe? Does he have one, do you know?"

"Not that I know of."

"We checked out the bank where he kept his checking account," the younger detective said. "They didn't have one for him. But actually I meant this part. 'Dig on Coleman, Garvey/CG Towers.' Does that mean anything to either of you ladies?"

This time the women openly exchanged glances, each looking puzzled but bereft of answers.

"Nope," Wynn said first.

"Not a thing," Mona agreed. "He used the word 'dig,' though. Maybe it had something to do with the research for his dissertation?"

Pulaski raised an eyebrow. "I thought he was

studying anthropology, digging up Stone Age tombs and such."

"Archaeology," she corrected. "Anthropology studies cultures, how they develop, change, and function. Archaeology looks at the things they leave behind and what the things can tell us about their lives and cultures. But Bran's interest wasn't specific to the Stone Age. In fact, his dissertation work focused on the Bronze Age, which came later."

"So how would any of that relate to Ronald Coleman, William Garvey, and their office tower downtown?"

She shook her head and shrugged. "It doesn't."

"Then why would your brother make a note that he needed to 'dig on' them?"

"My brother and I are close, Detective, but we can't read each other's minds."

The detective watched her intently. "You know Coleman and Garvey are pretty powerful people in this town, right?"

"I know they're rich, and I know they make the news a lot, but I really don't follow business issues. It doesn't interest me."

"Really." Jansen eyed her skeptically. "Just what is it you do again, Miss Powe? For a living, I mean."

Knox could read the defiance in his female's deliberate meeting of the human male's gaze.

"I work for myself, Detective Jansen. I make my own line of bath products using all-natural ingredients. I don't work for either of those men, either directly or indirectly, and I really couldn't care less about their businesses. I can't imagine why my brother would feel any different."

Sitting back in her chair, Wynn laid her hand over the

paper containing her brother's list and pushed it away from her. "I think it's useless to speculate on what my brother meant by a handful of words jotted down on a piece of paper months ago. Maybe he was aware of some sort of archaeological discovery on their property. Maybe he wanted to invest in their businesses. Maybe he just saw them on the news and something in the report piqued his curiosity about them. There's no way for us to know for certain."

Pulaski tapped his pen against his small notepad. "I thought you said Bran wouldn't have had the money to take a trip to France? If he couldn't afford that, how was he going to afford to invest in a business?"

"When he comes home, you'll just have to ask him," Wynn snapped.

There was a small, intense moment of silence as the humans at the table watched one another closely. Then the older detective snapped his notebook closed and pushed back his chair.

"Thank you for your time, ladies," Pulaski said, gesturing to his partner. "Keep the list. It's a photocopy anyway. I'm sorry we bothered you for something that didn't turn out to be significant. We'll be in touch if anything further develops."

The men stood and moved toward the exit. Wynn rose as well and followed them. "What about the rest of the things that you received in that envelope? Maybe something in that would give us a clue about Bran. I mean, there has to be a reason why someone sent it to you, especially now. Is there a way to find out where it came from?"

"We're looking into it. Like I said, there was no

return address and nothing to indicate who might have sent it."

"I'd be happy to take a look through it, and see if I can tell you anything."

"We're looking into it," Jansen repeated, yanking open the door. "Thanks for your time, ladies."

The men departed, leaving Wynn looking both angered and frustrated. She turned to her mother and blew out a breath. "And what the hell was that, huh?"

"Don't curse," Mona warned absently. "The whole thing does strike me as rather strange. I can't imagine what they were fishing for. When they called, I was so excited. I thought they must have found something, some clue about where your brother has gone."

The woman dropped her gaze to the tabletop, weariness dragging her shoulders down, making her suddenly appear every one of her years. Wynn saw her mother's posture and sighed, the anger apparently leaving her on the gust of air. Slipping into the chair beside her, she took the older woman in her arms and hugged her.

"I know, Mom. I'm sorry," she said. "I thought so, too. But he's out there, and he's alive. I can feel it, and I know you can, too. Whatever is keeping him from coming home, he'll be okay. Bran's a smart cookie. Remember that."

Mona clasped her hand over her daughter's arm and squeezed. The gesture became a reassuring pat as she visibly gathered herself back together and slipped on a mantle of calm and control.

"He's a good boy. When he can come back to us, he will." Nodding decisively, Mona shifted her gaze to Knox and offered him a bright smile. "Now it appears we have other matters to deal with right here under our noses. Please, Guardian, sit with us and let us know what we can do to serve you. Is your Warden nearby? I would hope that he, too, would feel welcome in our home."

Wynn looked away and rubbed the back of her neck, clearly avoiding her mother's gaze. "Uh, yeah, Mom, that's kind of the thing. Knox doesn't have a Warden at the moment."

"Don't be silly, Wynn. All Guardians have Wardens. Who else would wake them when we need their protection?"

"Wow, um, that's kind of a long story . . ."

"A story, hm?" Mona looked from her daughter to the Guardian and back again, her eyes gleaming with curiosity. "In that case, I'll put on a pot of tea."

"Do you have any cakes made?"

Mona looked away from the kettle and arched a brow. "Oh, it's like that, is it?"

"You have no idea."

"Cakes are in the tin. Best set out a plate, if we're to be here awhile."

Wynn rose and crossed to a cupboard, reaching up to withdraw a battered green tin with a scripted brand name printed on the side. "Oh, we will. I'll need milk for my tea."

Mona flicked on the flame under the kettle with an angry snap of her wrist and turned on her daughter. Knox continued to watch, fascinated by their interactions.

"That is it." The older woman braced her hands on her hips and glared at her daughter. "Wynn Myfanwy Llewellyn Powe, if you're in a situation that calls for cakes, and you want the comfort of milk in your black-as-tar-and-twice-as-strong tea, you'd better start telling me about it. Exactly how soon is the world going to come to an end?"

Wynn winced and slumped back down at the table. "We might have time to finish the tea?"

"Talk," Mona ordered. "Now."

Chapter Four

The headache made Wynn wish she'd never gotten out of bed—that morning more than a year ago, when she'd accepted the position as a research assistant to a professor at McGill University studying the properties of traditional healing herbs. If she'd just rolled over and pulled the covers up around her ears, she'd never have gone to Montreal, never have met Felicity, Ella, and their Guardians, and never have gotten dragged into the mess she had just somewhat meanderingly described to her mother.

Of course, her brother would probably still be missing, and the world would still be in imminent danger from the threat of the Order's latest plan, but what she didn't know couldn't hurt her, right?

Oh, wait. Total earthly apocalypse might end up stinging a bit, huh?

Her mother pushed away her tea. She'd stopped sipping somewhere around the time that Wynn described the hours spent performing a ritual to sever Fil from the bond of the demon mark left on her hand by a *nocturnis* spell. By the end of the long, convoluted story, which culminated in the security guard, the sprained ankle, and the appearance of Knox, the liquid had long since gone cold.

Her expression slightly dazed, Mona rose from the table and pushed Wynn's hair away from her face, angling it toward the light to reveal the bruises and scrapes from her fall. She ran a gentle finger over the red line at her daughter's throat and made a soft clucking sound. "I can't believe I missed this. You sit right here. I'll get the first-aid kit."

Wynn's mouth dropped open as she watched her mother step into the powder room off the rear of the kitchen. "That's it?" she demanded. "I tell you the Order have raised one of the Seven, the whole Guild—or what's left of it really—have gone underground, a Guardian popped up in the middle of an evil minion trying to kill me, and there are only four other people in the world who know the real extent of the situation, and all you have to say is you want to fix my booboos?"

"You watch your tone, miss." Mona reemerged carrying a white plastic box and a damp washcloth, which she set on the table before resuming her seat. "I heard every word you said, but we can only deal with one thing at a time. First, we patch you up, then we can talk about what has to happen next. I think getting in touch with your new friends in Canada is probably the right first step, but I doubt another five minutes is going to determine the entire course of the future. Now hold still."

Wynn glanced helplessly at Knox, but the big Guardian simply watched as her mother gripped her chin in one hand and began washing off the dirt and traces of dried blood the same way she had since Wynn was a baby. So help her, if her mother licked a thumb and used it to scrub at a stubborn spot, Wynn wasn't sure she'd be able to keep from decking her, no matter how much she loved the woman.

Then she'd turn around and deck Knox. The Guardian had been no help at all, barely uttering a word since they'd arrived at her mother's house. How the heck did he expect to save the world if all he did was sit around and watch what everyone else was doing?

He met her glare with a bland expression and nodded toward her right foot. "You should also allow your mother to tend to your ankle. You limped quite badly on the way from the car."

"My ankle is fine," she bit out, baring her teeth at him. "It only looks bad because I already hurt it a couple of weeks ago. I'll slap some ice on it, and it will be just peachy."

Mona finished smoothing ointment on her daughter's facial abrasions and gave her an imperious look. "A sprained ankle, hm? Come on, then. Let me see it."

"Mom, I swear, it's—"

Mona waited.

Sighing, Wynn surrendered and slid her chair back to allow her to raise her lower leg and rest her foot in her mother's lap. She knew that expression. It meant Mona Powe expected to be obeyed, and if she had to wait forever or unleash her mighty wrath on her child, she would. Given her fiery temperament, Mona usually went with wrath. Wynn had the memories to prove it.

"It's not so bad," Wynn said, unsure if she was trying

to convince her mother or herself. To be honest, the ankle hurt like a son of a bitch, but the entire day so far had felt like the steep drop of a roller coaster—fast, terrifying, and completely out of her control. Damn it, she should at least get to have a say over her own health and well-being, right? Even if it meant suffering the agony of an untreated sprain.

And dear Goddess, didn't that just make her sound like either the biggest idiot on the face of the earth, or a sugared-up three-year-old at nap time?

"Guardian, if it wouldn't be too much trouble, would you please go into the freezer and fetch me the bag of peas?" Mona looked up from examining Wynn's injury just long enough to flash the Guardian a charming smile. "I'm so sorry to impose, but I'd like to bring down this swelling a bit before I wrap the foot."

"Do not worry yourself." Knox rose and retrieved the item, passing it over with an elegant flourish. "It is the least I can do after you have received me so graciously into your home."

Oh, come on, Wynn thought, rolling her eyes beneath lowered lids so her mother wouldn't catch her. *Seriously with the chivalrous Knight of Yore routine?*

She hissed when her mother slapped the cold bag of vegetables onto her bare skin. She must not have hid the roll as well as she thought. Clearing her throat, she scrambled to get this whole debacle back on track.

She looked at Knox. "Did you leave my phone in the car? Because we probably should call Ella and Felicity, but I don't know their numbers off the top of my head. I need the contact list on my phone."

Knox reached into his pocket and set the device on

the table between them. "It is here. You will show me how it works, and I will initiate the contact."

"Are you certain there's no one else here in Chicago we should call?" Mona frowned as she wiped her hands on a dry dishcloth she had snagged from a drawer. "I know you said Knox appeared spontaneously, without a summoning, and that this is his first time in our world, but that just seems so crazy. I've never heard of anything like that happening before. I can't believe he doesn't have a Warden of his own waiting somewhere."

"Trust me, Mom, if he had a Warden waiting, I'd be the first one to call him," Wynn said.

Hell, she'd throw the Guardian at the Warden's head and run like hell. She'd already seen more than enough of what the Order was capable of; she wasn't exactly craving a closer look.

"But Ella and Fil both had almost the same thing happen to them, and in their cases, they know the Wardens for their Guardians had already been killed by the *nocturnis*. Even though Kees and Spar had been sleeping on our plane, they still should have needed Wardens to wake them up. Something has changed recently. The old rules don't apply anymore."

"No, I guess they don't." Mona bowed her head at Knox. "Forgive me, Guardian. A mother is never anxious to see her child drawn into a battle, even when she knows the cause is just."

Wynn jumped in before Knox could speak. "Sheesh, Mom, chill. It's not like I'm strapping on a sword and going out to chop the Seven's heads off. We're still rallying the troops. We know the Order is already active and working on a plan, but that's why we need to make sure all the Guardians who are already awake are on the same page. I was kidding when I said we only had time to finish our tea before the *nocturnis* struck. We'll be okay."

Knox ignored Wynn's speech and placed one large fist against his chest, directly over his heart. "I give you my word, Mrs. Powe, I will protect your daughter with my life. She will come to no harm that I can prevent."

Her mother beamed. "Thank you, Guardian. And please, call me Mona."

"If you will call me Knox."

And both of you can call me irritated.

Wynn grabbed the phone and dragged it toward her. "I'm calling Ella, and I'm putting this on speaker. We need to start getting our shi—" She caught herself and cast her mother an apologetic glance. "Ourselves together. The others need to know we have a third Guardian on hand. Maybe they can give us some advice on the Warden front. Maybe there is someone else in Chicago, and that's why you were able to be summoned. Maybe it was like some sort of remote-control thing. If any of us knows, it will be Ella. She's the least clueless among us newbies."

Pulling up the other woman's information, Wynn initiated the call and then sat back while the phone rang. On the third tone, Ella answered.

"Wynn? Thank goodness. Kees and I talked to the others, and we think we have an idea for you to try. It might sound kind of out there, but just bear with us."

Wynn cut her off. "Ella, before we get into all that, I—"

"No, really, just hear me out," the woman continued. "We all think that since the evidence of Fil and I waking up the guys points to things being really out of whack right now—"

"Ella, seriously, you need—"

"—it might be worth it for you to try summoning a new Guardian to replace the one that was destroyed. Now, I've been looking into the texts I was able to get my hands on, and—"

"El! I've already got one!"

"—from what I can tell—"

It took a moment, but eventually Wynn's interruption seemed to cut through her friend's urgent babbling. Ella fell abruptly silent, and there was a long pause before she spoke again.

"You what?"

Wynn leaned forward and spoke into the phone. "I've got a Guardian. He's sitting right here. Knox, say hello to Ella. Ella, meet Knox."

"Hello, Ella," Knox repeated obediently.

"Oh, my God. Hold on. Let me put you on speaker. Kees! Get over here. Wynn did it!"

They heard some rustling and the rumbling of words exchanged in the background, then Kees's deep voice flowed over the connection. "I am not aware of a Guardian by that name, Wynn. And Ella informed me that the Guardian you went to contact had been destroyed in his sleeping shape. A shattered Guardian cannot be woken. Are you certain you have not been deceived?"

Knox growled at the phone, glaring as if the device itself had somehow insulted him. "I am no liar. I am

Knox, Guardian and Protector, and I stand against the Seven with my brothers at my side. Who are you to challenge my honor?"

"Boys, please." Wynn held up her hands like the referee at a boxing match, which considering there was only one combatant currently in the room only served to make her look stupid. "Trust me when I tell you, Kees, that after having met two Guardians in real life, mistaking the third one when he's standing right in front of me is really not an option. Knox wasn't woken, though. He was summoned to replace the one the Order blew up. This is his first time around."

Wynn really hoped the squeal that followed her announcement came from Ella, because if Kees had made that sound, she feared for his testicles.

"Kees, hush. This means it worked!" Ella said, her voice all but vibrating with glee. "That is so awesome, the best news we've had in days. This means that we can probably still manage to gather all Seven Guardians, and if we're right about what the Order has been up to, we're definitely going to need them."

"Um, I hate to burst your bubble, Ella, but I don't follow your train of thought there. Yes, something summoned Knox for us, but I don't think it was me, because I have no idea how it happened. All I did was lie there and nearly get killed. I couldn't duplicate it if I tried. Not to mention that I wouldn't want to." Wynn reached up and touched the wound on her throat, which had thankfully turned out to be little more than a scratch. "And frankly, I can't recommend the experience to anyone else, either."

"It's okay. Fil and I had no idea how we managed to

wake these guys, either, but it still happened. It's fine. At least you've given us reason to believe it's possible. Trust me, at this point, that goes a long way."

"If you say so."

"I do." Ella's tone brooked no argument, but after a pause, it returned with sly amusement. "You do realize what this means, right, Wynn? You're one of us now."

One of us. One of us. The chant of the brainwashed villains from a favorite movie echoed in Wynn's head, and she shook it to clear it. "One of who? The idiots who think it will be fun to stand up against the ultimate evil and tell it, *Thanks, but we'd prefer not to be destroyed right now, if that's okay?*"

"Well, that, but I was taking about the new generation of Wardens. It's like in a store, you know? 'You break it, you bought it.' Only in this case, it's 'You wake it, you're in charge of it.'"

"In charge of it?" Kees rumbled.

"Relax, big guy. It's a figure of speech. I just mean that since Wynn was the one to witness Knox's summoning, that means she's his Warden now."

Wynn felt the impact of the words like a smack to the forehead. Her? A Warden? She wanted to laugh, but it really wasn't very funny. All her life, she'd felt like her destiny was to be a Warden, but now when the position had fallen on her shoulders, her only response seemed to be stunned silence.

"This is actually really great," Ella enthused over the phone. "You know so much more about the Wardens than Fil and I do, and your family is a total asset. You all can teach us so much. I mean, you're the only one in the group who actually knew the Guild and the Guardians existed before you got saddled with one."

"Well, sure, but the things I know aren't exactly practical or useful, El," Wynn said. She felt a stirring of panic at the thought of being viewed as some kind of expert on how to be a Warden. "I know the basic structure of the Guild and abstract overviews of Guardian history, but when it comes to hands-on work of the Wardens, I'm as clueless as you are. All that stuff is secret. Heck, Wardens in training have to take a sacred oath not to reveal what they learn to outsiders."

It had caused one of the few serious fights she and Bran had gotten into since they'd grown up. His training had fascinated her, of course, and she'd pestered him constantly with questions until he'd exploded. He had yelled about the need to restrict Guild secrets to the Wardens and called her a whiny baby who just couldn't stand the idea that he was privy to the knowledge she'd always wanted for herself. They hadn't spoken for almost two weeks, at least partly because she'd known he was right. She'd felt such jealousy over being denied entry to the Guild that she'd tried to use her brother as a back door into the secret society. It hadn't been fair to him, and it had taken a lot of swallowing of her pride to admit that and apologize for her behavior.

Bran had forgiven her and they'd moved on, but the jealousy had never gone away. Now, when someone was telling her she'd finally get the chance to be a Warden herself, it had to be in these circumstances, when no one was left to train her, the Guild was in ruins, and the threat the Guardians faced had seldom been graver. How was that fair?

"That's still more than we started with," Ella said. "Trust me, you're already a step ahead. Anything you can give us is going to help."

"If you say so." Wynn wasn't convinced, but arguing about it didn't appear to be doing any good, and they had bigger things to worry about at the moment. "As far as I'm concerned, though, Ella is still our Warden in Chief. You're the one with the plan. Now that I've got us another Guardian, what am I supposed to do with him?"

"Same thing as the rest of us. Our priority is still locating the remaining Guardians and making contact with any surviving Wardens we can find. At this point, it's all about amassing troop strength."

"Okay, so what have you been able to dig up since I last saw you?"

As Ella summarized her latest attempts to follow the obscure trails to Wardens in hiding and the information she'd been sorting through about statues that might or might not turn out to be sleeping Guardians, Wynn tried to focus on her words. It posed a bigger challenge than she would have expected. Maybe she was still off her game because of her late arrival into Chicago and the resulting lack of sleep, but at the moment, more than anything in the world, she just wanted to go upstairs to her old room, crawl into her old, twin-sized bed, pull the covers over her head, and sleep for a week.

Oddly, she didn't hear an opportunity for any of that mentioned in Ella's strategy briefing.

The sensation of eyes following her made her turn to glance at Knox. The Guardian watched her closely, almost as if she were a puzzle he wanted to solve. She could have told him there was nothing all that extraordinary about her, nothing to set her apart from any other witch. She didn't have the faintest idea why she had ended up drafted into this army of inexperienced and ill-prepared Wardens, so she had no hope of explaining it to him.

Goddess, yet another reason for her to wish she could just call Bran and tell him to get his butt over to Mom's house. He had all the knowledge and training that she and Ella and Felicity lacked. He would know what to do. Wynn? She hadn't the foggiest. All she seemed to know to do was what other people instructed—find the statue, come to the house, stick with the Guardian.

That last part stuck in her paw like a thorn. Her reactions to Knox's presence made her more uncomfortable than she could remember being in a long while. He made her body sit up and take notice, which was bad enough, but something about the energy he emitted intrigued her, tugged at her. It was the sort of visceral reaction that she had no hope of fighting and that scared her almost silly. Why was it happening? Was it because she really was his Warden? And if so, what did that mean?

Ella and Fil had mated to their Guardians, but that was so not an option in Wynn's mind. Nuh-uh, no how, no way. She was not about to let circumstances dictate one of the most important decisions of her life. That was why they called it that, because she'd be *deciding* that one on her own, thanks, and frankly she couldn't imagine tying herself to a Guardian. Ever.

Not only did the Guardians represent the Guild in a way, being the other half of the ancient alliance that had caused the Guild's formation in the first place, but they would always be tied to it. Wynn, if she got really lucky, could back out when this was all over. Well, she might be dead at that point, but if she survived to see the Darkness put down, the Guild would be able to rebuild itself and they could assign Knox a real Warden. You know, someone with a dick. Why would Wynn want to be tied to a Guardian, knowing that eventually she would be shuffled aside in favor of someone more suitable? It was one thing to be replaced, it was another to stick around and watch the person doing your old job for the rest of your life.

"While I agree that locating the rest of our brothers should remain a high priority," Knox interrupted, finally pulling his glance away from Wynn and focusing it back on the phone, "I believe it would be unwise not to first get a sense of the current situation here in this city. From what you all have said of your own experiences, while the threat from the Order as a whole does seem elevated, each of you faced a much more immediate threat in the area where you woke. I find myself inclined to believe I did not come here merely because of the Order's grand scheme. It seems likely the *nocturnis* must have something planned in this vicinity that requires a Guardian's skills to combat. Both Guardians who woke before me did so at times when the Order had an active plot to be stopped in their city."

Ella sighed. "Damn. You're right. It only makes sense. I mean, if Guardians are supposed to wake only at times of a threat, it would have to be a specific threat. Otherwise, they'd never sleep, because the Order always has the same goal stewing along in the background. I can't believe I didn't think of that."

"Your thoughts are already too crowded. You cannot

be expected to anticipate the Order's every move," Kees soothed his mate. "Knox, you make a good point. Wynn, are you aware of any obvious *nocturnis* activity in your area?"

"I just got back here from Montreal this morning, re-member?" Wynn shook her head. "This hasn't been my area for a long time now. I'd have to take a look around, poke under some rocks, do a little digging before I could even begin to answer that question."

"Perhaps that is where you should start, then."

Knox gave a dissatisfied rumble and frowned at Wynn. "You say you can think of no problems in your city, but I have been here only hours and already I can see one. What of your brother's disappearance? Do you not think this might connect to the Order in some way."

"Of course, it does," Wynn snapped. "It connects to the Order in the same way that all the missing Wardens connect to the Order. They've been trying to crush the Guild. We're all aware of that. "But if you're trying to imply that my brother is involved in this mess, you can—"

"I imply nothing. Your brother is a Warden, therefore he is allied with us against the *nocturnis,* but the police said he went missing quite a long time ago. Could his disappearance have marked the beginning of the Order's plans for this area being set in motion?"

Goddess, Wynn had never thought of that before. What if her brother's disappearance wasn't just like all the other missing Wardens? What if it had been a clue that something big was going to happen in Chicago and she had missed it? Hell, everyone had missed it.

During the bulk of the phone call to Canada, Mona

Powe had simply sat quietly at the table and listened. She had gotten up briefly to warm her tea, then returned to sip the brew while her daughter and the others discussed their situation. Wynn had noticed that at some point, her mother had reached out for the photocopy of Bran's list the detectives had left behind. If she had thought about it, Wynn might have assumed that her mother was simply seeking comfort in the familiar sight of Bran's writing after so long missing him, but when Mona began to frown and set her tea aside, the gesture caught Wynn's attention.

When she spoke, the older woman caught everyone else's. "Wynn, honey, take a look at this."

"Mom, we're trying to—"

"I know what you're trying to do, Wynn Myfanwy, I'm not an idiot," Mona snapped. "Nor would I interrupt your conversation for anything I didn't believe related to it. Now take a look at what I'm trying to show you."

" 'Mom'?" Ella repeated. "Wynn, is someone else there with you."

Wynn sighed, even as she followed her mother's pointing finger to the second item on her brother's forgotten list. "Yeah, sorry. Knox and I are at my mother's house right now. Of course, she already knows all about the Guild and the Guardians. Her name's Mona. Mom, obviously this is Ella Harrow and Kees, another Guardian."

"How do you do?" Mona murmured absently. "Wynn, do you see this right here? How the word 'salt' shows up so much darker than all the rest of the list?"

"Sure. That happens on photocopies. There's variation in the image quality."

"Not usually when the paper is flat and even and the copier is working properly. I think he wrote 'salt' in a different color of ink."

Wynn glanced up at her mother and blinked in confusion. "Why would you think that? Who would bother to write one word using a different pen from the rest of the list?"

"Maybe if he was using a blue pen for the main list and he wasn't talking about regular table salt."

Her meaning clicked into place and Wynn leaned closed to examine the paper more carefully. "You mean he needed black salt? You think that's why right above that he said he needed to call me?"

"It would make sense. Your brother knows no one makes black salt as effective as yours. You have a gift with protective and charms magic."

Ella's voice cut in to their side discussion. "Um, sorry to butt in, but we're kinda lost over here. What list are you all talking about, and what does it have to do with the situation with the Order?"

"This afternoon, the police came by to talk to us about my brother's missing persons case," Wynn explained. "They brought over a list he had made that was mailed to them along with some other things of his. They didn't know who sent them or why, so they wanted us to take a look. At first, I didn't think anything of it, but Mom just pointed out to me that maybe there is a connection after all."

"Because your brother wanted you to make him black salt?"

"Drive away salt, remember?" Felicity had used a batch Wynn had made during their adventures in

Montreal. "Very useful against demons and demonic energies."

"Oh, wow," Ella said, making the connection right away. "So maybe Knox is right and your brother was looking into some kind of *nocturnis* activity in your area before he disappeared?"

Wynn and her mother exchanged worried glances. "It's definitely possible. That's what Wardens do, isn't it?"

"It is," Kees rumbled. "Tell us what else is on that list."

Wynn read the whole thing for the rest of the group, and explained to the others that Coleman and Garvey were prominent businessmen in the local community with ties to officials in both government and the private sector. "If Bran thought they might be connected to the Order, he was walking a tightrope. A, because digging up dirt on those two wouldn't be appreciated and wouldn't likely go unnoticed, and B, because whether he was right or wrong, they aren't the kind of people the Guild can just make disappear."

"Could they be responsible for your brother's disappearance?"

The thought made Wynn's stomach tighten. "Do they have the capability? I'm sure they do. But unless they really are *nocturnis,* I can't imagine they'd have the motive."

"Well, it sounds like we need to figure that out," Ella said decisively.

Mona reached out and gripped her daughter's hand. "Knowing has to be better than not knowing."

"You're right." She blew out a breath. "Ella, is there any way you could look into the two of them? I know you're not even in the same country, but if there is something to this speculation, it might be better not to bring another member of my family to their attention by me poking around."

"No, you're right. I can absolutely handle some preliminary research. I'm getting pretty darned good at it, actually."

"Thank you."

"We should not take chances with anyone's safety. Kees, you will care for Ella while I look after Wynn," Knox said, surprising Wynn by reaching up to rest his big hand on her shoulder, almost as if offering her his own support and comfort. She knew he felt a duty to protect all of humanity, but he had no reason to care about her safety in particular. "We will do our own investigating here. Perhaps Bran left more clues behind for us. Now that we know what we are looking for, we should search through his belongings to see what we can find. If he knew what the Order had planned, we must discover everything he knew."

Wynn nodded. "Mom and Uncle Griff and I already went through everything, but we certainly weren't looking for anything like this. It can't hurt to take another peek."

"Then peek we shall."

Chapter Five

Dust tickled his nose and the scent of neglect flooded his senses. The apartment smelled of absence, of old fabric and unpolished wood, and it gave the rooms an air of sadness and abandonment that belied the warm colors and inviting arrangements. Even the bright morning light seemed dimmed.

"Mom and I renewed the lease on this place a couple of months ago," Wynn said, setting her keys in a bowl near the front door and crossing to push open the curtain on one of the windows flanking the battered sofa. "We wanted to make sure Bran still had his own place to head to when he came back."

The apartment occupied the second floor of a modest house in a residential neighborhood less than a mile from Mona Powe's dwelling. Wynn mentioned that her own home also sat only a few blocks in the other direction. It gave further evidence of the closeness of the family and their long history in the area. If something was going on here that a Warden needed to keep track of, one as entwined in the place as Bran Powe should have been the first to know.

Following Wynn into the space, Knox secured the door behind them and surveyed their surroundings. The house had been built in the early twentieth century, and evidence of original wood trim around the windows and doorways testified to the care of those long-ago crafts-men. It didn't appear to be a large apartment, but the main living space boasted several windows that let in good natural light, and the pale-colored walls contrasted with the dark oak floors and millwork to make the room look open and inviting.

To the right, a large, squared archway opened into what had probably been intended as a dining room, but from the looks of it Bran Powe had gotten more use out of the space by pressing it into double duty as an office as well. A battered wood-and-metal desk had been backed up to the wall beneath a curtained window, and its cluttered surface indicated that it saw a great deal of use when its owner was in residence.

Knox stepped through the arch and noticed a door off to the side.

"Bran's bedroom," Wynn explained, and he nodded.

Another door in the far corner of the room stood open, revealing kitchen cabinets and vintage linoleum-tile floors. Clearly no one had renovated anytime in recent memory, but despite its age, everything in the apartment appeared neat, functional, and well cared for. Knox might have expected much worse from a human single male in his mid-twenties who lived alone.

Turning back to face the desk, Knox gestured to the haphazard piles of paper and two sides of file drawers.

"I take it that if your brother recorded his research, the information would be somewhere in that?"

"Yeah, organization was never my brother's strong suit, though." Wynn made a face. "We'll have to go through everything. He had no filing system worth mentioning. He just piled everything together and then seemed to know exactly where to find whatever he wanted within seconds. When we were in school, it used to drive my mom and me nuts."

"Then we should get started."

Together, they crossed to the desk and looked down at the mountains of information. With a sigh, Wynn reached up and flicked the curtains open to let the light stream in. She also switched on the desk lamp for added illumination.

"Nobody's touched this stuff since right after Bran disappeared. Mom told me that she and Uncle Griff poked around to see if they could find anything to say where he'd gone, but they came up empty. She said she hasn't been over here in a couple of months."

Knox ran a finger along the top of a stack of papers and saw the trail of clean white he made in the layer of dust. "So it would seem."

"Ugh. If we don't get rid of some of that, I'm going to spend the whole time sneezing. Dust wreaks havoc on my allergies. Hold on. I think Bran keeps a can of compressed air in this drawer."

The prickling sensation at the back of Knox's neck had him reaching out to stop the human from touching the drawer's handle, but he was too late. As soon as her fingers curled around the cool metal, the trap was sprung with a flare of dark light and a whiff of sulfur and rot.

"Holy shit!"

Wynn jumped back as if she'd taken an electric shock, and nearly stumbled over the back of one of the three *hhissih* that had appeared when she activated the spell. Snarling, Knox grabbed her around the waist and swung her aside, setting her down between his big body and the wall. Already his first instinct was to keep her safe, no matter what the danger. The realization made him frown, but he would consider what it meant later. Right now, he must concentrate on protecting her.

"What in the name of Cerridwen are those?" she demanded, peering over his shoulder.

"Hhissih," he grunted. "Minor demonic attack dogs. They are not what I am concerned with."

"Well, I am! Look at them!"

Knox didn't have to. He knew how ugly the small, evil creatures were, with their simultaneously slimy and furry hides, wickedly sharp claws, and lack of any features other than black, lidless eyes. He knew there had to be mouths in there somewhere, because they possessed a vicious bite, but they were obscured in the blackness of the creatures' fur and auras. The things hissed and chittered as they darted forward and back, threatening but not attacking. They knew they could not hope to defeat a Guardian, nor could they get to Wynn with him in their way.

Dismissing the *hhissih,* he looked warily around the room until he spotted the real threat. There, in the corner near the door to the bedroom, he could see the air begin to grow slick and shimmery. Not waiting for the portal to open, Knox shifted, his human form disappearing and his natural, bestial warrior shape taking over.

With a fierce battle cry, he flung himself into the half-formed magical gateway. He could not be certain what waited on the other side, but he knew one thing absolutely—whatever it was, he would not allow it to harm Wynn Powe.

"Oh, holy gods on garlic toast."

Wynn watched Knox disappear into what looked almost like a heat mirage in the corner and wanted to scream in frustration. Then she looked at the three nasty black mini demons eyeing her like lunch and screamed for an entirely different reason. What the hell! The Guardian had left her alone with the minions of the Seven? And she was supposed to do what? Invite them to a game of canasta until Knox got back from his impromptu extra-planar vacation?

Fat ever-loving chance!

With no *Harry Potter* spells or wand handy, Wynn relied on instinct. Drawing back her injured foot, since it wouldn't support her weight anyway, she channeled her inner soccer player and let fly right into the nearest *hhissih*'s repulsive little belly. The thing let out a horrible screech that muffled her own cry of pain, but the sound was abruptly cut off when it sailed through the same portal that Knox had gone through.

Good. Let the Guardian deal with the little shit. That was supposed to be his job, wasn't it?

Unfortunately, the remaining creatures seemed to take exception to the loss of their compatriot. They took up the screech where the first one had left off and began closing in on Wynn. Hopping backward, she bumped into the front of Bran's desk and realized she had let

herself be backed into a corner. Cursing, she grabbed
the only useful item in reach and found herself warding
off the malevolent mini demons with the straight-
backed chair her brother used with his desk.

Great, now all she needed was a safari hat and a bull-
whip, and she could join the circus as a new take on lion
taming. *See the Magnificent Mistress of Magic Bravely
Face Down the Horrible* Hhissih *from Hell!* She ought
to get top billing for that act.

The monsters made practice lunges at her, chittering
and clacking and screeching when she shoved the legs
of the chair in their faces—or at least in the places where
their faces should have been. She couldn't really describe
the noises these things made. It sounded like a Foley
artist had gotten drunk in the recording studio and com-
bined the sound effects for scurrying cockroaches,
growling dogs, screaming owls, and clicking beetles into
one highly disturbing soundtrack. It made Wynn's skin
crawl.

Glancing over at the place where Knox and the first
hhissih had disappeared, Wynn saw only the same
strange shimmer, and damn it if it didn't appear to be
fainter than it had a moment ago. If the Guardian got
himself trapped in some other dimension and left her
here to get eaten alive by demonic tick–hyena hybrids,
she was going to kill him. Even if she died, she'd wait
to be reincarnated, then roll on up in her stroller and stab
him in the eye with her pacifier, if that's what it took.
The Guardian would pay.

Frankly, though, Wynn would prefer not to get killed
in the first place. Keeping the chair between her and the
creatures, she reached behind her for the drawer that had

started this whole mess and fumbled it open. After all, the trap had already been sprung. What more harm could she do?

Her hand searched blindly through the drawer's jumbled contents, brushing aside paper clips, getting jabbed by thumbtacks, and skipping over what felt like a deck of card or an outdated and discarded cell phone. Pushing the items aside, she patted through more detritus. She wasn't certain what she was looking for, since a sharp pencil or a letter opener might count as a weapon, but it would require her to get a lot closer to the *hhissih* than she found acceptable. She knew for certain she wouldn't find a gun in Bran's desk, and since she had no idea if a bullet would even work against a demonic minion, she didn't wish for one.

Just as her fingers closed around a smooth, hard cylinder about twice the size of a lipstick case, the *hhissih* to Wynn's left either lost patience or got too hungry to wait for its next meal. The thing darted forward, dodging Wynn's defensive thrust of the chair and managed to swipe its claws across her lower leg. Her jeans all but melted under the attack of the razor-sharp implements, and she felt a line of fire dance across her skin.

Damn it, the little shit had gotten her uninjured ankle. Great, now she could limp on both legs at the same time. Or was that just called falling down?

Hissing at the burning pain, Wynn brought the chair down on the monster's head and grunted in satisfaction when it yelped and darted backward. Using the chair as a crutch, she managed to boost herself up onto the surface of the desk and chanced a quick glance down at the small bottle she had pulled from the desk drawer. When she saw it, she wished her brother were here so she could give him a big fat kiss right on the lips. He had tucked away a jar of her own special version of goofer dust with his rubber bands and old gas station receipts.

Goofer dust proper belonged to the realm of hoodoo, which Wynn made no claims to practicing, but she did like to consider herself a modern and open-minded witch. Basically that boiled down to a more polite way of saying she was willing to borrow or steal any idea she thought would work in her own practice. In hoodoo, goofer dust usually—though not always—was blended from nasty stuff and made for a nasty purpose. Practitioners used ingredients like grave dust, powdered snakeskins, ground-up bones, and even dried manure to cause harm or illness to the target. Wynn, however, had come up with a unique version of the substance that she found effectively turned that ill intent into something that only harmed malevolent energy.

In the past, she'd only had cause to use it on negative spirits, since running into demons and their minions counted as a new experience for her. She could only hope it proved as effective on the *hhissih* as it had on poltergeists and shadow people.

Taking her eyes off the nasties for a split second, she uncorked the bottle, shook some of the powder into her palm, and blew a stream of air into the miniature pile. The puff lifted the dust and sent it billowing straight into the non-face of the black menace.

She caught the thing in mid-leap. Apparently, it had decided it had waited long enough, and the best way to get through her chair-leg defense was to go over it. For the space of a heartbeat, she watched in horror as it continued to advance, coming for her with claws and fangs and evil intent. Then, abruptly, it froze and dropped smoking and screeching to the ground.

Adrenaline and triumph rushed through her. Quickly she palmed more dust and blew a second lungful at the remaining *hhissih*. It, too, let loose an awful, high-pitched howl before it fell. Within seconds, nothing remained of the beasts but two gently smoking piles of stinking ash.

Wynn slumped on top of the desk, trying to convince her galloping heartbeat to ease off before she went into cardiac arrest. Her breath continued to stutter in and out in ragged pants, and she felt cold and clammy with the residue of panicked sweat drying on her skin. She'd never felt so frightened in her entire life, not even when she'd stood in a small, magically diseased island in the St. Lawrence River looking at an entire cell of *nocturnis* cultists. Then she'd had two Wardens and two powerful Guardians by her side. Despite the danger, she hadn't been alone, and she'd been so busy focusing on releasing Fil from her bondage that she hadn't had time to get scared.

Today, she'd had the time. And the inclination. And three very damned good reasons.

Without warning the shimmering air in the corner began to pulsate, appearing almost to bow out like a bubble of pressure. Wynn watched in horror, clutching the remaining goofer dust in one hand, just hoping whatever came out of that portal reacted to the magical powder the same way the *hhissih* had.

She felt a giant, soundless pop, like a huge break in the air pressure, and the bubble burst, spewing forth a disheveled Guardian in full battle mode. The portal winked out instantly, leaving Knox standing on her brother's carpet, wings quivering and fangs flashing. A black, liquid substance dripped off his claws and his chin, great smears of it coating his skin wherever it remained uncovered by the kilted loincloth all the Guardians wore.

Wynn stared at him for a second, waiting for her brain to catch up to the fact that this was a Guardian, not some noxious new demon beast intent on devouring her flesh. When the understanding finally sank in, her stare turned into a furious glower.

With her free hand, she picked up the nearest object—a stress ball in the shape of a cartoon germ she'd given her brother as a joke—and hurled it with all her strength straight at the Guardian's head. Since she used her off hand, the ball missed his eye, bounced off his shoulder, and tumbled to the floor, where it rolled quickly beneath a side table.

Even inanimate objects knew when to get out of the line of fire.

"You useless, disappearing, woman-deserting, job-not-doing, leave-the-human-here-to-die *asshole*!" she bellowed.

Knox eyed her impassively. "You are upset." His voice remained flat and uninflected. "Did something harm you?"

"Did something *harm* me? Well, it certainly gave things the old college try, boulder brain! Did you forget that you left me alone with three fucking demon spawn, you dip-twaddle? Was I not supposed to get harmed?"

"The *hhissih* represented a much smaller threat than

the creature attempting to move through the portal," he said, dropping his gaze to examine her wound. His brows drew together, but he didn't so much as wince at the blackened edges and sluggish bleeding. "My priority was to keep you alive, so I attacked the *shedim*. I knew the *hhissih* would be no match for you. Did you not dispatch one through the portal after me?"

Wynn opened her mouth to continue yelling, but his words finally penetrated her fear-driven rage. No match for her? Shit, how was she supposed to argue about being left to save herself when he informed her so matter-of-factly that he had every confidence in her ability to do just that? His vote of confidence hadn't just taken the wind out of her sails; it had furled them tight and dropped anchor for good measure. If just felt hypocritical to attack him for *not* treating her like some helpless, swooning damsel in distress.

But damn it, there had been a moment there when she actually *had* wanted to swoon.

"Fine," she snapped, not quite ready to give up her annoyance. "I dealt with the other two as well, in case you're interested. What did you go after, anyway? I never even caught a glimpse of it."

"Be glad you did not." Face grim, Knox blinked back into his human form, somehow managing to leave the nasty black drops—which she kind of assumed equaled the blood of something icky—behind in the transition. "The *shedim* are fierce and a thousand times more deadly than an entire herd of *hhissih*. I dispatched it, but it fought me with determination. It wanted badly to cross into this realm and taste human flesh."

"Um, ew. Thanks for that mental picture." Wynn

shuddered. "Did you manage to find anything out from it before you eviscerated it, or whatever you did to kill it?"

"I took its head. *Shedim* are difficult to kill in any other manner. They can regrow all other limbs if they are removed, and they can continue to fight even if every organ in their body is destroyed."

"Yeah, big ew. So what did you find out?"

The Guardian eyed her strangely. "I killed it, witch, I did not waste time in conversation with the creature."

"But if you didn't ask it any questions, how are we supposed to figure out who set the trap on Bran's desk? Because I'm pretty damned sure it wasn't my brother."

"Of course not. The *nocturnis* set the trap, of course. There is no doubt of that."

Wynn rolled her eyes and nodded with exaggerated motions. "Yes, I get that, but unless we find out the names or descriptions of an individual, we can't track them down, can we? We need information, quick draw. Isn't that what we came here to find?"

Knox had the grace to look vaguely uncomfortable. "I was not thinking of that. The *shedim* nearly crossed over. I could not allow it to harm you."

He fixed her with a look so intense, it made Wynn's breath catch in her throat. His black gaze pinned her in place, and she felt her heart rate speed up in response. Why did the Guardian do this to her? He made her feel like an awkward teen in front of the football captain.

Desperately, she dropped her gaze and tried to calm herself. She had no intention of bonding to a Guardian like Ella and Fil had done. In fact, she had no intention of remaining a Warden any longer than she had to. Somehow nearly thirty years of being discriminated against and told she wasn't good enough had sort of soured her on the idea.

Wynn would do what she had to do to get through the impending battle and then—you know, providing she lived through it—she intended to go right back to her comfortable old life where she was a witch, and the snobbish men were the Wardens, and never the twain did meet. Let them replace her with a man when this was all over. It would hurt a lot less if she was the one to leave, and if she flipped them the bird on the way out.

After a moment of fraught silence, she managed a business-like tone and moved to slide off the desk. "Fine. In that case, I guess we should get back to work. We came here to go through Bran's things, so that's what we'll do. You take the right-hand drawers, I'll take the left, and we'll meet up at the piles on top. Okay?"

The question ended in a pained yelp when Wynn put her feet on the floor and attempted to support her own weight. Between her sprained ankle on one side, further aggravated when she'd punted a certain *hhissih* into another dimension, and the wound left behind on her other lower leg by the second monster, her legs offered her all the support of overcooked spaghetti. They buckled under her, and she would have landed hard on the wooden floor if Knox hadn't darted forward and caught her in his huge, hard hands.

"Owowow!" she chanted through clenched teeth. She hadn't realized how badly she hurt until she'd moved and put weight on her abused limbs.

She also hadn't realized what it would feel like the first time Knox put his hands on her. Oh, she'd gripped his clawed, bestial paw when she'd been in his other form and she'd been trying to get him into her car and away from the scene of the crime in Lake Forest, but he hadn't touched her. He'd simply let her drag him along like a big stuffed animal. This time, he gripped her in return, his fingers closing around her waist to support her. His human hands gripped her gently but firmly, and the feel of his thumbs pressing into her stomach made things inside her clench and then go soft and hot and liquid.

Goddess, where did she get off being attracted to someone who wasn't even human, who was like the worst choice in the world for a lover, especially for a slightly bitter witch with a chip on her shoulder? It made no sense, but apparently no one had explained that to her endocrine system. One touch—a touch meant to assist, by the way, *not* to arouse—and her hormones all of a sudden took on the force and speed of a tsunami. What the heck was wrong with her?

And did she have time to make a list?

"Show me your injury," Knox growled, scowling down at her with his brows drawn together and his mouth set in grim lines. He looked like some kind of biker thug, with his shaved head, heavy musculature, and dark clothing. Wrap the man in some leather, slap on a goatee, have him straddle a Harley, and he'd look like he'd just ridden off the set of *Sons of Anarchy*. Charlie Hunnam's pretty, wavy locks had nothing on this guy.

Wynn opened her mouth to dismiss his request, to tell him it wasn't so bad. A lame excuse danced on the top of her tongue, but she couldn't force the words out. She'd be lying, and he'd know she was lying the minute he let her go. She couldn't even walk at the moment, so pretending she was fine just so she could assert some independence would be a pretty stupid move.

"I can't reach it," she murmured instead, and Knox turned to carry her back through the arch into the living room. He set her gently on the sofa and crouched at her feet.

"Show me," he repeated, his voice softer, but no less authoritative.

Reaching down, Wynn grasped the torn bottom of her jeans and rolled the denim up almost to her knee. There on her left calf, a long painful gash curled around her leg from about halfway down her shin on the right to just above her ankle on the left. The wound seeped blood along its shallow length, but more disturbing was the way the skin at the edges of the cut had begun to turn black with a faint, underlying tone of sickly green.

She felt herself go pale, literally felt the blood rush out of her head, and the room began to spin. Desperately, she drew in air and immediately leaned forward until her forehead rested against her right knee. She let out a soft moan and fought back the urge to let the faintness sweep her away.

Knox cursed, a deep, harsh sound in a language she didn't understand. It sounded tinny in her ears, but she caught the gist.

"The *hhissih* released its venom," he said grimly. "The wound is poisoned. We need to get you to a healer, someone familiar with demonic creatures. We need a Warden."

Wynn sucked in a shuddering breath and pushed hard

at the grayness at the edge of her vision. She didn't have time to pass out, damn it, and she sure as hell wasn't going to do it in front of the Guardian.

"Yeah, well, Bran's not here, is he?" she snapped, then immediately regretted it. "I'm sorry. He was the only Warden I know of in the city proper." Then memory teased at the corner of her mind, and she spoke again. "At least, he was the only active Warden. Maybe we can try someone else . . ."

"Who?" he demanded.

Carefully, hands and consciousness equally shaky, Wynn pushed herself back into a sitting position and met the Guardian's fierce gaze.

"My uncle Griffin," she said. "He was a Warden, but there was, um, an incident, and he had to retire, but he's the only one I know of who even comes close."

Knox frowned. "Wardens do not retire. They serve from the moment they begin training until the day of their death."

"Mostly, yes. But this is an unusual circumstance. Uncle Griff was never your average Warden, but if this thing's poison is going to kill me, he's definitely the one we should go to."

He held her gaze briefly, seeming to search for something in her eyes or her expression; then he nodded once and stood. "Very well. If this is who can help you, then we will go to him now."

He reached down and scooped Wynn up, holding her against his chest as he strode for the door. The sudden change of position brought back another rush of dizziness, but she fought it down. It felt so weird to be carried, a sensation she hadn't experienced since she'd been a tiny girl, but Knox's embrace felt nothing like her parents'. Even when he leaned down and pressed a kiss to her forehead, she didn't mistake a hint of the gesture for anything parental.

"You will tell me where to find your uncle, and when he has healed you, we will have a discussion, little witch." His voice rumbled out of his chest, and she could feel the vibrations through her skin. It sank into her bones like the heat from a bath and warmed her just as thoroughly. "You will always tell me when you are in need of care, do you understand? You will not wait until you collapse to alert me to your injuries. Never."

Still reeling from the touch of his lips to her skin, Wynn simply nodded and let herself go limp in his arms. Sometimes, it paid not to argue, even if it just meant saving up her strength for the next fight. She had a feeling more were headed her way. In fact, she suspected that she could cross running with the bulls in Pamplona off her bucket list. Chances were, she'd know what that felt like before too much longer, only it wouldn't be bulls chasing her, and broken bones would be the least of her worries.

Was it even possible to outrun the end of the world? And did she really have to be the one to find out?

Chapter Six

Unlike the rest of the Llewellyn Powe clan, Griffin Llewellyn had eschewed the old neighborhood of Dunning and headed as far south as Montclare, a whopping distance of under two miles away. His small home occupied a lot in the middle of a quiet street, complete with speed bumps that made Knox curse every time he hit one, which was often.

If she hadn't been gritting her teeth against the pain the jarring caused her, Wynn might have laughed at Knox's griping even as she marveled at the speed with which he had mastered the skill of driving. There had been no way she could have operated the brake and gas with her injured ankles, so she'd been forced to hand Knox the keys to her Toyota. He'd listened carefully to her instructions, then proceeded to guide the small car through the midday traffic with efficiency if not much aplomb. She could tell that if he were to take on the task very often, he'd work himself up to an epic case of road rage in record time.

"Right there." She raised her arm and pointed to the small house with the white porch and the brown shingles on the far side of the street. "You can pull into the driveway, just keep to the left."

Knox complied, parking the car, then coming around to lift her from the passenger seat without a word. He didn't even breathe hard as he toted her across the postage-stamp front lawn and up the brief set of steps to the door. Instead he held her snugly and nodded at the bell. "Alert your uncle that we are here. Your wound must be seen to quickly."

She had to lean forward to reach, but she'd barely lifted her finger from the button before she heard the shuffling of slippered feet on the floorboards in the hall. An instant later the front door opened and her uncle peered around the edge, his gray-streaked auburn hair disheveled and his dark-rimmed glasses balanced crookedly on his nose.

"I was wondering when you'd get here, young lady." He frowned and stepped back to swing the door wide. "Come in, come in. Onto the couch with you, so I can get a good look at this little mess you've gotten yourself into. Hurry up. Let's go."

He waved Knox inside and into the living room to the left of the entry. The Guardian appeared more curious than shocked by the man's rumpled appearance and odd behavior, and Wynn found herself grateful for that. For the last few years, a lot of people had started to shy away from Uncle Griffin, even people who had known him for years, and that bugged Wynn. He was the same sweet, loving man he'd always been, after all. It was just that these days his . . . eccentricities didn't do quite as good a job at blending into the background. They tended to stare people right in the face, and that made some of them nervous. Knox barely even blinked.

At the moment, Griffin looked like a cross between an absentminded professor and an escapee from a hospital ward. In addition to his disheveled hair and crooked glasses, he sported at least three or four days' worth of stubble on his ruddy cheeks. He had dressed, if you could call it that, in a pair of worn flannel pajama pants in a scarlet plaid pattern, topped with a faded University of Chicago T-shirt that had probably started off in the college's customary maroon but now looked more like a pale dusty-brick color. Over that he wore a knee-length bathrobe in a clashing plaid of cream, green, and gray. On his feet, shearling scuffs that had seen better days (probably during the Reagan administration) mostly covered up a pair of wool socks in the shade of muddy gray only achieved by failing to properly sort laundry.

Knox appeared not even to notice. He followed the man's instructions, gently depositing Wynn onto the center of a battered sofa with tweedy brown cushions and a brightly colored, hand-knitted Afghan draped haphazardly over the back. Wynn couldn't quite bite back the hiss as her sprained ankle bumped against the edge of the coffee table, and Knox mumbled another curse.

"Are you all right, little witch? Did I cause you some further injury with my clumsiness?"

"No, it's fine." She tried to reassure him, but her uncle shooed him away—literally made shooing motions with his hands at the hulking warrior—and took a seat on the coffee table in front of Wynn.

"Well, let's take a look at this, hm?" Griffin reached

for his niece's left foot and lifted it gently into his lap. "This is the right one, isn't it? I mean the correct one." He chuckled. "I *do* still know my right from my left, I promise. No matter what anyone says."

Wynn frowned. It was the correct foot, the one wounded by the *hhissih,* but she hadn't expected her uncle to know that. She hadn't even expected him to know she was hurt, but when he'd answered the door, he'd already seemed like he'd been expecting them to show up. Which was weird, since she hadn't spoken to him in weeks, definitely not since she'd arrived back in Chicago.

"That's the one," she confirmed, smiling at him despite the frown she couldn't quite smooth away from her brow. "How did you know, Uncle Griff? How did you know we were even coming here today?"

Griffin had eased back the hem of her jeans and angled her foot toward the light so he could examine the blackened gash. He made soothing noises when she tensed, ignoring the way the hovering Guardian stiffened every time Wynn expressed even the slightest discomfort.

"I saw you, of course," the older man explained. "I was in my workroom trying to fix that problem I've been having with my cuneiform translation spell when I felt that trap zap you. I saw the *hhissih.* Nasty little varmints, and I saw your friend here disappear." Griffin looked up to glare at Knox over his glasses. "I'm assuming you had a good reason for leaving my niece alone with three angry demon spawn, young man."

Despite Wynn's own reaction to that earlier, she felt her face heat at her uncle's behavior. "Uncle Griff, I was fine, but Knox isn't a young man. He's a—"

"A Guardian, I know," Griffin finished, turning back to her leg. "But he's still young to me. Heck, he's young to you, too. I'm surprised he's not still casting off granite dust, he's so new."

Wynn blinked at her uncle. "How did you know that?"

"Well, I saw that, too, didn't I? I see a few interesting things these days whenever I'm not looking." He set her foot down on the edge of the coffee table and patted her knee. "I need to get some supplies from my workroom if I'm going to tackle that. You and your pet rock can wait right here."

He bustled out of the room without sparing either of them so much as a backward glance.

"Pet rock?" Knox repeated, his tone suspiciously bland.

Wynn shrugged and rubbed one hand nervously against the rough weave of the sofa cushions. "Uncle Griffin is . . . a little different."

"I can see that. It perhaps explains why he is no longer a Warden, but it does not explain how he became one in the first place."

She sighed. "He wasn't always like this, and trust me, if the Guild had let him stay, he'd still be a Warden today. When I say he retired, I should have said it was a forced retirement. They booted him out, gave him no choice. He was devastated."

Knox frowned. "I have no recollection of such a thing having ever happened in all the centuries of the Guild's existence."

"Yeah? Well, how would you know? You're like a day old."

"I might be newly summoned, but I have access to

the collective memory of our kind. I know all of the history of the Guild of Wardens, as well as of the Guardians ourselves, and I know that never before has a Warden been relieved of his duties for anything less than the betrayal of his oaths. Is that what your uncle did?"

"Of course not." Wynn glared up at him, furious that he would even imply such a thing. "How dare you! My uncle has an enormous sense of honor, and being a Warden was a family legacy he took a lot of pride in. He loved his job. He just—"

"I just made a really stupid mistake."

Griffin reappeared in the entrance to the living room with an armful of bottles, tins, and other assorted items. Sighing, he dropped them all onto the coffee table and looked at his guests with an expression of sadness and regret pulling at his features.

"It's sweet of you to defend me, Wynn-ding, but I know better than anyone else that I got myself into this mess." The man resumed his seat on the tabletop and reached again for his niece's foot. "I made the wrong choices, and it's up to me to live with the consequences."

Griffin drew a soft white cloth and a corked bottle of what looked like water from the things on the table. He wet the fabric and began to clean Wynn's wound as he spoke.

"You're not blind, and I don't think the Light would send us a stupid Guardian, so I'm sure you've noticed that my niece is a witch. If you've met her mother, you'll have seen that her mother is one, too."

Knox grunted. "I have. They share a similar energy profile, though I would guess they each possess different strengths."

Griffin nodded. "Like I said, not dumb. All the women in our family are witches. That's the way it's always been, and I imagine that's the way it'll always be. I've heard stories of the occasional girl baby born without much more than a streak of particularly good luck, but they're always the exception, and always the result of a bad match between the parents. The Llewellyn women breed true."

Wynn listened to her uncle's story and tried not to whimper as the blessed water began to burn while it washed over her injury. It felt almost like acid being poured onto her skin. She looked down, expecting to see it bubble and froth like some chemical experiment gone wrong, but she saw nothing unusual. Damn it, if she was going to suffer, she should at least get some visible proof to point to when people asked how she felt.

Knox took a good look at her face and shifted, stepping forward to stand beside her right shoulder. Reaching down, he lifted her hand in his and pried open her clenched fist. Pressing their palms together, he squeezed gently and gave her a small nod. She hoped he meant that she could squeeze back, because that's exactly what she did. Every time the blessed water scorched across the wound, she squeezed the Guardian's hand tighter until if he'd been human, she'd have feared she was hurting him. Luckily, he was a quite a long way from human. She figured he could take it.

She knew her uncle saw their hands link, but he didn't look up, just set aside the water and reached for another bottle. She hoped to the Goddess this one contained something that wouldn't make her feel as if she were being sliced open all over again.

"So, I grew up surrounded by witches, powerful women, but I never had even a fraction of the magic they had," Griffin continued. "I mean, I had enough for the Guild to accept me as a trainee, don't get me wrong, and I made a pretty quick study when it came to learning how to use what I had. The Guild helped me out, taught me how to tap into the power of the Light so that I could perform whatever spells were necessary for me to do my job. But I just kept thinking back to my mother and my sister and my aunts and my grandmother, and I couldn't help but remember how easy they all made it look. All of these women around me didn't just *do* magic, they *were* magic."

"Uncle Griff, why didn't you ever tell us you felt that way?" Wynn reached out with her free hand and squeezed her uncle's shoulder.

"Heavens no, I couldn't do that. Explain that I spent my life eaten up with jealousy for the people I loved most in the world?" He shuddered and made a face. "No one wants to shed that kind of light on themselves, sweetheart. We all want to look like we're good people, even when we're consumed by bad thoughts."

Wynn squeezed harder and gave him a stern look. "None of that makes you a bad person, Uncle Griffin. It makes you human. Don't you think I've spent my life jealous of Bran because he got to be a Warden instead of me? I wanted to join the Guild so badly, but they never let me in. Does that make me a lousy person?"

"Of course not, but it doesn't make me look any better in comparison." Griffin set aside the second bottle and reached for a bowl, into which he poured regular water from a small pitcher and the contents of several small plastic bags. "I knew you wished you could use your talents for the sake of the Guild, and I knew there had to have been other women in our family who felt the same way, but it didn't stop me from wishing I had what they did. So I tried to get that power for myself."

Wynn frowned as she watched her uncle mix the contents of the bowl into a thick paste that he began spreading over a length of gauzy fabric. "What do you mean, you tried to get it for yourself?"

His mouth quirked in a wry half smile. "Don't worry, pumpkin, I was never so far gone that I actually tried to steal anyone's power. I was jealous, but not evil. I figured that the secret to the Llewellyn women's power had to be encoded into their DNA, specifically in the pairing of the double X chromosomes. Having two copies must somehow unlock the magical potential in the genes. I figured if I could just understand how that worked, I would be able to find a way to unlock it in my own X chromosome. Like tapping into an underground water source—I knew it had to be there, so all I needed to do was figure out how and where to sink the well."

Knox made that unhappy rumbling noise in his throat, like a dog growling, and scowled down at Griffin. "What did you do, human?"

The older man sighed and laid the poultice he'd created over the wound in Wynn's leg, securing it with more gauze to bind it in place.

"I came up with a spell," he admitted after a long, uncomfortable pause. "I thought I could break down the barriers that held the magical potential in place and let it out. Into me. But I made a mistake."

Wynn shook her head. "Why didn't you ever tell us

this? We thought the Guild had betrayed you, kicked you out because your magic started to become . . . unreliable."

"That's exactly what happened, pumpkin. And I didn't tell you for the same reason I already mentioned—I didn't want you and your mother to know how jealous and shallow and selfish I'd been. I couldn't stand to have you look at me with pity or, even worse, with anger."

He took a deep breath and wiped his hands clean on a scrap of cloth. "The spell backfired. Instead of breaking down the barriers keeping the magic contained in the X chromosome, it erected all sorts of new barriers against tapping into the magic of the Light, the way the Guild had trained me to do. It's like every time I try to cast a spell now, the magic has to go through a maze to get to me. Sometimes it makes its way through without a problem, but sometimes it gets lost and nothing happens. And sometimes it smacks up hard into a dead end, and whatever I was trying to do goes haywire. And for a really fun twist, every once in a while the spell doesn't work but I get a vision instead, like I had of you two. No matter how you look at it, magically, I'm completely unreliable. Useless."

The words penetrated only a little at a time, like tea leaves cast on top of water—they absorbed the liquid slowly before gradually sinking to the bottom. Wynn thought back to the first time her uncle had told her about leaving the Guild. He had lied, obviously, but she couldn't hold on to anger. Instead she just felt sad and a bit disappointed.

"You told us you were forced into retirement after an assignment went wrong," she finally said, speaking softly as she tried to keep any hint of accusation from tainting her tone. "We thought they were being so unfair to you."

"I know, Wynn-ding, and I'm sorry." Griffin bent his head and busied his hands gathering together his supplies. "It was always my fault that they set me aside. I brought it on myself."

"You are wrong."

Knox's voice dropped like a stone into the awkward atmosphere. Both humans turned to him with surprise in their expressions. Wynn thought her uncle had almost forgotten the Guardian was there, but Wynn had simply not expected an opinion from him that didn't support the Guild's position.

"What do you mean?" she asked.

Knox kept his focus on her uncle. "I do not debate your responsibility for your own predicament, human. Clearly you did start in motion the events that led to the damage your abilities have incurred, but you are not to blame for the actions of the Guild toward you. Those were wrong, and the Guild alone must bear responsibility."

"The Guild was wrong?"

Griffin sounded as surprised by that pronouncement as Wynn felt. From everything she had ever read or heard or assumed, the Guardians and the Guild had always moved in lockstep, each providing the other with unconditional support. It had seemed necessary for the entire operation. They needed to maintain a solid front against the machinations of their enemies. But now a Guardian, regardless of how long he had existed, had voiced an opinion of dissent? How weird was that?

"Of course they were," Knox affirmed with impatience. "It might be true that certain functions within the Guild require the reliable use of magic to perform—serving one of my brothers, for instance; magic is required to oversee their waking, sleeping, and summoning. But many other duties exist that would not suffer for the lack of spell-casting skills. Wardens are scholars, the keepers of the knowledge of our kind. This requires many, many hours of record keeping, organization, research, and other mundane tasks."

He fixed his attention on Griffin. "You swore an oath to serve the Guild for the remainder of your life, and they should honor that oath by valuing your service, no matter what form it takes. You should simply have been assigned to duties more suited to your change in abilities, not tossed out of the Guild as if you no longer served any purpose whatsoever in their ranks."

Wonder began to tug at the corners of Wynn's mouth. "That's almost exactly what I said when Uncle Griff told us he'd been retired. Only, you know, a little less formally."

Knox nodded at her. "You have a surprisingly logical mind, for a human. And a female. And a witch."

The smile faded before it ever emerged. "Gee, I'm flattered," she snapped.

The Guardian ignored her. "Wynn has told me that the Guild headquarters were destroyed and most of the Wardens gone into hiding. What can you tell me of this? Why have you not disappeared as well?"

Griffin shrugged. "Why bother? The Wardens who have gone underground are in fear for their lives. They believe the *nocturnis* are attempting to exterminate them in order to get them out of the way for some huge strike against the Guardians. Since my powers have become so unreliable, no one perceives me as a threat anymore. I have no reason to hide. No one is coming after a crazy old man who can't even maintain a simple illumination spell, when he can cast one at all."

Wynn and Knox exchanged glances.

"Uncle Griffin," she said gently, "we have reason to believe that those Wardens are right. The Order is planning something big—in fact, they've already started on it. The Guild, the Guardians . . . heck, the whole world is in very real danger. Going into hiding might not be a bad idea, even for you."

For the first time since beginning his confession, Griffin met his niece's gaze straight-on, his forehead creased in a frown. "What does that mean, Wynn? What are you talking about?"

"I . . . discovered a few things about the Order while I was in Montreal, Uncle Griff. In fact, I had a run-in with some *nocturnis* that proved to be very enlightening. And pretty scary, too."

"Did they hurt you?" Griffin demanded, surging to his feet as if the villains were right there, just waiting to be beaten up for touching a member of his family.

"I'm fine," Wynn soothed. "Well, aside from what you just saw, but things really are pretty bad out there. There's a lot that's been happening that we've all been overlooking. It's time to start paying attention." She gestured toward Knox, looming over the both of them with his forbidding scowl, his bulky arms crossed over his powerful chest. "Hence the reappearance of a Guardian. Well, of three Guardians, really."

Griffin went very pale, very quickly. As the color leached from his face, he sank almost bonelessly back onto the coffee table. "Three Guardian have awakened? Wynn, tell me what's going on. Please. Maybe there's some way I can help."

"Oh, we need your help, all right, but this is a long story, and it might take a while. Do you have anything to drink? And maybe an ibuprofen? I kind of have a headache, to go along with all the other aches, and by the time I'm done filling you in, I wouldn't be surprised if you have one, too."

Chapter Seven

It took hours to get the whole story out, as well as about a gallon of tea, another gallon of soda pop—which Knox declared appalling after one brief taste—and half a dozen reheated pasties. It might have gone faster, but Griffin had a lot of questions. Frankly, Wynn didn't blame him. She had a lot of questions herself, and she was caught up right in the middle of the whole damned mess.

When she finally finished the story with her version of the attack in Bran's apartment and their arrival on her uncle's doorstep, she felt wrung out, Knox looked grimmer than the Reaper, and Griffin had his face propped on his palm with his fingers fisted in his already disheveled hair.

"This is a bad thing, Wynn-dixie," he muttered, shaking his head and wincing every time the movement yanked at his own hair. "This is a very, very bad thing."

"Yeah. We figured that much out on our own, actually."

"There hasn't been one of the Seven to reach this plane since the fourteenth century. You've heard of the Black Death, right? Well only a fraction of those deaths were actually caused by the plague virus. Most of the millions fell at the hands of Shaab-na."

"The Unclean," Knox agreed. "It enjoys spreading disease and watching humanity suffer as they multiply its contagion among themselves."

Wynn shuddered. "That's . . . pretty gross. But that wasn't the one we think they brought through. Fil's mark and all the rest pointed to one called Uhlthor."

"The Defiler." Griffin made a face. "Not really much of an improvement. That one started the fall of the Roman Empire before the Guardians turned him back, and he hadn't even made it all the way through to this plane."

"Ugh. Why do these demons even still exist? Why didn't the Guardians simply destroy them the first time, instead of locking them up in some sort of interdimensional prisons? I mean, they had to know the Seven would continue to make trouble over the centuries. Why not just take care of them once and for all?"

"The Seven cannot be destroyed. Not by any means." Knox cupped his large hands around his cup of water and brooded. "They are the embodiment of the Darkness. There has always been Darkness, just as there has always been Light. Neither can ever be completely destroyed, only driven away or contained, because neither can exist without the other. Without Darkness, there is no Light, and vice versa."

Wynn made a face. "That sounds like a pretty lousy deal to me. It would be a lot simpler not to have the threat of the end of the world hanging over our heads for the rest of eternity."

Knox looked at her, his mouth quirking. "But if there were no threat, there would be no Guardians, little witch. Would you prefer that I did not exist as well?"

She knew the question was meant to tease her—and hey, who knew the Guardians could have a sense of humor?—but something inside her took it way too seriously. It wailed in protest at the idea of no Knox, and Wynn had to step on it hard to keep it from breaking out.

What was happening to her? Sure, hearing the big guy take a stand against the Guild made him all the more attractive to her. (Did that really have to be possible, by the way? She had already felt the water rising over her head as it was.) But he still couldn't erase his ties to the entire organization. He was a Guardian, and the Guardians needed the Guild as much as the Guild needed the Guardians. They were inextricably entwined, which meant neither of them could ever be on her side.

She tamped down the butterflies his words had set loose in her belly and turned back to her uncle. "Well, then, I guess the only good thing to come out of this conversation so far is Uncle Griff. Before this, I was afraid to ask you for your advice and help with any of this. I didn't want to bring up something that might be painful, and honestly, the way you've been behaving over the last couple of years . . ."

She blushed and looked away. How was she supposed to tell her uncle that they had all believed he was losing his marbles? He'd become so reclusive, and his behavior so erratic, it had seemed almost as if he had begun to sink into senility. That he remained lucid and still in possession of his memories and training made him an asset they desperately needed.

"No, don't be embarrassed, pumpkin," he said, grasping her hand in his. "I completely understand. I've been in a rough place, but getting this all off my chest has helped enormously. I'm sorry I led you to believe you couldn't rely on my help when you needed it, but I hope that's changed now. I want to do whatever I can to help you face this threat. I mean that."

Wynn squeezed his hand in return. "I know you do, Uncle Griff. Thanks."

She managed a grin when she thought about someone else who would be pretty excited to have an actual, trained Warden on their side, no matter how little magic he could actually perform. "I can definitely promise that Ella especially is going to love meeting you. She's been trying to train herself as a Warden with basically nothing more than a few books and some common sense. Having you to answer her questions is going to make her day."

"However I can help."

Wynn actually managed a laugh. "Well, now that you mention it . . ."

"Tell me."

"We sprang that trap today because we went to Bran's place looking for some more information. The police brought this to Mom yesterday." Shifting, Wynn reached into her pocket, pulled out her copy of her brother's list, and showed it to her uncle. "Knox thinks—and I have to agree with him—that for him to be summoned to replace a destroyed Guardian means something big must be coming to Chicago. It fits the pattern of what happened with Kees and Spar in Vancouver and Montreal. The problem is that we have no idea what it might be, and we thought maybe Bran might have been looking into something that could point us in the right direction."

Griffin scanned the list, his brows furrowed. "Your brother never mentioned this to me, but things weren't the same between us before he left. Not since I left the Guild. I'm not certain what any of this means, but I'm more than willing to do a little digging and see what I come up with."

Disappointed, Wynn grimaced. "Thanks. Whatever you find will be more than we have right now."

She had been hoping that her uncle knew something that could keep them moving forward. She hated feeling like she was just sitting around and twiddling her thumbs. Of course, considering she could barely stand on her own two feet at the moment, maybe that was all she was good for. Despite the painkillers she had downed, her sprained ankle still ached like a sore tooth, although the pain in her head had faded to a dull throb. Curiously, the fresh gash in her leg pained her the least of all her injuries.

Twisting in her chair, she stuck out her foot and examined the bandaged limb. Her uncle followed her gaze.

"How does it feel?" he asked.

"Better," she admitted, faintly surprised. "When you were treating it, it felt like it was packed with red-hot coals, but now I can barely feel it."

"The poultice is drawing out the poison. It needs to stay on until dark, then you can remove it and burn it. If the blackness is gone from around the edges of the skin, you can just start treating it like any other cut. If not, I'll apply another round of the poultice. Even if the poison is gone, expect it to take a bit longer than normal to heal. *Hhissih* venom is nasty stuff. Stitches probably aren't strictly necessary, but once the poison's gone, you can go get it sewn up if you prefer."

Right, because letting someone come at her skin with a needle and thread—or worse, a stapler—always made the top of her to-do list. Wynn shook her head. "I'm sure it'll be fine."

A yawn ambushed her, stretching her jaw almost to the breaking point, and her hand shot up to cover her mouth. "Sorry. I don't know why I'm so tired. It's barely four o'clock."

Knox stood and crossed to scoop her out of her chair. She couldn't tell if it was the sudden change in altitude that made her dizzy, or the feel of his arms closing around her.

"You have faced several dangerous situations in the last day, and been injured repeatedly in recent times," Knox reminded her. "To feel exhausted is only natural. You should rest for the remainder of this evening. Tomorrow is soon enough to return to our digging."

Griffin stood as well and gestured vaguely toward the stairs. "You're more than welcome to stay. In fact, if you're too tired to drive, I wish you would. I know your place isn't very far away, but I'd worry if you left now. Plus, this way I can check your leg later and make up another compress if you need it."

Knox shook his head. "I will drive her to her dwelling. I thank you for your care of your niece and for your food and assistance, but I will care for Wynn now."

Griffin looked confused, and Wynn offered him a tired smile. "It's okay, I promise. Knox actually drove us here, so I'm sure he can manage another short trip back to my place. I really do appreciate the offer, but I've already been away from home too long. I just got back yesterday, and I've barely managed to set foot into my own house. I'd honestly rather go home. I promise to call if the cut doesn't look completely clean."

"All right, then. If that's really what you want." Her uncle didn't sound entirely convinced, but she didn't blame him for not wanting to argue about it. After all, not only had he called her stubborn as a mule a thousand different times over the years, but she had a gigantic, mythical warrior on her side. Uncle Griffin pretty much had no chance at all against those odds.

Plus, a small, very annoying voice at the back of her head whispered, this was her first chance to be really alone with Knox. Mona hadn't let them leave her house last night, but having your mom under the same roof as the man who attracted and fascinated you kind of put a damper on any thoughts of getting to know each other better.

But this time, if they went back to her house, they would be all alone. All alone with this crazy, magnetic force pulling them together. Who knew what might happen?

Of course, that all depended on Knox sharing in the attraction. Goddess, she really hoped he shared it. It would be mortifying to find out she was the only one feeling this way, thinking this way.

Fantasizing this way.

Sneaking a peek up at the Guardian's face, she saw

nothing to tell her either way in his set, impassive features. He might as well have still worn his stone form for all the clues his expression gave her. His eyes, though, almost glowed with a hot spark of awareness, and when he turned that gaze on her, she shivered in his arms.

"Do not worry, little witch," the Guardian murmured, bending his head until his breath stirred her hair even as his voice stirred something a lot lower down. "I will have you home soon, and I will always ensure your safety, as well as your warmth."

Boy, did she believe that one. Heat was not something lacking when he was near. Common sense, on the other hand, seemed to do an impressive disappearing act. She knew letting herself get involved with a Guardian was the last thing she needed. She just needed to keep reminding herself of that and ignoring the rapid beating of her heart and the restless emptiness in her belly.

A Guardian lover is the last thing you need, Wynn Myfanwy, she told herself sternly.

Too bad it was the very first thing she wanted.

Knox liked his witch's home immediately. The walls of the main rooms were painted a pale shade like watered honey, creating a warm and inviting atmosphere the minute he stepped through the door. Her furniture as well looked designed for comfort over fashion, with deep cushions and fabrics that invited a lingering touch. It all reminded him very much of the woman who lived here.

She shifted uneasily in his arms, and he glanced down at her. She wore the expression he had come to realize indicated that she was thinking and thinking hard. He could track the deepness of her thoughts by the deepness of the small furrow that formed between her eyes, directly above the bridge of her small nose, when she concentrated. He found the expression enchanting, but he could not be certain about her thoughts. He had a feeling he might not be so charmed by those.

He set her down where she indicated, in a chair much too large for her small frame, yet much too small for him to sit beside her. Had she chosen it deliberately? He wondered as he slid an ottoman into place beneath her injured feet to keep them elevated above the floor.

Standing, he stared down at her, wondering at what kept that quick, sharp mind of hers so preoccupied. She had said barely a word to him since they had left her uncle's house, only the bare minimum required to direct him to her home. He found himself surprised to realize he already missed the sweet, light sound of her voice.

"I still believe you should be in your bed," he told her, knowing she would argue, but welcoming any excuse to hear her speak. "You need sleep to recover from your wounds, as well as to keep your mind sharp for our mission."

"And I still believe that lying around in bed before it's even dark out is a stupid idea." She scowled up at him, the expression more amusing to him than threatening. "I'll go to bed when it's time to go to bed. Until then, there are still things we can be doing to help us figure out what the Order might be up to."

He raised a skeptical eyebrow. "What sorts of things?"

She looked blank for a moment, as if she hadn't expected him to ask the question. Finally she managed to bluster, "All sorts of things. I could cast a divination spell. Maybe that would point us in the right direction?"

"First of all, in order to divine the intentions of the Order, you would at the very least need an object that has belonged to one of them," he told her, trying to hold back a smile. He knew she still experienced nervousness around him, but he could not tell if it had its roots in wariness of his strength or attraction to it. Or perhaps both. "And second, you do not possess the strength at the moment to divine more than the location of the nearest flat surface. You are exhausted. I can see that even if you refuse to admit it. You will do nothing tonight that requires you to expend further energy. Tomorrow is soon enough for whatever you wish to attempt."

"Hey, you're the one who pointed out that the Order must have big plans for something around here, and I for one want to be ready for it. What if they make another attempt to harvest souls to feed to their pet demon? Don't we need to be ready so we can stop them?"

"We will be ready. An evening of rest will not change that. Whatever the *nocturnis* are planning, it will not happen tonight. I would be able to feel it if the threat were so imminent. You have time to regain your strength."

"Fine," Wynn pouted.

Knox had to hold back a grin at the adorably cranky expression, because he knew his little witch would not appreciate it. She would interpret it as a sign that he found her laughable, when he simply could not contain the pleasure she brought him just by being herself.

Schooling his features into serious lines, he gazed down at her. "Your uncle provided us with food and drink, but do you require further sustenance?" he asked politely. "I would be happy to provide you with whatever you need."

She eyed him for a moment, still pouting, but he thought he saw a flush of color tint her cheeks before she cleared her throat. "I'm not hungry or anything, but I could use a couple of things for my right ankle. I need to get the swelling down again and rewrap it. You could fetch the tin of arnica balm from the bathroom medicine cabinet and some ice from the freezer. I can reuse the elastic bandage my mom gave me for support, but first I need to treat the injury."

"As you wish." He turned to comply with her requests, but out of the corner of his eye he could see more color rise in her cheeks. He wondered how he could have caused it with such simple words.

Gathering the items Wynn asked for gave him the perfect excuse to explore her dwelling. Her house was small, tiny really, with the living and kitchen rooms on one side and two small bedrooms on the other, separated by a bathroom. He poked his head in each door, noting that the second bedroom appeared to have been converted into a space for rituals and magical practice. The slightly larger bedroom opposite clearly belonged to Wynn. Her scent filled the space, woven into the fabric of her sheets and pillows, into the curtains, and even into the small, soft area rug that protected the old wooden floors from the weight of the large iron bed.

Picturing his little witch spread out on that bed, her skin bared to his touch, her curvy body opened for his delight, nearly made his eyes roll back into his head. There would be time enough for such fantasies later, though, and even more time to turn them into realities. For now his witch was in pain and needed the remedies she had asked him to collect.

The bathroom smelled almost as strongly of her as the bedroom had, despite the tiled floors and walls. The slick porcelain was a poor conductor of scent, but she bathed in this room, and the lightly perfumed soaps and lotions with which she cleansed herself lingered in the air. He detected subtle hints of musk and lemon balm, sweetgrass and myrrh, all underlined with the unique freshness that made up Wynn's natural female scent. He could stand here for hours just breathing her in, but he forced himself to retrieve the labeled tin of balm from the cabinet and return to the other side of the house to rummage through her kitchen.

Spotting a clean towel hanging from the handle of the oven, he snagged it and filled it with ice from the freezer. Gathering it up with the balm, he retraced his steps into the living room and perched on the edge of the ottoman in front of her.

While he'd wandered, she had turned up the both legs of her jeans, leaving her pale, shapely calves exposed. The left was still mostly covered by the gauze that held her uncle's poultice in place, but she had removed the beige elastic from around her right ankle, baring her bruised and swollen flesh to the air in the room. Gently, he balanced the improvised ice pack on the swollen joint, placing a soothing hand on her leg when she hissed at the sudden cold.

"Thank you," she murmured, her gaze fixed on his hands. She seemed fascinated by the contrast of his bronzed fingers against her much paler skin. He also found the sight intriguing, but not as intriguing as the silky texture against the roughness of his callused palms. He stroked experimentally and felt her muscles ripple even as she drew in a shaky breath.

"Wh-what are you doing?" she asked, her voice trembling.

He lifted his gaze and found her watching his face now. Her brown eyes were wide and wary, her cheeks tinged a rosy pink.

"I am touching you," he replied calmly, though he felt far from calm. He felt tense, restless, and . . . hungry.

"But why?"

"Because I wish it." His hand slipped higher, stopping just above her knee, fingers sneaking beneath the fabric of her jeans to curl around the soft flesh of her thigh. He squeezed gently, relishing the way her roundness gave slightly under his strength. He wanted to slide his hand farther, to tear away the cloth that hid her from him, but he restrained himself. He did not wish to frighten his witch into fleeing from him.

Still, his fingers crept almost without his volition another inch up her leg until her hand slapped down and pinned them in place. "Stop it," she whispered.

Knox shifted forward, bracing his knee against the cushion beside her hip and looming over her, like a cloud blocking out the sun. Her eyes widened and her breathing grew fast and shallow. He could feel her tense, but he hesitated, unsure if she felt arousal or fear. He would not wish for his little witch to be afraid of him. He wanted her to desire him as strongly as he desired her.

Closing his eyes, he lowered his head until his face hovered only a breath away from the tender curve of her neck and drew in a deep breath. Her scent filled his head, nearly making him dizzy with the rich smells of Wynn and heat and thick, intoxicating arousal. His witch wanted him. He fought back a roar of triumph.

"I said stop," she repeated, bracing a hand against his shoulder and pushing weakly against him. She protested verbally, but she did little to back up her words.

"But I want to touch you, little witch," he breathed against her throat, watching the way her pulse jumped beneath her tender skin. "I want to touch you, to feel you . . . to taste you . . ."

Unable to resist, he pressed the flat of his tongue against the enticing spot where her neck and shoulder met and felt her quiver beneath him. The scent of her desire flooded his senses, and he wanted nothing more than to claim this woman, to sink inside her and feel her close around him, all slick heat and breathless welcome. In a rush, he shifted, gripping the back of her head in his hand and holding her in place as he seized her mouth in a crushing kiss.

Her first response was to moan and press against his shoulder, but that lasted barely an instant. In the space between heartbeats she melted, softening beneath him, parting her lips and welcoming him inside the sweet haven of her mouth. He surged forward like a conqueror, invading to the heart of her and wallowing in the rich, addictive flavor he found there.

Fierce possessive instincts overtook him. Some primal part of him howled and writhed and demanded that he make Wynn his. The insistence of its ranting surprised him, and the small part of his logical mind that hadn't completely shut down at the feel of her viewed the phenomenon with suspicion. It instructed him to remain calm and rational, to remember his duty to humanity as a whole and not lose himself in the baseness of his desires. It whispered not to give the human power over him, to remember that she was just a woman, and he was sworn to put the battle against the Darkness above all else.

The beast wanted to rip the logical voice into small, bloody pieces. *Remember,* it insisted, *remember that only a female, only a woman of power, can ensure that the Guardian remains to protect the world. Remember that without their mates, the first of our kind turned their backs on the world. Remember that and claim the witch. Make her ours.*

His fist clenched without thought, tugging at the handful of hair tangled about his fingers and drawing a yelp of surprised pain from his female. Abruptly, she slammed the heels of both hands hard into the cluster of nerves at the front of his shoulders. The sharp blows didn't hurt him, but they did register enough discomfort that he lifted his head to look down at her, his lips curved in a warning snarl.

"Get off me," she growled, matching him bared teeth for bared teeth. In another moment, he might have found her attempts at ferocity amusing. Now they just confused him. She wanted him, the beast insisted, wanted him almost as badly as he wanted her, so why was she pushing him away?

"I said. Get! Off!"

This time, he felt a jolt of energy behind her shoves. She still lacked the power to physically move him—he was easily twice her size—but the force broke through the urgent lust clouding his mind, and he eased back a few precious inches.

"That was a really bad idea," she stated, her voice eerily calm and filled with tangled undertones of anger, fear, desire, and frustration. "I think it would be best if we each got some space and took a little while to cool off. I'm going to go into my bedroom, and I'm going to lock the door."

He made an instinctive noise of derision, and she firmed her lips.

"Yes, I know a flimsy little lock, not to mention a thin wooden door that wouldn't keep you out if you wanted to come inside, but I'm trusting you to honor what the lock represents." She eyed him warily, forcing him to back off as she edged forward in her chair and prepared to rise. "I'm telling you I want to be alone and as a Guardian, I expect you to respect that."

Before she could stand, Knox snatched her up in his arms yet again and strode toward the bedroom. Immediately, Wynn shrieked and began to struggle.

"I said, you need to leave me alone, you asshole!"

She didn't waste time pounding at his heavy chest and shoulder muscles the way stupid women apparently did in films. No, she curved her fingers into claws and went straight for his vulnerable eyes. Lucky for him, she was so much smaller than he that all he had to do was stretch his arms out and crane his head to the side to put them out of her reach.

It required every ounce of his self-control to carry the squirming hellcat into her bedroom and deposit her gently atop the patterned duvet. Then he had to dig deep into untapped reserved to force his hands away from her tempting body and take a step backward when he wanted nothing more than to strip her naked, crawl on top of her, and show her exactly why time apart was not going to do either of them the slightest bit of good. The witch belonged to him, she was his mate, but pride and honor both demanded he let her come to that realization on her own.

Wynn pushed herself up on her elbows and fixed him with a glare so sharp he was tempted to check himself for nicks and cuts. When she spoke, her voice all but vibrated with fury.

"Listen to me right now, mister," she hissed. "I don't care who you are, I don't care what you are. If you lay one hand on me again without an engraved fucking invitation I will make you wish you'd just been turned back to stone, do you get me?"

Knox felt his fists flex and release, flex and release at his sides and reminded himself sternly that arguing with his witch would provide neither of them with satisfaction. She had demanded time alone, and as her mate, it was his responsibility to give her what she asked for.

Plus, if he didn't step outside and get away from the way her scent permeated her entire house, he would lose his last grip on sanity. He would not go far, because to leave his female alone and undefended simply was not possible for Knox, but he could watch her well enough from outside. Perhaps the fresh air would allow his muscles to relax and the painful erection she had conjured to subside before it caused him irreparable harm.

But before he went, he needed to make one thing clear.

"Do not threaten me with a vengeance you have no intention of carrying out," he growled, knowing his eyes must be glowing with the force of the struggle inside him. He was a Guardian after all, and his soul was formed of magic. "You may struggle against me as fiercely as you struggle against yourself, but we both know what is inevitable. You will invite me to touch you again, little witch, and soon, because we are mates, and the Light itself has formed us for each other. Believe me when I tell you, there is no power on earth that can deny a bond forged by fate."

Not waiting for a reply, not even pausing to see her react to his harsh decree, Knox spun on his heel and left, drawing her front door softly closed behind him.

Chapter Eight

Wynn huddled in the center of her bed for what felt like hours, brooding. Well, she ended up huddling and brooding, but before that she took more than a few minutes for swearing, kicking, yelling, pouting, and denying. After that, she settled on brooding.

What on the Goddess's green earth was the matter with her? What had she already told herself? Getting involved with Knox would qualify as the height of stupidity. After all, she had already predicted the outcome. If she let herself get involved with the Guardian, she would also tie herself irrevocably to the Guild, which meant watching as they eventually—inevitably—pushed her out of her accidental Wardenship and replaced her with someone they deemed more suitable. Why would she want to set herself up for that kind of pain? Would the Guardian really be worth it? Would any man?

No, she knew perfectly well that getting tangled up in a relationship with a Guardian had about as much potential upside for her as getting tangled up in a thicket of blackberry bushes—it would waste her time, cut her up, and leave her with nothing much to show for it but the memory of a few tasty moments in time. How was that worth it?

We tasted him just a minute ago, a sly voice inside her head responded. *How was it not worth it?*

Wynn winced. The fact that Knox went to her head like whiskey and knocked her off balance like a shake table were not facts she cared to dwell on just now. No, she'd rather think about what she needed to do to extract herself from his existence as quickly and painlessly as possible. Of course, achieving the painless part already felt like it might require fairly heavy doses of morphine.

She placed all the blame for this squarely on Knox's shoulders. Not only were they a heck of a lot broader than hers, but he was the one who had started it, with his addictive kisses and mouthwatering scent and all those yummy, cut muscles that just made her want to run her tongue over the creases between them and—

Crap on a cracker. That train of thought needed to head off a cliff and fast. Not helpful.

As caught up as she'd gotten in her brooding, the chiming of her cell phone from the pocket of her jeans made her jump high enough that the bounce had her sprained ankle yelping a protest. Gritting her teeth, Wynn tried to ignore the fresh twinge and answered. "Hello?"

"Wynn, awesome. It's Fil. How's it going down in the southland?"

"The southland?" Wynn rolled her eyes at her friend's foolishness, but she couldn't help her lips curving at the sound of her friendly voice. "Well, the cotton's coming up, but the magnolia trees just aren't blooming like they used to."

Fil chuckled at the sarcastic reply. "So much for the good old days, right?"

Wynn frowned. "How are you feeling these days? Still on the road to recovery?"

Fil had taken a hell of a beating during the events in Montreal. She'd been in the hospital for days dealing with a severe concussion, several broken bones, and multiple stab wounds. She was lucky to be alive.

"Ugh. Yeah, it's turning out to be longer than the road to redemption. And I have to tell you, out of everything, I really didn't expect the broken collarbone to be the worst, but it really is. I never realized how much of my upper body the stupid thing impacts. It sucks. I'm stuck in a stupid sling for at least a couple more weeks, but everything else is a lot better."

"Progress is progress, right?"

"I guess," Fil grumbled, then perked up. "Hey, listen, I talked to El last night and she caught me up on what you found. I have to say, nice going. Managing a summoning is more than we pulled off, and we really couldn't afford to lose a Guardian right now, so, well done, you."

"Accidentally, unintentionally, and completely unconsciously done, you mean. I have no idea what happened, Fil. One minute my life was flashing before my eyes, and the next the guy who tried to kill me was dangling off the claws of a live-action gargoyle. If I really had something to do with it, it's beyond me what it was, so don't go getting any ideas that I might be able to repeat the experience."

"Why on earth would we think that?" Fil sounded honestly baffled, which wasn't a terribly Fil response. The independent art restorer generally attacked life with an ask-no-questions and take-no-prisoners sort of outlook. "You only get one Guardian, sweetie. That's kinda how it works. Each Warden wakes up—or in your case, summons—her own fella. One per customer."

Wynn made a face. "And what's the return policy like?"

Fil chuckled. "No backsies. I take it your granite head is giving you fits already? Do what I do—agree with everything he says, smile real pretty, then go do whatever you were planning anyway. They're so overprotective that they're usually so busy being happy you're home safe that they forget to be all that mad about it. Give it a try."

Wynn groaned and flopped back into the pillows. "Gods, Fil, how did I get dragged into all this? I was perfectly happy with my life the way it was, when the Guardians were a totally abstract concept. Like Great-Uncle Eugene, the one you see in the family photo album now and then, but you'll never have to meet because he died before you were born. I wanna go back to that."

There was a brief pause. "Sorry, sweetie. I suppose it's my fault you got dragged into this. If I hadn't needed someone to get rid of that mark on my hand, you'd still be back there."

For the space of a few seconds, Wynn allowed herself to believe that, then she sighed and admitted the truth. "No, I wouldn't. I'd still be from a family full of Wardens, my brother would still be one of them, and he'd still be missing—just like ninety-eight percent of the rest of the Guild. It might have delayed the inevitable if I hadn't met you, but eventually I would have ended up right where I am. And I have to say I feel both very mature and hostilely bitter to admit that."

"I can't say I blame you. So does this mean your Guardian really is giving you fits? What has he done?"

"In the last thirty hours? Oh, besides saving my life, charming my mother, bullying my uncle, and carrying me around like a bale of hay, not all that much. Things have been a little hectic around here."

"Really? What's been happening?"

Blowing out a deep breath, Wynn pursed her lips and began a recitation of all the events between discovering the shattered remains of the former Guardian to Knox carrying her out of her uncle's house and back to her own. If she left out a few minor details, like the electrifying lust arching between them and the almost-sex they'd engaged in on the chair in her living room, she told herself it was only in the interest of brevity and clarity. Like a movie being aired on network television, she'd edited for time and formatted the story to fit her screen.

"Oh, wow, that is really, really fantastic news," Fil gushed when Wynn finally wound down. "I mean, not about you respraining your ankle or getting your other leg sliced up, because that part sucks. And I know what I'm talking about because I got caught in a *hhissih* fit, too, and I didn't even get envenomated, but I know how those suckers hurt. But actually, when I said fantastic, I was talking about your uncle. Having a real-life Warden in our corner is going to make a whole bunch of this mess so much easier, Wynn. Really. El is going to be over the moon when she hears."

"Well, I'm glad we managed to do something positive, but we're still left with a bunch of questions. Most important, what is it the Order has planned around here? Knox is right, there has to be something, something significant enough that fate decided to send a Guardian to handle it."

"Yeah, I'm thinking that's the not-so-good news in all this. You guys don't have any theories yet?"

"Nothing solid," Wynn said. "So far, all we've got to go on is the theory that my brother might have sensed something before he disappeared. If that note was significant, maybe Coleman or Garvey is involved with the Order. I just don't know how we're going to find that out. I doubt they wear cool club jackets when they go out, and they aren't the sort of people you run into on the street and strike up a conversation with."

"There's always a way, Wynn. I know you'll find it. Hey, maybe you'll take up some after-hours work, or do a little B and E, like El and I did. You'll think of something."

"Yeah, provided I can start thinking straight again," Wynn mumbled, staring up at the ceiling.

"What was that?"

Wynn signed. "It was nothing. Never mind."

"No, that wasn't nothing," Fil insisted. "Is it just the situation stressing you out, or is something else going on? I'm your friend, Wynn. You know you can talk to me about anything."

And the weird thing was, Wynn did know that. She'd only met Felicity a matter of a couple of weeks ago, but already she felt as if they'd known each other forever. Maybe it was like being in the army together—

friendships formed in combat tended to be tight ones that lasted a lifetime. Wynn just wasn't sure if she was ready to talk about her feelings for Knox with herself, let alone with anyone else, no matter how close they were.

"Come on, sweetie," Fil coaxed over the phone. "Let me help. Tell Dr. Fil what's going on."

That at least earned a snort of laughter, followed by a low groan as Wynn squeezed her eyes shut and pressed a hand to her throbbing temple. "Goddess, Fil, I think I'm losing my ever-loving mind. There is something seriously wrong with me. Being around Knox is making me crazy. I'm not kidding. He just—"

"Makes you wonder if killing him would hasten the end of the world, or kissing him would."

Wynn's eyes popped open and she blinked up at the ceiling, whispering, "How did you know?"

"Aw, sweetheart, I know because that's the way this whole thing works," Fil said gently, her voice kind but tinged with laughter. "Ask Ella. It's practically programmed into these guys' DNA to drive us up a wall. The only thing we can do is hold on to something so we don't fall and hope we can get in a couple of good kicks to their thick, rock-filled heads once in a while. That's what being mated to a Guardian is, for better or worse. No pun intended."

Wynn made a fist and pounded it into the mattress beside her hip. "We are not mates," she growled. "I am not mated to a Guardian. I refuse to be."

Fil snorted. "You really think you get a choice?"

"Of course I get a choice! I've got free will, don't I? I should get to decide who I'm going to fall in love with."

"Hm, maybe you should. But let me ask you something. Have you ever tried to fight against your fate? And how has that worked out for you?"

Wynn maintained a stony silence.

"Look, sweetie," Fil sighed, "I'm not really the person to go to for relationship advice. I was the one who thought Spar was going to leave me right up until he basically laughed in my face. And me lying there in a hospital bed. But I digress. What I'm trying to say is that sometimes things are just meant to be the way they are."

Wynn hmphed.

"Okay, let me try again. Ella and I have a theory about all this, about the current mess with the Order, about the Guild, about multiple Guardians waking up. Did she mention it to you?"

"No."

"Okay, then I will. Now, you know more about the Guardians than Ella and I did when we first got involved, so you've heard the legend about the first Guardians and the seven women of power."

Wynn grunted in acknowledgment. Of course she knew the story. Everyone who knew the history of the Guardians knew the story.

Early in the history of humankind, the Darkness threatened to take over the world. Desperate to save themselves and their people, a group of extraordinary magic users had banded together and used their power to draw forth from the Light protectors who would battle against the evil and keep it from destroying them. Those protectors had been the first Guardians, seven mighty warriors, born of magic, with the strength to tear apart the Darkness and imprison the Seven demons spawned by the rift. Once they achieved victory, the

Guardians, knowing that the Darkness could never be
fully destroyed, had allowed the magic users—the found-
ers of the Guild of Wardens—to put them to sleep, en-
casing their magic in frozen shapes of stone until the next
time the Darkness chose to threaten humanity.

Over and over, the cycles of sleeping and waking had
played out, but the Guardians who protected humanity
never grew to know those they defended, and so their
stony hearts had not cared about the humans for whom
they fought. After many battles, their apathy had led
them to ignore a summons from the Wardens for the
first time in their existence. With no Guardian capable
of defending humanity, the Darkness had threatened to
take over the whole of the earth. Then one day a woman
of power had knelt at the feet of a Guardian and prayed
to the Light to wake the protectors of humanity once
again. To the shock of the male members of the Guild
of Wardens, the Guardian had broken free of his statue-
cage and claimed the woman as his mate. Once again,
humanity began to hope the Darkness could be defeated,
so another woman of power stepped forward, and the
same thing happened again, over and over, until Seven
Guardians had claimed seven human women of power
for their own.

Filled with the need to protect their new mates, and
consequently to protect humanity as a whole, those first
Guardians once again beat back the Darkness and
emerged triumphant from the battle. But when peace returned and the Wardens attempted to send the Guardians back to sleep, they refused to be parted from their
mates. The Guild had been forced to release them from
their service and summon new Guardians to take their

places. From that point on, anytime a Guardian had found his true mate and claimed her as his, the magic released him from his service and granted him a mortal life to live with his beloved.

That was the story, anyway. For the sake of Ella and Fil, who truly loved their Guardian mates, Wynn hoped it was true. She hoped that when they won the battle against the Order and its master, the Darkness, the big warriors would be freed and allowed to spend the rest of their lives with the women they loved. Whether it would really happen that way remained to be seen. After all, the Guardians weren't required to return to sleep until whatever threat caused their awakening had been vanquished. Clearly, they hadn't yet reached that point.

"Good," Fil continued. "Because if you know the story, you know that you can draw a few parallels between the circumstances described in the legend and what's going on around us right now."

"I can?"

"Of course you can. These are desperate times right here, girlfriend. We might not have Guardians who refuse to awaken, but we have a situation where they can't wake up normally. We don't have the Wardens to do it anymore. If the personal Wardens of any of the Guardians are even still alive I'd be astounded. So once again you have a set of circumstances where someone else has to wake them up. Have you maybe noticed that those someones so far have all been women?"

Wynn made a noncommittal sound.

"Well, they have been, and Ella and I have talked about that. We believe that other than a Warden, only the mate of a Guardian can wake him, and his mate has to always be a woman of power. Ella had the ability to channel magical energy, I can see magical energy, and you're just a big ol' witch. Add up big ol' witchiness along with you managing to summon Knox like pulling a rabbit out of a hat, and what do you get? Mates. I'm sorry, sweetheart, but we're pretty sure that's the way this thing works. If you didn't start out as a Warden and you still ended up with a Guardian, then you are that Guardian's mate. It's a done deal."

"Can I fold?"

Fill laughed. "Sorry, hon. You gotta play the cards as they fall."

Wynn groaned and thumped her head repeatedly against the pillows. If only they had been a brick wall instead. What she wouldn't give for a good bout of un-consciousness right about now. "Okay, can I just refuse to think about it for now? I'm pretty sure that if my brain has to deal with anything else at the moment, it's going to start leaking out my ears."

"Oh, sweetie, you can try avoiding it forever, if that's what you want, but don't be surprised to find it coming back to bite you in the ass. And don't say I didn't warn you."

"Well, since my ass is about the only part of my lower half that doesn't have a current injury, some nice teeth marks will blend in just fine."

Wynn cracked the joke to keep from cracking up. Fil's theory about mating a Guardian was the last thing she wanted to hear, because it meant she was damned if she did, and damned if she didn't. If she stuck to her guns and kept Knox at a distance then walked away when this whole thing was over, she'd be cutting herself off from the one person in the whole world meant to be her perfect soul mate. But if she allowed herself to accept their mating and build a relationship with the Guardian, she'd have to stand by and watch her pride be trampled by the misogynistic bastards of the Guild who would shove her aside in favor of their chosen Warden.

Then of course there was the possibility that she didn't even want to acknowledge, the deep dark fear that ran underneath her entire understanding of who and what the Guardian were. What if Knox took her as a mate not because he loved her or lusted for her, or whatever you called it when a Guardian took a mate, but because mating her meant he would never have to be trapped in the stone sleep of a peacetime Guardian? What if all she really meant to him was a get-out-of-jail-free card?

She shoved the thought back and tried to focus on the phone conversation. She couldn't share that fear with her friend. Hell, she wished she didn't have to share it with her own subconscious.

Fil laughed. "In that case, you give it all you got, Wynn. I never said that just because he's destined to be your mate, you shouldn't make him work for it."

Working around it still held greater appeal for Wynn, but she kept her mouth shut. As long as she had Fil on the phone, she should get some business taken care of.

"Not to change the subject or anything—" Subtle. Very subtle. "—but I wanted to make sure that you and Ella got connected to my uncle Griffin. I've already told him about you, so let me give you his number. That way maybe you and Ella can arrange a conference call or something and you can both ask him any questions you need urgent answers to. After that, I'm sure he'd be happy

to help you guys get an organized plan together to keep
your Warden training moving along."

Fil followed the switch in tracks without a word.
"Great. What about you, though?"

"I can grab him anytime I need him," Wynn answered
vaguely. She spoke the truth as far as it went; she didn't
need to start another argument with Fil about how she
wouldn't need Warden training if she wasn't actually going to be staying with Knox over the long term. Maybe
Fil was right. Maybe Knox was her fate and there was
no point fighting against it.

But then again, what if she was wrong?

The women exchanged a few more bits of information, Fil promising to have Ella update Wynn on anything they dug up about Coleman and Garvey, and Wynn
in return assuring her friend of regular communications
on the situation in Chicago. When she finally ended the
call, Wynn felt wiped out and no less confused than
she had before Fil's advice. Maybe sleep was what she
needed.

Her sprained ankle throbbed uncomfortably, and
she revised that plan. Arnica balm, rewrapped elastic,
more ibuprofen, and then sleep. Now, that felt like a plan.

Easing herself up and out of bed turned out to be less
painful than Wynn had feared, which improved her
mood at least a little. The fact that she was able to hobble
back to the living room to fetch the supplies Knox had
abandoned there earlier helped even more.

Slowly, Wynn crossed to the chair, taking note of the
relative silence in the house. No place in a major city
was every truly silent, what with traffic and outside noise
pollution and the constant electric buzz of modern liv-

ing that hummed from refrigerators and other appliances. But it was quiet in her familiar space. Dark had fallen recently, casting the room in shadows. She considered turning on a light, but she knew the layout of her place so well, she really didn't need one. Plus, the dark reminded her that she could take the poultice off her leg now. It also emphasized Knox's continued absence, but Wynn tried not to think about that.

Settling back into the ottoman she'd left earlier, Wynn once again pulled up her jeans and reached down to unwrap her ankle. A quiet tinkling sound from the direction of the kitchen stopped her.

Her first thought was to call out Knox's name. After all, he should return to the house at some point, so maybe the sound had come from his opening the back door and letting himself inside. She even parted her lips, but something inside told her not to make any noise.

Her heart immediately began to race. Wynn tried to tell herself she'd imagined the breaking-glass sound, but her instincts were screaming at her that something was very wrong, and Wynn had very good instincts. Over the years, she had learned that when she ignored them, bad things happened.

Easing slowly back to her feet, Wynn kept her eyes on the kitchen doorway as she began to sidle toward the hallway and her ritual room beyond. Her entire house had basic wards, but if someone was breaking in, they had obviously gotten through them. The ones around her ritual room were a lot stronger. She'd be safer behind them. Years of ritual practice had left the space inside those four walls heavy with magical energy, too, and all her tools and supplies lived in that room. If she was going to have to defend herself, that was where she wanted to make her stand.

A shadow moved in the kitchen, and Wynn spun to dash toward the hall.

If her ankle had cooperated, she might have made it. Instead, the abused joint collapsed mid-turn and sent her tumbling to her hands and knees on the smooth oak floors. Her instincts continued to scream at her, so she didn't waste time trying to get to feet that wouldn't support her. Instead, she put her head down and crawled as fast as she could across the ten-foot space.

The intruder caught her just inches from her sanctuary. She felt a looming presence, then a steely, gloved hand closed around her shoulder, and Wynn screamed.

She didn't just scream, though, because just screaming was for wusses and dead girls. Twisting her body, Wynn flipped onto her back, closing a few precious inches of the gap between herself and the threshold of her ritual room. Even as she tumbled, she also swept her legs into the knees of her attacker. The unexpected blow upset the man's balance and sent him to the floor with a thud and a muffled curse.

The instant she finished the kick, Wynn channeled her momentum into a roll that took her into the room on an angle, with her torso crossing over the magical barrier and her legs still caught outside. She felt the energy bisecting her waist in a tingling line and scrambled to drag her legs in after her. The man in the hallway grabbed her swollen ankle in a painful grip and began trying to drag her back toward him.

Not just no, but hell to the ever-loving no.

Wynn caught her slide by slapping her hands up

against the doorjamb and locking her elbows tight. No way was she going to let this bastard get her back out into the hallway where she had no hope of defending herself against his much greater strength. In her ritual space, physical strength took a backseat to the strength of a pissed-off witch and the gods and goddesses she served. The intruder could overpower Wynn easily, but she'd like to see how he would fare against Cerridwen. If anyone could use a fundamental transformation, it was this jerk. In fact, if he ended up as a salmon, she was broiling his ass for dinner.

A glance over her shoulder revealed little about her attacker. He was definitely male, broader in the shoulder, narrower in the hip, and at least six feet tall. He wore all black clothing, looking almost like a refugee from a SWAT team, with fatigue-style pants and some sort of tactical vest over his long-sleeved shirt. Between those, the gloves, and what looked like a black ski mask, she couldn't catch so much as a glimpse of skin, leaving her with no way to identify him to authorities. Not that calling 911 was her first priority. She didn't think this really fell under the jurisdictions of the local cops.

This had to be the work of *nocturnis*. No one else she knew of wanted her dead—at least, not that they'd mentioned—and it seemed a bit too coincidental that anything else could account for two violent attacks on her person in two days. She just wasn't that unlikable.

Her arms began to tremble under the strain of bracing herself against the force of the man trying to drag her into the hall. She knew she couldn't hold on indefinitely, so she needed to go proactive. Drawing up her free leg, she bought it down hard directly into the bastard's face. She heard something crunch, then heard a voice muttering some pretty nasty language, but the grip on her sore ankle barely loosened. Time to release the kraken.

Drawing in a lungful of air, Wynn tilted her head back and yelled, very loudly, the name of her inconveniently absent Guardian. The fact that she'd sent him away didn't excuse him not being here when she was attacked, and she wanted him back to clean up his mess.

And no, logic held no meaning for her in that moment. Only survival did.

Knox appeared almost instantly, so quickly she knew he must already have sensed trouble and decided to return. One minute, she felt herself sliding inexorably out of her ritual room at the hands of an enraged attacker, and the next a huge, menacing form filled—no, *overflowed*—the hallway behind them, gigantic wings half unfurled like midnight sails becalmed on a windless sea. She heard a roar and a curse, then the pressure on her ankle abruptly released and chaos and vengeance descended.

You know, she'd actually started to look forward to that salmon dinner. Now she figured she might want to make some alternative plans, because it was starting to look like an enraged, fanged, razor-clawed Guardian was not going to leave any pieces big enough to bother with.

Freed from the intruder's grasp, Wynn scrambled on her hands and knees across the threshold into her ritual room. A few quick motions had the wards recharged and up to full strength. They glowed briefly before settling back into invisibility and allowing her to watch the events in the hall without obstruction.

Yikes. She almost wanted to cover her eyes. Knox appeared to be playing with the intruder like a cat playing with its dinner. He struck repeated blows to the man in black, claws shredding through fabric and skin with equal ease. The intruder never seemed to manage a single strike on the larger, faster, and infinitely more powerful Guardian. Quickly, fatigue began to take an obvious toll on the man, and he stumbled, barely able to catch himself with a hand braced against the wall.

Wynn saw Knox reach back, saw the man's death reflected in his dark, glowing eyes, and cried out, "Stop! Knox, don't kill him!"

The Guardian turned his fury on her, the flames in his eyes threatening to burn her to ashes. "Again you ask me to stop when a human servant of the Darkness has dared to harm you. Enough. It is right that the Dark one should die, and you will not deny me my right as the victor to spill his blood into the earth."

Instinct had her taking a step back from the Guardian's fury, but she refused to show him fear. Instead, she squared her shoulders and glared at him. "Maybe not, but I'll sure as hell deny you the right to spill it on my hallway floor. I'm not cleaning up that mess. Besides, think for a minute. We've been wondering what the Order has planned for us here. Why not just ask them?"

Knox snarled, his lips drawn back over gleaming, three-inch fangs, but he followed her pointing finger to the swaying figure of the masked intruder. He clearly lacked the strength to run, but Wynn would bet he still had the strength to talk. Given the correct motivation, of course.

She could see the internal war Knox waged with

himself. His thirst for the man's blood filled the air so thickly, she could almost taste it, dark and bitter and coppery-sweet. But he was more than a killing machine, more than a dumb beast incapable of reason and strategy. He knew she was right to want to gather whatever information they could from the intruder. And she knew he wasn't going to like being denied his prey.

With a disgusted growl, Knox seized the human by the scruff of his neck, easily lifting him to dangle a foot off the floor. His other hand ripped off the mask concealing his identity.

Wynn gasped in shock.

In the dim light filtering in through the windows, she could make out the familiar, formerly attractive features of Detective Jansen. Formerly attractive because it was hard to find anyone appealing after you found out they were a sociopathic servant of evil, though the broken nose, swollen, blackening eyes, and bruised, lacerated skin didn't do him any favors, either.

"I know you," Knox rumbled, his voice deep with fury and menace. "You are the one who investigated my female's brother and pretended to uphold human laws."

Jansen curled his lip and spat in Knox's face. "Screw you, Guardian. The Seven will go free and the earth will weep for the rest of eternity."

"You're *nocturnis*. Did the police give you a good cover story, you piece of shit?" Wynn demanded, stepping right up to the threshold of the door. "Is your partner part of the Order, too? How many of you are there on the force?"

"Pulaski is an idiot," Jansen sneered. "He's worthless to the Order. The Hierophant seeks men of vision, not useless bureaucrats who wouldn't know what to do with power if it fell into their laps."

The Hierophant. Wynn had heard that title before, and it hadn't spelled very good news last time, either. The elusive figure was the high priest of the entire Order of Eternal Darkness. He called the shots, made the plans that the *nocturnis* carried out. If they could find him, maybe they could cut the head off this viperous snake.

"Is the Hierophant here in Chicago?" she demanded. "Where can I find him."

Jansen laughed. "You can't, you stupid bitch. The Hierophant is beyond your pitiful understanding."

Knox shook the detective so hard, Wynn swore she could hear the teeth rattle in the man's head.

"Tell her!" the Guardian commanded.

Jansen just laughed again, his grin a distorted rictus of evil disguised as humor. "The Seven are rising, and there's nothing you can do to stop them. All hail the Defiler! May he shit on your bloody corpse."

Then the *nocturnis* clenched his jaw, and foam began to pour from his mouth. His body went stiff as a board, then shook with wild seizures for long, horrible seconds before he finally collapsed limp in Knox's grasp. The Guardian released him with a disgusted sound, letting the body fall to a heap on the hallway floor.

"He is dead. The coward took his own life with some sort of poison."

Pale and shaking, Wynn stepped into the hall and peered down at the dead detective. "He must have used a suicide pill. Maybe cyanide? I think that's what the Nazis and all those foreign spies supposedly used." A chill raced through her and she wrapped her arms around herself, searching for a hint of warmth. "What a nasty way to go. It looked painful."

"He deserved pain," Knox growled. "Though it enrages me to be deprived of the pleasure of inflicting it myself."

"Whoa, calm down there, big guy." Wynn held up a hand and shuddered. "No mayhem and torture in my house. At least, no more mayhem, and definitely no torture. Though it would have been handy if you could have gotten him to answer some questions. We need to know what the Order has planned, or at least where there cell is operating out of. This may have been our best chance to get that kind of information, but a dead guy isn't going to tell us anything."

Knox scowled and crouched down next to the body. "You would be surprised by how much the dead *can* tell us," he said cryptically.

Wynn felt a jolt of surprise. "What? Do you mean you can make him talk? That's impossible. First, because Guardians can't cast spells, and second, because what you're talking about is necromancy. And you and I both know that performing necromantic spells is like rubbing yourself in demon-bacon and telling them to come and have a little taste."

Knox glanced at her sideways and began rummaging through the dead man's pockets. "I had something a bit simpler in mind, little witch. Something more like this."

He held up a small scrap of patterned fabric, barely bigger than the palm of her hand. In the dimness of the unlit hallway, she had a hard time determining the color or pattern woven into the cloth, but she could clearly see that it emitted a clear red glow, barely deeper than pink, but translucent and steady. Someone must have cast some sort of magical spell on the thing.

What sort of spell would someone cast on a tiny little rag like that? She took a step forward to get a closer look and the light around the fabric flared brighter. It took a second for Wynn to make the connection, but when she did, her stomach performed an acrobatic two and a half twists in the pike position.

"That's part of my shirt," she whispered. "I ditched it yesterday when the security guard grabbed me in Lake Forest. He got hold of the back of it, so I shrugged out of the shirt and took off. I figured better for him to catch my shirt than catch me."

She looked up into Knox's grim, beastly face and saw the way his nostrils flared with anger and his lip curled over dagger-sharp, wickedly long fangs. In his Guardian form, his features looked like they really had been hewn from granite with the blade of a battle-ax. There was nothing clean or pretty about them. They were harsh and brutal and incredibly reassuring.

"I should never have let the minion live." He spat the words through clenched teeth. "He should have died at my hands, then the *nocturnis* scum would not have had a weapon to use against you."

Wynn lifted a hand and placed it on his broad, bare shoulder. His skin retained the gray color and rough texture of his sleeping, statue-like form, but it radiated a surprising heat against her palm. "I'm the one who told you not to kill him. At the time, figuring out what to do with a dead body seemed like a bigger risk than letting him live, so it's my responsibility. Besides, I don't think that's a weapon; I think it's a tool. And I might have a way to make it just as useful to us as it was to him."

"What do you mean?"

"I think they put a tracking spell on that," she explained. "That's why the light got brighter when I got closer to it. Jensen probably used it to find me. The security guard at the Van Oswalt estate never knew my name, so even if he gave a heck of a description of me to the rest of the *nocturnis,* Jansen might not even have known I was the one poking around the old statue when he first saw me. Though unless he was as dumb as he looked, he must have recognized you at my mother's house. Still, the Order wanted to track down whatever woman had worn that shirt and gone looking for a Guardian, so they used the fabric to create a spell to track me down. It would have led Jansen right to me, but most good tracer spells also report back to the person who cast them."

Immediately Knox closed his fist around the glowing fabric and surged to his feet. "Then we must destroy it. We cannot continue to lead the *nocturnis* straight to you. It puts you in too much danger."

"Relax, big guy. We're not going to just sit back and wait for the Order to find us. We're going to use the spell to find them. Come on."

Beginning to smile, Wynn turned and led the Guardian through the wards and into her work space. Her right ankle still caused her to limp, but she noticed with a sense of gratitude that she felt barely a twinge from the cut on her left leg. Thank the Goddess for small mercies, she supposed.

She caught a glimpse of the shiver that coursed through Knox when he passed through the magical barrier into the room behind her, but she knew he wouldn't be stopped by it. After all, he intended her no harm, which was what the wards had been designed to prevent, but he was sensitive to magic, so he had felt their presence.

"Bring the cloth over here."

Wynn stopped beside a long, rough-hewn table at the far side of the small former bedroom. She had salvaged the table from an abandoned barn years ago, during some exploratory teenage road trip into the country. She couldn't tell exactly when it had been made or who had left it there in the half-demolished barn to rot, but she'd known the minute she'd touched it that she had to have it. The wood called to her, full of earthy power and sweet, nourishing memory. Someone had built the piece with love and care, and many loving preparations had graced its surface. Once Wynn brought it home and cleaned it up, she had immediately begun using it for all her magical and herbal preparations, and the energy of the piece had only grown stronger.

The center of the table's surface she always kept clear so she had room to work, but jars and baskets, boxes and a small chest of drawers sat along the rear edge, pressed up close to the wall under the window. The containers held everything from herbs to feathers to small stones and bits of string—anything she might use in her magical work. More items filled two tall bookcases in opposite corners, and she crossed to one of these to retrieve something before returning to place her burden on the table's work surface.

"What do you intend to do?" Knox rasped, eyeing her with suspicion. "I will not allow you to place yourself at risk. If what you propose is dangerous, we will find another way to locate the Order's hiding place."

Wynn smiled. "Magic is an inherently risky business, Knox, but I can assure you," she hastened to add when he began to growl at her, "what I'm going to try is about as safe as it gets."

He didn't appear all that relieved, so she gestured to the object on the table. It was a small box, about half the size of a shoe box, constructed of what looked like scraps of wood. A small round knob of faceted glass, like something you might find on a cabinet door, protruded from the top, but it bore no other markings or identifying characteristics.

"This is a mirror box," she explained, "or at least, my version of one. Different examples of the same principle have been used in all sorts of magic practices, from witchcraft to hoodoo to root work to a whole bunch of others. The basic idea is to reflect magic back on itself. For example, if you think an item is cursed, you might place it in a mirror box intending that the negative energy would reflect back on whoever cast the curse. Sometimes I think the boxes get a little out of hand. Like when people crack the mirrors, or use poppets in the boxes to represent people they want to harm. Me, I just want to get a clear reflection of the source of that tracing spell."

Wynn grasped the tiny knob and lifted the lid off the box. Inside, it appeared to be the same rough, unadorned box it looked like from the outside, but when she showed him the underside of the lid, he could see the smooth, unbroken surface of a single glassy mirror.

"The mirror turns the magic back on itself, and the wood is salted to prevent any energy from leaking out. Hold on while I get one more thing."

She felt his eyes following her while she pulled a scrap of paper from a nearby stack and used it to line the bottom of the box. "Sometimes, the information about the source of the magic shows up in dreams, but other times it gets recorded on the paper. Either way, with a little luck, this spell will turn around in here and tell us not just who cast it, but where we can find them."

"And you are certain this will not cause you any harm."

"Like I said, the mirror reflects the magic back into the box, and the salt in the wood keeps any odds or ends from escaping." Wynn nodded to him. "Go ahead. Drop it in."

Reluctantly, Knox let the tiny piece of fabric flutter down into the box and watched while Wynn fit the top firmly into place. "The knob on top is also a kind of indicator. When the spell has expended all its energy and finished the trace, it should light up to let us know." Then she stepped back and crossed her arms over her chest.

"What happens now?" Knox asked after a moment of silence.

"Now we wait."

Chapter Nine

It took a barrage of threats, intimidation, bullying coercion, bribery, and the judicious use of physical force before Knox managed to get Wynn to go to bed and actually rest. The little witch tried to fight him, but exhaustion eventually overpowered even her stubborn streak.

He waited until he was certain she slept before he retrieved the body of the *nocturnis* detective and carried it into her small backyard. There, screened by trees and the tall wooden fence, he shifted into his natural form and launched himself into the air. He flew through the concealing cover of clouds out to the center of Lake Michigan before dropping the foul burden and letting it sink into the dark water. Whether he inflicted a few fresh cuts and scratches to entice the aquatic denizens to feast should concern no one.

Oh, he had no doubt the human authorities would take an interest in the disappearance of one of their own, but with no evidence of foul play, they would not get far. Nothing connected the detective back to Wynn any more than to the dozens of other cases he must have worked in his career. She would be in no danger.

Taking care to remain unseen, Knox made the return trip with speed, touching down behind Wynn's house a little over an hour from when he had left. As he let himself in through the kitchen door, he noted the broken pane of glass through which the *nocturnis* had gained entry. It took him some time to find what he needed to temporarily seal the hole. In the end he retook his human shape and used some clear plastic material and strong, sticky tape he found tucked into one of the kitchen drawers. It made no difference in security, of course—only replacing the half-glass door with something in solid steel would—but it would keep insects and the evening chill out.

Satisfied with his handiwork, he replaced his supplies and locked the door. He noticed then that his witch had a red string tied around the knob with keys dangling from the ends. He recalled seeing the same sort of thing at her mother's house. When he concentrated and looked closer, he noticed a faint glow coming from the keys and decided it must function as some sort of protective charm. Too bad it hadn't jolted the *nocturnis* straight in the ass.

He moved silently through the quiet house, drawn inexorably to his witch's side. The darkness of the bedroom where she lay meant nothing to him, as his night vision nearly equaled the acuity of his sight in the daytime. Wynn lay on her side beneath a fluffy covering, one arm curled beneath her, and the other tucked up so that her fingers curled in a loose fist beneath her chin. She looked innocent and so very fragile, and Knox felt something shift inside him as he stood above her and watched her breathe.

He knew he should concern himself with nothing more than neutralizing the threat to humanity posed by the *nocturnis*. For that reason alone had he been summoned from the nothingness of endless potential. He existed for no other reason than to battle against the forces of the Darkness, and yet he knew that if he had to choose between saving the world and saving this one small female, he would not hesitate to let the world sink into the abyss.

The knowledge made him uneasy. It ran contrary to the very core of his being, and yet he could do nothing to change it. Was this what those first Guardians had felt? he wondered. When they had grown bored with protecting a species for which they had no feelings, with which they shared no connection, was this what they had felt when they had woken to find their mates standing before them? He thought it must be, for he understood in his core that if his little witch asked him to take on the Darkness itself single-handed, he would do so just to please her.

It shook him, the thought that any creature should hold such immense power over his very existence, not because he feared she might abuse that power, but because he knew that he, a creature of such strength and ferocity, could be humbled by such a soft, tiny, weak little being. It made no sense.

No, *weak,* he realized, was the wrong word to describe his little witch. Fragile she might be, with her bones that easily snapped, her soft flesh that so quickly tore, and her short mortal life span; but at the core of her existed a strength he could feel every time she was near. It twined with the magic inside her, but he knew it existed separate from that power. The two fed off each other, her power greater because of her strength, her strength increased by the power she wielded. It all left him with a sense of awe and a burning desire to touch that inner magic and bathe in its bright, hot light.

Unable to resist the temptation, Knox gently seized a handful of fabric and drew back the covering that concealed her. She had removed her torn and soiled clothing before settling in to sleep, and now her soft, tempting curves lay before him, barely concealed by the pink scrap of cotton panties and the snug, gray tank top she wore over them. Her scent rose up to him, fresh and green and musky and sweet, and his mouth began to water. Like a lodestone, she drew him to her, and he followed helplessly, lost in the force of her magnetism.

He reached out, the need to touch her nearly unraveling him. With exquisite care, he traced the tip of one finger along the curve of her pale, shapely leg, admiring the silky smoothness of her skin and the warmth of her soft human flesh. Part of him wanted to seize, to grab and squeeze and stroke and taste, but another part wanted only to tend to her, to have her sleep and regain her physical strength for the battle he knew loomed before them. He might not know what the fight would entail, when it would begin, or where it would take place, but he could feel it coming deep in his bones.

"You know, in human society, it's considered impolite to molest a sleeping person. In fact, it's seen as pretty creepy."

His gaze shot to her face and found her regarding him

through dark eyes heavy with sleep but lit with amusement rather than indignation. He felt himself relax slightly and continued to explore the fascinating contours of her calf and thigh. "Then as you are now awake, I may continue without fear."

Wynn rolled to her back, her gaze searching his features, for what he did not know. If he could have given her what she sought, he would gladly have done so, but instead he simply held her gaze and allowed her to look.

When she spoke, her words caught him by surprise. "Do you really believe that fate can chose a mate for you? Just pick one out of the billions of humans walking this earth, plunk her down in front of you, and she would be the perfect match for you? No questions asked?"

He turned the question back on her. "You do not believe this is possible?"

She huffed out a soft breath. "I don't think I want to believe that. I prefer to think that we carve our own paths in life. To think that in the end, we have no choice about something as fundamental as who we spend our lives with . . . that scares me."

Knox hummed and laid his palm fully against his witch's skin, curling his fingers around her delicate knee. "I prefer to think that the Light designs for us the one being who most suits us, then offers us the chance to be together, knowing that no other would bring us half as much joy and contentment."

"I never would have pegged you as such a Pollyanna."

"I presume this means you think my outlook is simplistic and overly positive." He shrugged. "I find myself hard-pressed to believe otherwise when I am presented with such beautiful evidence to support my theory."

"Oh, smooth," she said, her tone wry. "Flattery is not going to distract me, though. How can you be content with just leaving it up to fate?"

Knox sighed and sank to sit beside her hip, his weight depressing the mattress and bringing her even closer against him. "How can I not? I knew from the moment I saw you that you belonged to me, that I must protect you with my life, and that if you were to be taken from me, nothing in existence, not even the Darkness itself, would stop me from getting you back."

He saw something flicker in her eyes, something made up of equal parts pleasure and wariness. "You mean you wanted to fuck me."

He growled at her dismissive tone and the crude way she described his desire for her. For him, having her would be so much more than a mechanical release of lust. He did not want to merely "fuck" her, as she termed it. He wanted to claim her, to possess her and be possessed, to sink into her soul until neither of them could tell their own being from the other.

Of course, the hardness between his legs insisted that she did have a point.

"Of course, I want to fuck you," he admitted roughly. "I am male and you are female. We feel attraction for each other. To want to satisfy that attraction is natural. But physical desire is only a small part of what I feel for you. My emotions for you are much more complex than simple lust."

"I didn't think Guardians were known to be emotional. You're supposed to be warriors, not exactly a touchy-feelyb unch."

Something colored her voice, uncertainty and a touch

of hope well hidden behind her bluster and sarcasm. He raised a brow and pinned her with his gaze. "You think because I take the form of stone that I have no more feelings than a rock?"

Wynn sighed heavily and lifted an arm to drape over her eyes, shielding her from his regard. "I don't know what I think. I'm too damned tired to think anything right now."

"Then do not try to think." He leaned forward, taking advantage of her temporary blindness to swoop in and hover his mouth over hers. "Simply feel."

He seized her lips before she even knew his intent. One minute his deep voice rumbled over her like the purr of a big cat, raising the hair on her arms and tightening her belly with a restless ache. The next, he took her mouth like an invading barbarian and the world around her dissolved in a rush of heat.

Already he tasted familiar, rich and dark, with a faint, intoxicating bitterness, like coffee and unsweetened cocoa. His flavor seeped into her until she began to crave it like a drug. Instead of pushing him away—she knew, oh but she knew she could push him away—she found herself raising her arms and twining them around his neck, pressing him closer until he settled over her like a blanket, heavier and warmer and so much more satisfying than her down-filled duvet.

His weight pressed her into the mattress, and she felt him brace his arms on either side of her, caging her within his embrace. Instead of making her feel trapped, it made her feel safe and protected, and she knew she was an idiot for thinking it. She was an idiot for allowing this kiss, for craving it, for aching to feel his body moving over her, around her, inside her, because if she surrendered to him there would be no going back. Allowing the Guardian to claim her meant giving herself to him forever.

How could she do it? Already, thorny tendrils of obligation and loyalty and human decency had twined around her to bind her to the Guardians and the Guild and the whole messy defense against the machinations of the Order. Bad enough that she had to work with the organization she'd resented for so long in order to put a stop to the *nocturnis*'s plans for her city, but to tie herself permanently to the very reason for that organization's existence seemed to her to qualify as a special form of insanity.

But then again, how could she not do this? Never in her life had Wynn felt anything like the electricity that sparked between her and Knox. If she could bottle it, she swore she could put ComEd out of business. Nothing in the world had ever felt so perfect, so right, and so damned exciting. This Guardian had lit a need inside of her that was fast taking her over. She craved him like air and water. If she pushed him away, how could she know if she would ever find this again?

How could she possibly live without it?

Groaning against his lips, she let herself dissolve. She sank into him, let him soak her up and make her a part of him. She knew now there would be no going back and prayed to the Goddess who watched over her that she wouldn't come to regret the decision.

In for a penny, in for a pound, her grandmother had said. Running her hands down the hard, muscular plane of his back, she found the hem of his dark T-shirt and snuck her fingers beneath. His skin felt hot and smooth, like flame itself, and she could feel the strength of him as his muscles flexed under her touch.

She had only seconds to savor the tactile sensations before he reared up above her and tore the cloth from his own back. Capturing her wrists in one large hand, he pressed them to the pillows above her head. "No distractions, little witch. I get to touch you first."

She might have protested, if she could have caught her breath, and if the sound of his tearing through the stretchy fabric of her top hadn't sent her head spinning with excitement. Wide-eyed, she gazed up at him, saw his mouth curve into a predatory grin, and felt the tip of something sharp as a knife slip beneath the fabric at her hip. She looked down just in time to see a razor-edged claw slice through her panties before the talon disappeared, leaving lean, callused fingers to glide over her sensitive skin.

"So pretty," he rumbled in a voice as deep and dark as the heart of a mountain. He brushed the scraps of cloth away from her skin and sat back on his heels, dragging his gaze over her like another caress.

Wynn shivered uncontrollably, not from cold, but from the heat building up inside her. He made her feel hot and wild and needy, and now that she had given in to the desire, all she wanted was to feel him inside her, because nothing less would sate it.

She didn't know if the man himself had caused this ache, or if it was a side effect of the bond fate had forged between them, despite all her protests. She wasn't even sure it mattered. Either way, she couldn't deny the way she ached deep inside, empty and needy, or the way she grew hot and slick between her thighs. She couldn't deny him, not anymore.

His huge, callused hand followed the path of his gaze, stroking the soft curve of her cheek and down over her throat. He skimmed across her collarbone and lingered at her breasts, palm cupping the weight of her, gently kneading until her breath grew fast and uneven.

Knox never hurried, giving each aching mound the same treatment before continuing his journey lower. Rough skin teased across her belly, making her quiver and tug impatiently at his grip on her wrists. He held her easily and refused to be rushed.

He pressed on the soft curve of her belly, and Wynn waited for the flush of embarrassment she always felt that she had never had a flat, trim stomach. It never came. How could it when he stared at her with heat so intense, she wondered that her skin didn't burn? Nothing but desire and deep appreciation shone from his eyes, and Wynn found herself relaxing, even pressing her curves against his hand, like a kitten begging to be stroked.

Knox obliged her, stroking out to her hip and squeezing with relish. Her mind immediately flashed her the image of both hands gripping her there, lifting her into his heavy thrusts, fingers leaving dark, possessive bruises on her skin. The thought only made her hotter, and she wondered if her hair might begin to smolder against her pillowcase. It would hardly surprise her.

As his fingers continued their journey of exploration across her body, she felt herself begin to tense, her body bracing itself for the moment when he reached the aching, needy flesh between her legs. She squeezed her eyes shut and felt her hips tilt upward without any prompting from her. Her breath froze in her chest as time swirled to a stop and she waited, waited, waited for that moment of exquisite torture.

It didn't come. Instead of sliding his fingertips through the tiny nest of curls over her mound and sinking into the slick folds beneath, she felt a confusing brush of something much softer, something that drew her brows together as she tried to process the unexpected touch. It came again, stirring gently against her skin before something soft and wet and hot touched her and sent her wits scattering.

Knox didn't bother to tease her with rough, knowing fingers. Instead, he went straight for the kill, pressing his mouth full against her and licking a path of conquest over her trembling core.

Goddess, he was going to kill her.

Wynn cried out, unable to bite back the sound, but it only seemed to urge him on. He tormented and consumed her, lapping and stroking and nibbling until her cries became pleas and her pleas a breathless entreaty for mercy. Her lover appeared to have none, driving her relentlessly into the maelstrom of pleasure. She felt like a bit of flotsam caught in the torrent of raging floodwaters. She shuddered and shook, arched and writhed, all while he skillfully tightened the cords of her desire until they snapped.

Her body bowed off the bed, shoulders and heels digging into the mattress, a scream breaking from her and echoing though the small room. She heard it as if from a distance, knowing it must have come from her, but unable to comprehend. She'd never made a noise like that in her life, but the rawness in her throat and the burning in her lungs told her no one else had done it.

He didn't even wait for the echo to fade. Crawling up her body like a predator capturing its prey, he cast a shadow over her, blocking out the light until all she saw was him. His eyes glowed, flames leaping and twisting behind the obsidian surface. She had an instant to drown in them before his mouth crushed once more against hers, and she drowned in his need instead.

She tasted herself on his lips and tongue. The flavor startled her, then annoyed her because all she wanted to taste was him. She dove deep, tangling her tongue with his, searching and exploring until the mocha essence of him exploded over her senses.

Her hands clutched at him, tugging him closer. If she could have crawled inside his skin, she would have. Even that wouldn't have gotten her close enough. She needed to be part of him, needed him to be part of her. Then his hips twisted, lunged forward, and suddenly he was.

He sank inside her, long and thick and harder than the stone he was carved from. She hissed at the slow burn as her body stretched to accommodate him. She'd gone a long time without a lover, and never had she felt so full, so complete as when his body joined with hers and froze, each of them savoring the power of the moment.

Knox tore his mouth from hers and raised his head to stare down at her. She wanted to look away, but she couldn't. She felt him sinking inside her soul even as he eased his hips back, slowly withdrawing from her body. Panic raced through her and she flung her legs around his hips, gripping him to her, desperate for him not to leave. He rumbled something dark and comforting and eased back in, soothing away the fear and inciting the need all at once.

She wanted to speak, wanted to tell him how good it felt, how perfect and exciting and erotic she found the sensation of his cock forging inside her, but she had no breath to form the words. Instead, she just whimpered and moaned and clutched at his shoulders, lifting into his steadily more powerful thrusts.

Her fingers slid up to the back of his neck and tugged, trying to bring his head down to hers. She wanted to fill herself with the flavor of him. She whimpered, and he took mercy, claiming her mouth again in a desperate kiss.

Desperation filled everything, every sound, every movement. They strained together, their bodies moving to a primitive rhythm, but she didn't know if they were struggling toward orgasm or toward something less tangible and more spiritual. For her part, she only knew that she needed more.

She breathed him in and found herself suddenly starved for oxygen. Tearing her mouth from his, she tilted her head back and gulped down great lungfuls of air. Even that smelled and tasted of him. He was everywhere, inside her, above her, around her, and yet still she couldn't get enough of him.

His breath rushed moist and hot against her cheek. She could feel his lungs working like a mighty bellows even as he continued to piston inside her. The tension in her womb ratcheted tighter, and then he shifted. His powerful thighs pushed her legs wider, his hands drew her hips higher, and his cock slid deeper, nudging her heart up into her throat and shattering her into a thousand pieces.

She felt like a field of stars, or the aftermath of a supernova, all twinkling light shining so brightly, she knew she could blind anyone who dared to gaze on her. She knew, but she didn't care. She felt infinite, powerful, not just filled with pleasure but like pleasure itself, and she clung to Knox as he roared in triumph and poured himself into her, giving herself back to him a thousand times more intense.

He collapsed over her. She barely felt it. His weight meant nothing, but the feel of his hot, sweat-sheened skin pressed all along her body made her want to purr. Nothing could have felt better. She wanted to wear him like a new skin, never losing contact between them.

Basking in the bliss, she concentrated on the only thing she understood, breathing in and out and letting the stardust settle back beneath her skin until she ceased to be the nova, and once again became human.

Human, and limp, and wrung out with exhaustion.

Eventually Knox shifted, and Wynn's fingers tightened against his shoulders, trying to keep him in place. Of course, her strength was no match for his, but he seemed to understand her desire to preserve their connection, because instead of moving off her, he rolled them across the bed until he lay on his back with her body draped bonelessly over his.

Her brain had begun to fill with a thick, sticky fog, like smoke flavored with molasses. Half a thought flitted through her dwindling consciousness, something about words. Maybe stringing them together into thoughts? No, she was too tired for that. Words could wait.

Everything could wait. Her world may have just changed for all eternity, but it would still be there, waiting to be dealt with when she woke up.

At least, she thought it would.

Chapter Ten

Knox woke, braced for another struggle. He feared that his little witch's surrender had been the whim of a moment, inspired by the cover of darkness and the haze of exhaustion. To his mind, their lovemaking had only sealed their bond. He had claimed his mate and would not, could not, now turn back. But how would Wynn feel about that? Would she once again try to deny their mutual destiny? He knew his female to possess the determination to try.

Cautiously, he turned his head and peered down at the small figure curled against his side. Her tousled head rested on his biceps like a pillow, and she had one hand tucked under her chin, the other resting lightly on his chest. Their legs tangled together beneath the concealment of the fluffy bedcover. To him, it felt like the best way to awaken, but he could not predict Wynn's reaction.

He nearly snorted as that thought struck him, but stifled the urge to prevent waking her. That could very well turn into a truism for his future—he could never predict what his mate would think or do or say from one minute to the next. On the one hand, it tormented him, because her unpredictability made protecting her that much more difficult; on the other, he knew he would never fall victim to boredom with a certain gorgeous witch by his side.

One hand reached up to brush a tangled curl behind her tiny, delicate ear. He wanted to trace the whorls with his fingertips, but again he felt loath to wake her. She looked so peaceful snuggled against him, and he feared peace might soon run in short supply.

When his hand shifted back to his side, he saw her eyes drift open. He found himself holding his breath, waiting to see if she would pick up the fight against him, or if she had truly given in to the bond between them and accepted him as her mate.

He should have known his witch would forge her own path.

Her mouth quirked up as she ran her gaze over his face. "Don't worry." Her voice was husky with sleep, deeper than usual, and the impact of it shot straight to his groin. "I'm not going to attack you, and I'm not going to pretend last night never happened. But I am going to tell you that we have more important things to deal with than this—" She gestured to where their bodies twined together under the duvet. "Whatever this is. So I'm going to concentrate on those right now, and I would appreciate it if you did that, too."

Inside him, Knox's beast snarled its displeasure. It wanted her total surrender, needed her to admit she belonged to him. It urged him to take her again, to overpower her with the force of his claim until she could no longer deny or avoid or ignore the bond between them. His rational side, however, knew that Wynn would respond to such a show of force by digging in her heels and refusing him with even greater determination. The only way he could hope to win her was by letting her come to him on her own.

No matter how badly that rankled.

He forced himself to nod and felt her relax against him. Closing his arms around her, he cuddled her to him and ran his fingers though the warm silk of her hair. "We must make a plan to move forward, then."

She sighed, her breath tickling over his skin like the brush of a feather. "Yeah, but I don't know how. I don't even really know what direction to look in. I get that you wouldn't be here if there weren't an immediate threat in this area, but Goddess only knows what it is. I feel so disconnected after being away for so long, like there could be clues all around us, but I wouldn't recognize them even if I looked."

He tightened his arms around her. "You cannot assume responsibility for an entire city all on your own, little witch. You are too small to carry such a heavy burden."

She tilted her head to glare up at him. "There you go with the 'little witch' thing again. What did I tell you about that?"

Knox grinned unrepentantly. "What can I say? You have bewitched me."

He saw her struggle to hold on to the irritation, but in the end she dropped her head to his shoulder and chuckled. "Smooth, big guy. Very smooth."

He pressed a kiss to the top of her head. "I try."

"Yes, you're very trying," she agreed wryly. "I'm serious, though. I honestly haven't got a clue about where to start looking. I mean, we can talk to Uncle Griffin again, see if he's noticed any unusual activity, but since the Guild pushed him aside, I don't think he's been as tuned in to tracking *nocturnis* activity. He became pretty withdrawn when it happened."

Knox recalled the conversation with his mate's uncle and the shock he had felt at the way the Guild dealt with such a long-serving member. In his understanding, the Guild did not operate in such a fashion. Hearing that had made the back of his neck itch. It simply felt wrong. He wondered if perhaps something more lurked behind that story.

"There is no sin in that, but he may have noticed more than he realizes. We will speak to him again," he told her, bringing his attention back to the matter at hand.

"Other than that, I'm not sure what else to do," she admitted. "I mean, I'll keep an eye on the mirror box, and as soon as the spell runs its course, I'm hoping that will tell us something. I didn't dream anything, though, and if the caster was even moderately powerful, it could take days before it fades. The downside of the mirroring is that reflecting the energy back on itself can feed it for a while, so it takes longer to peter out."

"Then as you said last night, we will wait."

She blew out a breath and made a face. "I hate waiting."

Knox turned his head, knowing she would not be able to miss the heat flaring in his dark eyes. "Perhaps you simply need something to distract you," he murmured.

His little witch went still, then her mouth began to curve. She ran slim, soft little fingers across his bare chest to cup his face in her hand. It look little pressure to urge him closer.

"Perhaps I do," she breathed against his lips. Then he touched her, and both of them had trouble breathing for the next little while.

They settled into a holding pattern over the next week. As Wynn had predicted, prodding her uncle's memory yielded nothing, but he appeared younger and more energetic than he had in years, thanks to his conversations with Ella and Fil. Feeling like a Warden again through helping guide their training had given him a new lease on life. It made Wynn happy to see it.

Of course, very little else did. The lack of a target for her restless energy made her cranky. She'd gone from the adrenaline rush of the battle in Montreal to the attack in Lake Forest to the break-in by the *nocturnis* detective, and now all she could do was pace around her house and wait for something, *anything,* to show her what to do next.

And Knox, unfortunately, wasn't helping. Oh, he distracted her often enough. Since she had given in to him that night and let herself be seduced, the big guy couldn't keep his hands off her. She felt hard-pressed to protest, considering how incredible the sex was between them, but the growing intimacy only made her more uneasy. A part of her knew it didn't matter anymore, that the decision to accept him as her mate was moot. It was fact, no turning back. But she couldn't push back the feelings of doubt and anxiety. She'd spent too long resenting the

Guild and the Guardians to happily commit her life to loving one.

He, of course, didn't see the problem. Why would he? Things continued to fall into place just the way he wanted them, at least where she came in. He didn't understand her problem, why she felt the need to struggle against something that for him appeared so black and white. To tell the truth, she could barely understand, either. Maybe she only continued to fight because fighting was all she knew.

Either way, a week passed with plenty of sex and absolutely no clues as to what they needed to do next. Wynn busied herself with work, trying to build up a stock of her wares so she would have plenty on hand when she met with her local clients to tell them she was back in town. Not having to ship things in from Canada for her long-standing clients made a nice change of pace, but she still needed to give herself a good head start before she started taking any new orders.

So she ground and boiled and distilled, mixed and measured and tried not to stare intently at the clear glass knob atop the mirror box. It made her uneasy that the spell still hadn't fully dissipated, because it indicated that whoever had cast it had a hell of a lot of power at his disposal. Thinking of all that energy concentrated in the hands of a *nocturnis* cultist did not make for the best night's sleep, that was for sure.

The one good aspect of all the waiting and none of the doing was that it gave her injuries time to heal. The *hhissih* cut on her leg had improved steadily since Uncle Griffin had applied his poultice. It had closed fairly evenly and was now scabbed over. It looked like hell and it itched even worse, but it wouldn't be long before only a scar remained. According to Griffin, *hhissih* venom meant the wounds always scarred.

Getting her ankle back in shape proved a bit trickier. Sprains healed with notorious slowness, but she made sure to baby it, applying ice and castor oil packs for the swelling, and treating it several times a day with arnica balm, massaging the herbal remedy in well. She practiced gentle range-of-motion exercises and kept her weight off it until it could support her comfortably. All in all, it had healed fairly well. She should probably avoid entering any races or playing hopscotch for a while, but mostly things were getting back to normal.

By the time the following Friday rolled around, Wynn felt about one step away from breaking down and throwing a royal, screaming hissy fit. She didn't know who her target would be, or what would finally set her off, but she felt like the inside of a pressure cooker without a release valve in sight; once she exploded, things were going to get messy.

Just after dinner that evening, as she loaded the dishes into the dishwasher while Knox wiped off the table, her cell phone rang. Assuming it would be another call from her mother, checking in on her, or from her uncle to discuss his developing lesson plans, she scooped her phone up one-handed and pressed the ANSWER key before pinning it against her shoulder.

"Hello," she said absently.

"Wynn, it's Ella. I think I may have found something interesting."

Immediately Wynn stiffened, and the phone went skidding off her shoulders to bounce off the run in front of the sink and go skittering under the overhang of a lower cabinet. She dove after it, snatching it up and immediately pressing it back to her ear. "Sorry! I'm so sorry! Hello? Are you still there."

"I'm here," Ella reassured her. "What happened?"

"I dropped my phone." Wynn waved frantically at Knox to get his attention, then crossed to his side and pulled out a chair at the small table. "Knox is right here, though. Can I put you on speaker?"

"Go ahead. I've got Kees with me, as well."

Excitement trembled through her fingertips as she laid her phone faceup on the surface of the table and activated the speaker function. "You there?"

"Still here. Hey, Knox. How are you?"

"I am well," he rumbled.

"Yeah, yeah, we're all good," Wynn interrupted impatiently. "El, can the small talk. You said you found something?"

"I said I may have found something, emphasis on the 'may.' It's not exactly what you'd call a smoking gun."

"Well, what is it?"

She heard Ella draw in a deep breath. "Okay, so I've been digging like a terrier for any information that might link those two guys you mentioned—Coleman and Garvey?—anything to tie them to the Order."

"And you found something." Wynn's heart leapt with excitement.

"Not a bloody thing. Those guys are like Donald Trump minus the sleaze—hugely successful, ridiculously wealthy, and universally respected."

"Shit. How does that help us?" Wynn felt her heart begin to sink.

"It doesn't. You really have to let me tell this story, sweetie, or we'll be here all night."

She heard Kees chuckle in the background and winced. A warm hand covered hers, bringing with it a layer of tranquility that only Knox could offer. Maybe it was because he was so big, but he always seemed so unruffled, just having him near helped her remember to breathe.

"Sorry," she said sheepishly, reaching inside for her own sense of calm. "Go ahead, El."

"Thanks. So, neither of these guys has any obvious ties to the Order. I mean, belonging to a cult of demon-worshipping lunatics is not something anyone generally brags about at Starbucks, you know? But Coleman and Garvey don't even flip my radar. No ties to known *nocturnis,* not even through secondary investments, and nothing to suggest any interest in the occult, the Guild, Guardians, gargoyles, or the ancient Enochians. They look completely clean."

"Please tell me you have a 'but' coming."

"Sweetie, I've got buts coming and going." Ella's grin was practically audible. "The one thing I found out about Coleman that interests me is that he's rumored to be quite a collector of primitive art and artifacts."

Wynn frowned. "So?"

"So, apparently when he and this Garvey fellow broke ground for their big office tower in Chicago, there was a bit of a delay in construction because of some items that turned up while the crew was digging the foundation."

Oh, that made Wynn's Spidey-sense start to tingle. "Items like what?"

"Well, I couldn't find a complete catalog, but most of the articles I read alluded to them being Native American in origin, which might have made me shrug them off, but then I ran across this." Ella paused and the sound of rustling papers drifted over the phone connection. "I have an article here that says that Ronald Coleman donated many of the artifacts to a local museum, but he decided to keep an otherwise unremarkable item for himself, as a memento of the dig. It also says that he brought the item to the archaeology department of the University of Chicago for authentication and analysis. Wynn, didn't you say your brother was a grad student there?"

Wynn nodded, feeling suddenly off balance. When Knox squeezed her hand and nodded toward the phone, she remembered that her friend couldn't see her and cleared her throat. "Yeah. Yes, Bran is pursuing his doctorate in the archaeology department there. Do you think it means something?"

She asked the question, but her gut had already tightened, and the hair at the back of her neck had begun to prickle. A little voice inside her whispered that this meant something important indeed. She just had no idea what that might be.

"It's hard to say," Ella replied cautiously. "I mean, it could be nothing. It's not like it's a direct connection to the Order, but I'm not a real big believer in coincidence anymore. I find it strange that this Coleman guy's name keeps popping up, especially when it pops up in relation to your brother, who has gone missing and who is a Warden on top of it. If the Order was becoming especially active in your area, or planning something big, and your brother got wind of it, wouldn't he have tried to look into it? I think it might be worth a conversation with Coleman, either way. The worst that can happen is you get a little more info on what Bran was up to before his disappearance."

Wynn stared down at the table and tried to corral her stampeding thoughts. "Talking to the guy is easier said than done, El. Ronald Coleman really is a lot like Donald Trump here in Chicago. He's not the kind of person you can just walk up to and start talking with. I'm sure I'd have to make an appointment to see him, and I have a feeling I'd have to have a good reason even to get on his schedule. It's that kind of thing."

"There are ways around this kind of obstacle," Knox said, voice deep and hard and intimidating. "Any wall can be breached. Every defense has its weakness."

"I'm putting my foot down at breaking and entering," Wynn said, shooting him a glare. "What worked for Fil—who almost got blown up in the attempt, by the way—does not work for me."

"What about something else then? Maybe some kind of ruse." There was a pause while each of them pondered the idea. "You know, if you were a couple of inches shorter, we could just get you a green uniform, and you could go in selling Girl Scout cookies. No one turns away Girl Scout cookies."

Wynn rolled her eyes. "El, when I was thirteen, people thought I looked twenty. I don't think that at twenty-nine I'm going to be passing for thirteen."

"It was just an idea," Ella grumbled.

"I think you would look very cute in one of those uniforms, Wynn," Kees teased, and Knox growled in obvious displeasure.

Wynn shushed him. "Down, boy."

Kees only laughed. "Fear not, brother. I have my own mate. I have no interest in courting yours."

"You would court death," Knox grumbled.

"I'll try and think of something." Wynn rushed in to try and drag the conversation back on point. "I know Coleman is always in the papers for showing up at some charity event or another. Maybe I can find someone who could score me an invitation to something like that."

"That could work," Ella agreed, sounding encouraged.

"We will think on it," Knox said, leaning forward into the phone's speaker, "but in the meantime, I have another topic I would like to discuss."

Something in the Guardian's voice made Wynn take notice. She frowned as she studied his expression, as hard and closed as usual. The man could make a killing on the poker circuit.

"What troubles you, brother?" Kees asked, clearly picking up on his fellow warrior's tone of voice.

"I know that Ella has begun communicating with Wynn's uncle regarding their studies in the art and skills needed to be a Warden," Knox began. "Have you spoken to the man as well, brother?"

"I have not. No more than a few exchanges of greetings, at any rate."

"But you are aware that he was once a member of the Guild?"

"Once a member," Kees scoffed. "The Guild is not

some kind of social club where one belongs only as long as one pays for the privilege. Once a human becomes a Warden, he remains a Warden until death."

"I share that belief, and it is one I never conceived would come into question. So I find myself troubled by Griffin's assertion that he was forced into retirement due to his backfired spell."

"As do I."

Wynn frowned. "What are you guys saying? Do you think there's something hinky going down at the Guild?"

"*Was* something 'going down,' as you put it," Knox corrected. "From all I have seen and all you have told me, the Guild as it once existed is no more. I believe the evidence suggests that trouble was brewing there long before the fire you say destroyed the Guild offices in Paris. In fact, if I were pressed, I would speculate that the fire itself speaks to those issues. How does one burn down a building populated entirely by powerful magic users?"

"One uses traitors to ensure the victory." Kees's voice came over the connection, rough and grim.

"Exactly."

Just the idea of it made Wynn's entire world shift on its axis. The thought of a corrupt Guild operated on a level so contrary to everything she'd ever heard, everything she'd ever been taught growing up, that her mind literally boggled (not that she knew precisely what "boggling" entailed, but the sound of it seemed to fit the circumstances). She expected to feel a surge of triumph. After all, she'd hated the Guild for long enough, always called them archaic and closed-minded and uninterested in the things that would truly make them stronger.

Shouldn't she be happy to have all her dire pronounce-
ments confirmed?

So why did she feel so . . . hollow? Wrung out and
somehow saddened?

A whistle came from the phone before Ella spoke.
"Wow. Okay. Yeah, that's like a really big accusation to
throw out there, fellas. What actual proof is there to support that?"

"This is something I would ask you to look into,
Ella," Knox said. "Your ability to find information
has impressed me, and I am certain you have the best
chance of finding evidence to either support or dis-
prove my theory. Your skills make you the obvious
choice."

"Sure, because reading through old newspaper articles and sifting through the metaphorical rubble of a
centuries-old building owned by a millennia-old organization are soooo the same thing," Ella griped.

"If you cannot do this, I am unsure anyone could."

"And heap on the pressure there. Nice. Thank you
very much."

Kees's voice came through, quiet and soothing. "I will
aid you, of course, sweet. Do not worry."

"In the meantime, Wynn and I will find a way to
speak with this Coleman human. Perhaps he can lead
us to the Order, or to Wynn's brother. Either would be
useful."

"Okay," Ella agreed. "Good luck, guys. Keep us updated."

"You too."

The call ended, and Wynn had the worst feeling
that luck alone wouldn't be enough to save any of

them. Where was a little divine intervention when you needed it?

For the first time in her life, Wynn almost wished she'd spent her extracurricular time in high school on the drama club instead of the gardening team. Sure, she could grow tomatoes juicier than an orange and basil with leaves the size of dinner plates, but she had no idea if she could pull off the masquerade she and Knox had dreamed up.

After considering and discarding several ideas to gain them an audience with the millionaire, including the charity event ambush, Fil had suggested a ploy she herself had used in the past—posing as a reporter. Or in this case, a freelance magazine writer. Apparently, all you had to do was tell someone you wanted to do a feature on them for *Fortune, Forbes, Time,* or *Newsweek,* and folks couldn't wait to ask you over for coffee. Weird, right?

Wynn was impressed by how quickly her cover story had gotten her an appointment with Coleman; his secretary had bent over backward to work her into the schedule. Knox, however, was less than enthusiastic.

"I do not like it," he had said. And repeated. And reiterated. And harped on. Ad nauseam for the previous ten days. His objections stemmed from the fact that her story provided for only one cover, which meant she'd be conducting this interview on her own. Somehow, she didn't think a freelance writer bringing a bodyguard to an interview with a high-powered businessman would fly. Knox would have to content himself with escorting her to and from the CG Towers building.

Every time the subject of her being out of his line of sight for even five minutes—let alone the hour she had blocked for the interview—came up, he uttered a menacing growl and began pacing like a caged lion. She might have been touched if the whole alpha-male display didn't drive her up the nearest wall.

"I still do not like it."

Wynn rolled her eyes and begged for patience. "I know, Knox. I know you don't like it. Fil and Spar know you don't like it. Ella and Kees know you don't like it. Uncle Griffin knows you don't like it. In fact, I think the International Space Station knows you don't like it. Unfortunately for you, you're going to have to lump it. This is the best idea we have for getting info on Coleman. Not only does it let me ask him questions without rousing his suspicion, but I can also get a read on him. I'm not Fil when it comes to reading auras, but I have a spell that will let me know if he's got any power of the magical variety. If he does, it adds to the evidence he's hooked up with the Order. Knowing that will be invaluable. It will actually give us a start on tracking them down."

Knox grunted and continued to stare at her from where he lounged on the bed, as if he could intimidate her into changing her mind and calling the whole thing off. It was way too late for that. The interview was scheduled for the next afternoon, and Wynn was currently rummaging through her closet trying to put together an outfit that said, *professional freelance magazine writer* instead of *hippie herbalist witch with a tendency to spill things.* She hadn't expected quite as big a challenge.

She had her choices narrowed down to a pair of plain,

black pants that could maybe pass for business trousers if she actually ironed them, and a coral sweater set a well-meaning and absolutely clueless aunt had given her for Yule and that she hadn't gotten around to returning until it was too late. It was either that or a shirt dress that actually belonged to her mother and that Wynn had picked up at the dry cleaner's with the intention of returning it the next time they saw each other. That had been before she went to Montreal, but she had kept forgetting. Luckily, she and her mom wore about the same size, but the deep-green color really looked much better with Mona's auburn hair and cinnamon-freckled skin than it would with Wynn's plainer coloring.

"We should have thought of a story that would allow me to be in the room while you question the human."

"And I shouldn't have put off figuring out what to wear until eleven o'clock the night before," Wynn muttered, only half listening to his complaints. After all, she'd heard them just over seventy-five billion times in the last few days.

When Knox spoke again, his voice sounded much closer. In fact, she could feel the vibrations of his snarl against her ear. "Do not dismiss my concerns for your safety. Not only are you my Warden, little witch, but you are my mate. And I grow weary of reminding you of that fact."

She tried to spin around to face him, but his hard hands closed over her upper arms and held her in place. She shivered as his breath whispered against her skin and felt the familiar, uncontrollable spread of heat that washed through her every time he got close to her. She felt like Pavlov's dog, only instead of drooling at the

sound of a bell, she drenched her panties at the touch of
a Guardian.

Well, the touch of one particular Guardian, anyway.

Wynn braced a hand against the closet door and tried
to control her trembling. She failed miserably, of course,
but at least she could tell herself she'd tried. One of his
big, rough hands slid down her arm, left inconveniently
bare by the pajama tank top she had changed into in
preparation for bed. She didn't know why she kept bothering to put on pajamas since Knox routinely had her
naked ten seconds after her butt hit the mattress (and
sometimes well before she got anywhere near it), but
old habits died hard. He wrapped his arm around her
waist and tugged until her back nestled against him.
His erection pressed into the small of her back, hard and
insistent.

"What do I need to do, little witch, to get you to
admit that you belong to me?"

Wynn swallowed hard. "I belong to myself, Knox.
This is the twenty-first century. Doesn't your vast store
of universal knowledge include an overview of the term
feminism?"

His other hand left her arms to stroke up over her
shoulder and across her collarbone. His fingers cupped
over her throat, not threatening, but possessing and protecting. "I do not doubt your intellectual or spiritual
equality with me, mate. When I say you belong to me,
it is only because I belong so utterly to you, as well."

Wow. If words like those didn't melt a girl's knees,
nothing would. Wynn had to lock the pesky joints in
place to keep from sliding into a puddle at his feet. "You
know how I feel about the mating thing."

"I know you resist the truth, but I do not understand your reasoning, little witch. Not even remotely." He lowered his head and dragged his lips across the curve of her neck, sending her nerve endings into a tumultuous riot state. "How can you deny something so clear? So obvious? So perfect?"

He punctuated the questions with a series of little nips that had her pussy clenching and her eyes drifting shut on a moan. The man could play her like a guitar—one pluck to her strings, and she would vibrate in tune for hours.

Her fingers closed around the arm at her waist, gripping it in a vain attempt to steady herself. His muscles might as well have been made of steel bands, or the granite of his sleeping form. They gave not a millimeter under pressure, no matter how tightly she squeezed.

Despite the gentle strength of his embrace, Wynn felt squeezed enough for both of them. Not physically, but emotionally, as if a fist had closed around her heart and begun to exert a steady, inescapable pressure.

Every time he spoke this way, the fist tightened. When he expressed his feelings for her—always here like this, while he touched her or made love to her—he used words of possession and passion. He told her they belonged to each other, that she was his, that he was her mate. And he made love to her like a starving man, as if he couldn't get enough of her.

Wynn had never had so much sex in her life as she'd had since meeting Knox, but no matter how many orgasms he drew from her, each one left her wondering. Not about his desire, but about his emotions. Was it

enough that he clearly wanted her? That he felt possessive and protective and jealous?

Not for her, it wasn't. None of those things equaled
love, and without love she would always wonder if he
wanted her for her, or if he simply wanted not to turn
back to stone. She didn't blame him for wanting to avoid
the magical slumber of his kind, but she wasn't willing
to spend the rest of her life with him just to avoid it. If
she tried, her heart would be what turned to stone. She
just knew it.

"It's not denial," she said, trying to make her voice
come out strong and certain, instead of weak and whim-
pering. "It's realism. No one can force us to be together,
Knox. Not even us."

Without warning, Knox shifted his grip and spun her
to face him, pressing her back against the closet door.
The doorknob thumped against the wall behind it as their
weight forced the collision. The Guardian lifted her up
until their eyes were level and held her there while he
growledh isd ispleasure.

"Why do you say these things?" he demanded.

His eyes burned with that eerie inner fire, and when
his lip curled back she could see the tip of his fangs, as
if his natural form had bled into his human shape. His
skin hadn't gone gray, and he hadn't sprouted wings, but
Wynn knew he teetered on the edge of losing control.
She didn't fear he might hurt her, though, so she couldn't
make herself back off.

"I'll keep saying them until you start accepting them,"
she snapped back. "You don't get to determine the future for both of us, Knox. You can't force me to accept
you."

Abruptly, he set her back on her feet and took a step back. His expression went from furious to incredulous in an instant. "You would accuse me of forcing myself on you? When have I done this? When have I ever harmed you? You have wanted me as badly as I have wanted you."

"Relax. I'm not talking about you abusing me, you idiot. I'm just saying that I don't buy into the mate thing, and you can't make me. I won't let myself be forced into a relationship by some ridiculous notion of destiny. I make my own decisions."

"And you have decided you do not want me." His voice went flat and the fire in his eyes flickered out as if it had never burned. All emotion drained from his face, and the Guardian once again looked as if he had been carved from stone. Only the gray tinge to his skin was missing.

For some reason, the sudden transformation rocked Wynn. Unconsciously, she reached for him and was stunned when he moved away from her, deliberately avoiding her touch. "Knox . . ."

He shook his head and turned his back on her, taking heavy measured steps toward the bedroom door. "You have made yourself clear. I will not trouble you. You should sleep. Tomorrow's task is an important one. You will need to be rested and ready. I will see you in the morning."

Before she could open her mouth to speak, to apologize, to do anything, Knox left the room and shut the door softly behind him. The quiet click echoed in Wynn's head with the loudness of a gunshot, but she felt the impact of the bullet in her heart.

Chapter Eleven

Wynn checked her borrowed shoulder tote for the nine millionth time. Usually, she carried a battered canvas messenger bag filled with herbs and potions and magical supplies all lumped together with her ID, money, and the detritus of her everyday life, but today she needed to project the illusion of professionalism, so the black leather laptop carrier *cum* designer handbag had been pressed into service. She had nightmares about scratching it before she could return it to the friend who had lent it to her, but she was trying to ignore them. She had enough to worry about without those piling on.

She had left Knox sitting at a table outside a chic café in the atrium of CG Towers. On the one hand, she'd felt relief at putting some distance between them. He had barely spoken to her since the scene in her bedroom last night, and being anywhere near him made her feel as if she'd simultaneously kicked a puppy and turned into one before getting kicked herself. She hadn't been trying to hurt him; she'd simply been trying to protect herself from getting hurt. Unfortunately, she was discovering that his coldness caused her plenty of pain, so she appeared to be screwed either way.

On the other hand, every step she took away from her Guardian and toward the offices of Coleman Enterprises made her wish fervently that she'd included Knox in her cover story. Just having him by her side made her feel safer, a feeling she'd somehow grown accustomed to over the last couple of weeks. Now she found herself almost missing his coldness, because at least feeling his stony presence meant he was close by. This whole solo-investigating thing sucked as far as Wynn was concerned.

Hoping to distract herself from her bout of nerves, Wynn forced herself to take in her surroundings. CG Towers had officially opened its doors while she had been in Montreal, after two years of lightning-fast construction, so this was the first time she had visited the gleaming skyscraper located just a short block off the city's famous Magnificent Mile. Clearly designed to impressed, the main entrance gave into the atrium, a shining, marble-covered wonderland populated by a buzzy big-name chef's latest restaurant, the gourmet coffee-serving café where she'd left Knox, and a handful of very high-end boutiques selling women's shoes and handbags, luxury perfumes and bath products, and ridiculously expensive shaving supplies. She also spotted a branch office of a major regional banking company, and what looked like an old-fashioned luxury stationer. She felt like she'd stepped into an episode of some television show dedicated to making average Americans completely discontent with their own lives.

The elevator that carried her up to the sixtieth floor
sported copper-clad doors and an interior paneled in real
wood with large, framed mirrors on each of the three
stationary walls. Her delicate black flats sank into car-
peting so deep, it tempted her to kick the shoes off and
curl her toes in the pile. She resisted the temptation.

When she saw the digital numbers over the doors flip
to 60, she wiped a damp palm on the leg of the black
trousers she'd worn (the dress had seemed too Donna
Reed) and gulped in a last deep breath.

Showtime.

The elevator doors slid back, opening not into a hallway, as Wynn had expected, but into a large, sleek lobby.
Straight ahead, a curved counter, high enough to conceal
all but the head of any person seated behind it, shone
the burnished gold of antique maple. High on the wall
behind it, hammered copper lettering spelled out COLE-
MAN ENTERPRISES, LLC. Lush green plants in large copper pots flanked the desk, and a sinuous modern vase
adorned the surface. From its neck rose a frond of fern
so dark and green it looked almost black and a single,
enormous lily, easily the size of a soccer ball, in an
aggressive, vibrant orange.

As she stood there taking it all in, the figure behind
the desk rose and looked at her with bland politeness.
"May I help you?"

For a minute, Wynn wondered whether anyone ever
noticed the woman, especially in the shadow of that os-
tentatious bloom. Wynn hadn't, not until she spoke. The
woman wore a plain gray suit, the kind with a jacket that
wasn't meant to be removed. It fit her beautifully, obviously well tailored, but it made about as much of a fash-

ion statement as oatmeal. Her shoes and jewelry appeared equally high in quality and equally low in impact. With her hair pulled back in a sleek chignon, her fair skin and subtle makeup, the woman almost seemed as if she wanted to be invisible, which struck Wynn as odd for someone guarding the door of an important company.

Trying to act like a writer (Should she lock herself in a garret? Toss back some absinthe? How was she supposed to *do* this?), Wynn pasted on a smile and strode toward the desk with confidence she certainly didn't feel.

"Hello," she greeted, striving for breezy warmth. You know, like Tahiti. "I have a two o'clock appointment with Ronald Coleman. I'm Lynn Lewis."

Her cover identity. Fil had helped her put it together, and she had argued against the alliteration, but Fil had said it was perfect. Only real people had names that were almost stupid but not quite, according to her. Plus, *Lynn* sounded enough like *Wynn* that it should limit confusion and the possibility of mistakes.

"I'll let his assistant know that you're here." The invisible woman's response to breezy warmth, apparently, was robotic efficiency. Maybe she was one of those people who disliked the tropics. "Please, make yourself comfortable."

Wynn followed her gesture to a set of leather armchairs elegantly grouped around a low table to the right of the desk. Offering a polite smile, she headed that way, but she didn't intend to sit. At this point, she had built up so much nervous energy, she was surprised her feet still touched the ground.

Rather than sitting, she used the time to peruse the two paintings that decorated the waiting area. Both were

landscapes, one an impressionistic, brightly colored in-
terpretation of the Chicago skyline. Wynn found it pleasant but unremarkable, and found herself wondering what
Ella or Fil would think of it. They were the art experts,
not her.

The second painting also fell in a style Wynn would,
with her lack of any knowledge of art schools or peri-
ods, label impressionistic. To her that meant the artist
had portrayed a scene that was easily recognizable for
what it was, but not precisely what a camera might cap-
ture. In this case, the picture showed a hilltop around
dusk, at least if the dark blues and greens and purples
that dominated the color palette were anything to go by.
The perspective appeared to be from someone standing
at the top of the hill, looking back on the path he had
climbed to the summit. Trees blanketed the sides of the
hill and seemed to close in on the viewer, the feeling of
being surrounded by them so vivid Wynn swore she
could almost hear their leaves shushing in the night
breeze.

Really, the image was perfectly ordinary and un-
threatening, just a nature scene of an out-of-the-way bit
of forest. Something about it poked at the back on Wynn's
mind, though, and she found herself vaguely uncomfortable the longer she looked at it.

"Ms. Lewis?"

Startled, Wynn turned to find herself looking at another woman in beautifully tailored clothing, but the
similarities ended there. Ronald Coleman's assistant, or
so she assumed, wore a trim, short jacket in a deep shade
of scarlet with black fabric buttons and a touch of black
embroidery on the mandarin collar. She paired that with

trim black trousers and black, strappy pumps that probably cost more than Wynn's mortgage payment. Her smiling mouth had been painted a slighter darker red than her jacket, and her glossy dark hair had been styled in an abbreviated bob and just skimmed the angle of her jaw.

"Mr. Coleman is looking forward to speaking with you," she said, extending a hand with smooth, fair skin and neatly trimmed nails painted an unobstrusive pinky-beige. "I'm Jacquie Remington, his personal assistant."

Wynn collected herself and shook the other woman's hand. "I'm looking forward to talking to him, too. I think a lot of people are going to be interested in what he has to say."

Look at her, telling the truth in a way that meant nothing at all like it sounded. *Bring on the polygraph, bitches.*

"His office is this way." Jacquie led the way back past the reception desk and down a wide, well-lit hall paneled in more aged maple with copper accent pieces. "Can I get you anything to drink before you go in? Coffee? Tea? Water?"

"No thanks, I'm fine." If you didn't count the anxiety-induced nausea, that was.

Forcing herself to be calm, Wynn reviewed her story in preparation for meeting the man himself. She just needed to stick to her cover, and everything would be fine. Besides, what could happen? If she screwed up, Coleman might throw her out of his office, or maybe even call security to have her escorted from the building, but it wasn't like he was going to sacrifice her to Satan right there on his office desk. There would be a bazillion witnesses, and even if they all worked for him, she couldn't believe not a single one of them would have a conscience. She would be fine.

Plus, if she so much as screamed, she knew that mad at her or not, her three-hundred-pound Guardian dog would fly in through those plate-glass windows and tear apart anyone who tried to hurt her. So there.

The hall ended at a smooth, solid door with a knob made of burnished copper. Wynn found herself hoping like hell someone had coated it with a glossy coat of something tarnish-resistant; otherwise she had to assume that Coleman's payroll included a full-time knob polisher just for this door.

Wait, did that sound dirty?

She bit back a giggle that smacked of nervous hysteria as Jacquie paused to knock lightly on the expanse of burnished glossy maple. Someone inside called a greeting, so the assistant opened the door and followed its arc, leaving space for Wynn to step into the room beside her.

"Mr. Coleman, this is Lynn Lewis, the magazine writer," she introduced smoothly. "Ms. Lewis, Ronald Coleman, founder and president of Coleman Enterprises."

Ronald Coleman stepped out from behind a desk consisting of a huge expanse of tempered glass supported by twin columns of the same maple that appeared over and over throughout his office. His hand was already extended as he stepped forward, his smile wide and bright and consciously charming. In his dark pin-striped suit and pale-blue silk shirt worn without a tie and open at the collar, he looked like a politician playing at casual Friday.

Wynn attempted to inject some enthusiasm into her

smile and only hoped she did half as well as he did. She shook his hand briskly, noting his cool, smooth skin and the platinum watch that glinted at his wrist.

"Ms. Lewis," he greeted her jovially, "what a pleasure to meet you. Please, please come in. Have a seat."

He ushered her to one of two modern club chairs positioned in front of his desk, his head turned to look back at his assistant. "Coffee, Jacquie, please."

Wynn didn't bother to protest that she couldn't swallow much more than her own spit at the moment. Somehow she thought it might not go with her professional reporter's persona. "Thank you so much for agreeing to spare me this time, Mr. Coleman. I know what a busy man you must be, but that's one of the reasons I think people will be so fascinated to learn more about you."

Wow, she'd done that pretty well, Wynn thought, settling back in her chair and using the excuse of digging a notebook and pencil out of her bag to force in a another calming breath. Maybe she really could pull this off. Then she realized she'd forgotten the small voice recorder Fil assured her no modern interviewer went without, and she dove back into her bag to retrieve it.

He gave a hearty chuckle. "'Fascinated' might be taking things a little too far, Lynn. Do you mind if I call you that? Please feel free to call me Ron."

"Lynn is fine, thank you, Ron." She forced a smile and made a show of balancing the small recorder on the arm of her chair between them. "I hope you don't mind if I record. It guarantees the accuracy of quotes and keeps me honest with the little details."

She didn't bother to mention the small spell she'd put on the device, which would hopefully allow it to record any sounds that might be present in the energetic range, meaning things inaudible to the human ear but characteristic of magical energy. Just because she couldn't see something, after all, didn't mean it wasn't there.

"No, not at all. Feel free. I'm an admirer of accuracy, especially when it keeps me out of trouble."

He chuckled again, and Wynn found herself trying to figure out if he really found himself that amusing, or if he thought appearing so good-humored would contribute to her portraying him in a more flattering light in the story she was supposedly going to write.

The office door opened again, and Jacquie reappeared bearing a rectangular wooden tray with a petite silver coffee set and two cups. She set it on the small table between their chairs, flashed a smile, and retreated without a word. How efficiently subservient.

Wynn took the opportunity to tap into the spell she had cast on the way over that would allow her to see any signs of intrinsic magical power in Coleman's aura. She absently accepted a cup of coffee and focused all her attention on him while he prepared his own.

She couldn't say precisely what she had expected to see when she looked at Ronald Coleman through the veil of her spell. Part of her hoped he would light up her magical vision with the tainted red glow of a true-believer *nocturnis.* After all, it would shorten their search considerably if they found a link to the Order in the very first place she looked. Even a tinge of magical energy, the kind that wafted up from someone with minor abilities, like intuition, or expanded empathy, or a fortune blessing, might have made her feel a little better. At least it would have made this whole charade worth the effort.

But when she looked at Ronald Coleman, Wynn saw absolutely nothing. To her eyes, as well as to her powerful spell, the man appeared completely ordinary, about as magical as American cheese. And for this she'd practically given herself an ulcer.

Lowering her eyes, she took a sip of coffee, then set the cup aside. She hadn't wanted it to begin with, and now she didn't want to waste any more time here than she had to. With a blink, she let her spell dissipate. Time to get this interview started. Maybe if she could manage to work in a few questions about his artifact collection and the consultation he'd hired Bran's department to do she could salvage at least something from this gigantic waste of time.

Picking up her notebook and pen, she forced herself to smile at "Ron" and appear interested. "I hope you don't mind if I jump right into this, but I know your time is valuable, and I have a lot of questions for you."

Coleman sat back with his cup and saucer and waved for her to proceed. "By all means, Lynn, let's have some fun."

His odd phrasing and his toothy smile almost gave her pause, but she had too much to remember about conducting a believable interview to let herself get distracted. Fil had coached her for hours on what to ask, what to make notes on, how to respond and just make herself look like she knew what she was doing. Thankfully, Fil had spent a lot of time with an actual newspaper reporter in her past, so she had been able to offer some useful tips.

Over the next forty minutes, "Lynn" asked her subject dozens of questions, covering his background and the formation of his company, through his early financial successes, and on to his recent partnership with William Garvey.

"This is actually one of the costs of working with Bill." Those teeth flashed again, white and even in the man's lightly tanned face. "He can't stand media attention, so all of this fun stuff ends up falling onto my plate."

She found herself growing more comfortable with her role as reporter as time wore on. It helped that Coleman so obviously relished talking about himself. It wasn't difficult to interview a man who answered every question not with a simple statement but with an anecdote, a personal opinion, and a piece of avuncular advice.

He became especially verbose when she asked about his charity work, perhaps because he honestly enjoyed helping others—or maybe because he wanted the good publicity his overt generosity brought him. Wynn knew she should be ashamed of her own cynicism, but as relaxed as she had begun to feel in her cover, she felt no corresponding ease with the man himself.

She had no justification for it, of course, because she'd seen that he couldn't possibly belong to the Order of Eternal Darkness, not as magically void as he appeared, and he'd neither done nor said anything offensive or even inappropriate. She just couldn't seem to make herself like the man. Maybe she really was prejudiced against the wealthy.

Finally, as their scheduled hour together drew to a close, Wynn found the opportunity to steer the conversation toward the man's collection of artifacts. He was finishing up a story of the initial problems and delays he had encountered in the building of CG Tower, which provided her with the perfect segue.

"I read about the permit delays that resulted from the archaeological finds on the site," she said, smiling with something she hoped look like sympathy. "But I also heard that some of the objects unearthed proved to have significant value to academics and to the area's original native communities. As a collector of antiquities yourself, didn't you feel a sense of excitement at stumbling over such a treasure trove right here in your own front yard?"

"Of course, of course," Coleman nodded. "It's always exciting to be a part of the rediscovery of history. I just wish all of our investors had shared in my personal enthusiasm."

She forced a laugh. "Understandable. Tell me, though, weren't you tempted to keep any of those artifacts for your own collection? I imagine things like that can be nearly irresistible."

Wynn had leaned forward and tried to make her tone sound teasing and conspiratorial, but she thought she saw something flicker in Coleman's expression that made her wonder if she'd come anywhere close. Then he smiled again.

"We collectors are a greedy lot, but the real value in any artifact is what it can add to the existing body of knowledge about its creators," he said, his tone ringing with sober sincerity. "I felt—the whole investment team felt—that it was only right to donate the items to the proper parties who could evaluate and study them for that very reason."

"That's an admirable stand to take, Ron." She sat back, trying to remove any pressure that might have unsettled him and praying she hadn't screwed up her chance to find out anything she could about Bran. "You should be applauded."

"Now, let's not get carried away." He laughed and pushed to his feet, his coffee cup long since abandoned on the table. "I did add one or two items to my private collection, only after the experts assured me their value for the academics was nominal." She watched as he crossed to a cabinet built into the wall beside his desk. "I've always liked having my very favorite pieces where I spend the most time, so over the years I've taken to keeping them here in the office. My wife calls me a workaholic."

Coleman pulled out a panel cleverly concealed in the woodwork trim and revealed an electronic keypad. She was too far away to see the code he punched in, and he had angled his body for privacy regardless. The keypad beeped, and she heard the quiet click of a lock disengaging.

Reaching up, Coleman pulled open the cabinet doors to reveal a glass-enclosed display case with a series of shelves containing precious objects from throughout history. Strategic spotlights highlighted the treasures, flicking on automatically when the cabinet opened.

"Please, come have a look," he invited, waving her forward with a smile.

Setting her notebook aside, Wynn stood and joined him in front of the display. Once again, she found herself wishing she knew more about art than she did about identifying useful medicinal wildflowers.

She recognized the materials of some of the items on the shelves; that was pottery, that looked like bronze, and that appeared to be woven from a mix of grass and bits of leather. She could even guess from the appearance of one or two pieces where they had originated. The squat, human figure with the delicate features and ornate decorations probably came from somewhere in Asia, and the leather-and-grass weaving struck her as African in origin. But for all that, she really couldn't have given a reliable report on any of it. All she knew was that the items all appeared old, well cared for, and quite likely valuable. With such a collection of ancient objects, likely valued by many generations of people, she would have expected at least one or two to give her the sense of power, but she felt nothing. Not even traces of energy drifted through the glass enclosure.

"This is very impressive," she managed to murmur, hoping that made an appropriate response.

"As a said, these are just a few favorites," Coleman said modestly. "Some parts of my collection are always out on loan to different institutions, here in the state or overseas, but some things just have too much meaning to part with. Actually," he added casually, "that little beauty right there was found just under where the restaurant downstairs now sits. It's the one item I kept from the tower dig."

Wynn followed the tip of his finger to a small, circular object on the second shelf of the cabinet. Lucky for her, it was at the right height for her to look down on it, so she got a good look at the surface. Not that she figured her view mattered all that much; she still had no idea what she was looking at.

The object appeared to be made of blackened metal, like wrought iron, chipped in at least two places on the edge, with a hole in the upper right-hand quadrant. She supposed it could have been a piece of jewelry, or even a coin, though it looked a little big to carry around in a pocket. The face of it appeared so worn, she couldn't make heads or tails of what had been engraved there, though she got the impression that something had been.

Was this what Coleman had brought to the university for identification? It had to be, didn't it, if it truly was the only item from the site that he had kept?

Wynn forced herself to remain calm, to act casual. "I thought I heard that you made use of a variety of local experts to help you identify the items you uncovered in the dig. Was the local Native American population useful in that capacity?"

She felt his eyes on her, but she wasn't sure she could keep her expression under control if she looked straight at him, so she pretended fascination with the small disk.

"Somewhat," he replied. "I also made use of the local academic community. The University of Chicago is, after all, an amazing resource to have in one's own backyard."

"Of course," Wynn agreed, tamping down a surge of excitement. "And who did you speak to there?"

She held her breath and waited for the answer.

"The head of the department there is Dr. Antonio Pallandano. A brilliant man. He was a great help through the entire dig."

His reply came so naturally, so casually, that it took a moment for the words to sink in. Then she had to fight for the self-control not to give any indication of her disappointment. So much for their lead on Bran's where-abouts. This whole effort had yielded nothing but dead ends. She'd have gotten just as much useful information by consulting a Ouija board.

She struggled to maintain her professional facade as she began to wrap up the interview. A few more random questions about the businessman's leisure activities—golf (natch), sailing, travel, oenology—coupled with an inquiry about what message he hoped people would take from reading his story eased her into a graceful exit. She thanked Coleman profusely for his time, nattered on about which magazines had supposedly expressed a desire to see her story submitted, packed up her useless supplies, and attempted a graceful exit.

She thought she had made it, overwrought nerves urging her to get out, quickly, before she lost control and did something stupid to blow her cover—the definitive evidence of her unsuitability for CIA recruitment. Her hand already rested on the knob of his office door when he called her name.

"Lynn."

Wynn froze. Her muscles wanted to tighten, her shoulders to creep up and forward into a defensive posture, and she had to mentally shove them back into place. She turned back toward Coleman with a smile plastered on her face. "Yes?"

The man stood in front of his desk, leaning casually against the thick glass surface. Holding up one hand, he showed her a small white square clamped between his first two fingers. White teeth flashed once more. "Almost forgot."

She held her ground while he ambled toward her,

trying to appear relaxed and mildly curious when her instincts kept urging her to get the hell out. He halted an arm's length in front of her and extended his offering.

"My card," he prompted in that same pseudo-intimate tone he'd used throughout their talk, as if they were old friends. "Feel free to call me anytime if you have follow up questions. And of course I'd appreciate a copy of your story. Once it finds a home."

"Of course," Wynn forced out, ordering her fingers to accept the card from him smoothly, not snatch it out of his hand like a relay baton. "Thanks again for your time, Ron. Our conversation really made me think."

"Me too. Me too," he murmured, stepping back as she pulled open the door. "Enjoy the rest of your afternoon, Lynn. Take care."

She murmured something appropriate—she hoped—and stepped into the hallway, breathing deeply of the relatively fresh air. Immediately Jacquie appeared from a neighboring door and smiled at her.

"Please, let me walk you out, Ms. Lewis," she said, gesturing back toward the lobby. "I hope your interview with Mr. Coleman went well."

Damn it, she would have to hold on to her charade for a little while longer. "It was great," she gushed. "Very informative. He's certainly an interesting man."

"Oh, absolutely. I've found working for him to be both challenging and very rewarding."

Oh, Wynn just bet she did.

Chapter Twelve

Wynn pretended to listen to the other woman's idle chatter as they made their way back to the lobby and the elevator that would take her to freedom. The tension in her body had begun to give her a headache, and her shoulders had tied themselves in knots even Gordias and his son would have been proud of. With one hand, she clutched the strap of her unfamiliar bag, simply to feel the sensation of holding on to something, while the fingers of the other had locked around Coleman's business card in a death grip.

Yeah, it was possible she might be in need of a good massage. Or, you know, some Xanax.

When she finally saw the copper elevator door close between her and Coleman Enterprises, she nearly collapsed in relief. As it was, she thumped back against the rear wall of the elevator and drew in such deep, desperate breaths, an observer might have assumed she'd just escaped drowning. Either that, or she was insane.

The trip down to the lobby seemed to take hours, but

within minutes she stepped out into the marble atrium
and looked around her for her Guardian. He appeared
at her side in an instant, cupping a hand beneath her elbow as he guided her toward the street exit.

"Well?" he grumbled.

Wynn shook her head. "I got nothing. Seriously. The
man was magically void. Not a hint of any power or any
connection to the Order. And worse than that, he didn't
appear to have any direct connection to Bran. According to him, he worked exclusively with the head of Bran's
department, not Bran himself. It was a lousy dead end,
and finding all that out nearly gave me a stroke. I am
not cut out for this sort of thing."

Hitting the sidewalk outside the building, the city air
assaulted them, full of car exhaust, the scent of asphalt,
food smells, trash smells, and the odors of perfumes, co-
lognes, and humanity itself. It all blended together into
an olfactory cacophony that to Wynn became the fresh-
est breath she'd ever inhaled.

She savored it for a moment, then blew it out on a
groan. "Goddess, that sucked."

Knox steered her toward the parking garage a couple
of blocks away where they had left her car. A glance up
at his expression told her that the results of her excursion
had pleased him no more than they had her. His features
were set in grim lines, his jaw tight, his lips pressed
firm, his eyes narrowed but still watchful as they moni-
tored the path ahead.

"I'm sorry this turned out to be such a waste of time."
She found herself apologizing, for what reason she had
no idea, but she did it anyway. "I was really hoping this
would be the big breakthrough we needed."

Knox grunted. "You say this Coleman had no direct contact with your brother, but I still find it curious his name appeared on Bran's list."

"Yeah, me too, but if Coleman didn't link them together, I'm not sure how we're supposed to manage it."

"Did the list not make mention of a box at a bank?"

The question seemed to come out of nowhere, and it took Wynn slightly aback. "Um, yeah, I think so."

He nodded, an abrupt jerk of his chin. "While I waited for you, I noticed a bank located in the lobby of Coleman's tower."

"Yeah, I saw that, too." She shrugged, then shot him a startled glance. "Wait, do you think that could be the bank from the list?"

He shot her a quick glance. "I recall that no box was found at the bank your brother habitually used."

"No, the police didn't find a safe-deposit box there, and Mom and I didn't find records of one anywhere else."

"If the box was secret, it would be foolish to leave such things where anyone might find them."

"You're right, we need to check. I just need to figure out how. Banks don't just give info like that out to anyone who asks. Maybe I can call—"

Whatever Wynn had intended to say next disappeared in the echo of a terrified scream.

"Oh, my God, that's a gun!" a woman shouted hysterically.

The warning hit Wynn at the same time as Knox, which occurred at the same time that a thunderous pop rent the air. Time seemed to slow as everything happened at once. She felt Knox's fingers close hard around her elbow and jerk her to the side. Air rushed past her, tickling her face, as he shoved her hard against the building next to them.

Reflex made her reach up and grab at him in an attempt to steady herself. One hand grasped his upper arm and the other clung to his shirt at the side of his rib cage while he put himself between her and the rest of the world. She saw the stark white of Coleman's business card flutter through the air as she lost her grip on it. Magic rippled against her, and she felt the Guardian's muscles flex next to her fist. Her hand jerked and thumped against his ribs. To her surprise, she felt not the almost indiscernible give of his human skin, but the barrier of his Guardian flesh. Her eyes flew to his face. His features remained human, but the lines had sharpened into a chiseled profile halfway between his two forms.

She heard another pop, more screams, and heard Knox grunt. Then time slipped back into place and the world came back to her in a rush.

"Are you hurt?"

All around them, people shouted. The babble grew deafening even before the wail of a police siren joined in, screeching over the top of the racket.

Hard hands shook her, and Wynn's gaze shot back to Knox as he glowered down at her. "I said, are you hurt?"

She shook her head. "No. Fine. You?"

He ignored her inquiry and stepped back, not even half a real step, just far enough that he no longer smashed her against the wall of the building. "We must go quickly. The attention has frightened away the shooter, but he may come back for another try."

His hard grip propelled her forward. She almost had to jog to keep up with him as he pushed her down the nearest side street and made a beeline toward the garage. "Shooter?" Her brain had trouble focusing, and the word somehow made her goggle. "Someone shot into a crowd in downtown Chicago? In broad daylight?"

"No," Knox snapped. "Someone shot at you."

Wynn stumbled and nearly fell, only Knox's hold keeping her upright. "Wait, I wasn't shot." Memory rushed in, and her eyes flew to his massive form. "You put yourself in front of me! Knox, did you get hit? Are you hurt? Let me see."

She tried to wrestle out of his grip, but he subdued her easily and hustled her along to the end of the block. Turning onto the cross street, he hurried her toward the back entrance of the parking garage.

"I am fine," he growled, his gaze not on her but constantly scanning their surroundings, looking for threats. "I saw the man draw his weapon just before he fired. I was able to partially shift beneath my clothes. In my natural form, bullets cannot penetrate my skin."

The vise grip on her heart eased slightly. "Thank the Goddess."

"Do not relax yet. We are not out of danger. We must reach your vehicle and get as far away from here as we can, before more of Coleman's goons can find us."

"Coleman. You think he was behind this? But I told you, I sensed nothing in his office." She almost had to jog to keep up with the Guardian's huge stride, and felt a surge of gratitude she hadn't worn heels the way she'd contemplated doing. "Besides, I was barely out of his office five minutes. How is that enough time to take out a hit on someone?"

"It was enough time to make a phone call."

Wynn knew he was right and had to suppress a shiver. "Oh, my gods. But how could my spell have been so wrong? I've never had trouble with it before."

"There are many ways to cloak power, if one has the means and the ability."

They reached the second level of the parking structure with Wynn only mildly out of breath. Keeping up with the gigantic warrior had shone an unpleasant spotlight on her lack of physical fitness. She might need to invest in a gym membership.

The sight of her car, parked halfway down the inner row of vehicles, could not have been more welcome. Wynn sighed in relief and began to head that way, but Knox grabbed her and pulled her into the shadow of a cement pillar. Confused, she looked up to see him once again scanning the area, clearly checking to see if anyone might have followed them.

When his grip eased and he moved forward, she breathed a sigh of relief. "If Coleman did just have us attacked, then he must be involved with the Order one way or another. Maybe he wasn't cloaking his power, though. Maybe he doesn't have any and he's just, like, the money behind them. A financial backer. The *nocturnis* are famous for promising enormous power and riches to get people to join them. The original devil's bargain."

"It is possible, but it does not matter." Quickly, Knox unlocked the car and tucked her into the passenger seat. He slid in behind the wheel and had the engine running before she even had time to fasten her seat belt. "However he is acquainted with them, we have our link."

Wynn reached up and grabbed on to the roof strap

as he slammed the car into reverse and took off like a bat out of hell. Like a gargoyle out of a parking garage? Maybe that could be turned into a new catchphrase for something.

"No, we might suspect our link, but we have no solid evidence," she gritted out, clenching her teeth and squeezing her eyes shut as Knox shot out of the garage and forced his way into traffic. "We also don't know anything concrete about the connection, so I'm not sure how much just knowing he's involved really helps us."

Knox threaded his way through the downtown congestion at a speed that would have put a Hollywood car chase to shame. When he headed for the highway instead of taking the back streets toward her neighborhood, she almost applauded. At least on the interstate, his speed would count as merely reckless instead of suicidal.

"Hey, I'd remind you that getting pulled over when you don't have a license is a lousy idea," she managed to say, cracking one eye open just enough to confirm she was better off keeping them closed, "but at the moment I'd be satisfied with you just making really, really sure not to kill us both!"

They careened down the highway and zipped right past the exit that would have taken them back toward Dunning. She risked a glance at Knox, and saw him concentrating grimly on the road ahead, but she didn't think he had forgotten which exit to take. The Guardian had a mind like a steel trap. When he showed no signs of searching for an alternative route, but simply continued to drive, she ventured a question.

"Um, not to be rude or pedantic or anything, but, uh, where are we going right now?"

Knox kept his eyes on the road, for which she gave a quick prayer of gratitude, and eased off the accelerator a bit, bringing her car into within fifteen miles per hour of the actual speed limit. She swore the little vehicle actually shuddered with relief.

"I did not wish to lead any pursuit directly to your home. You would be easy enough to find without us dropping a trail of bread crumbs."

Wynn felt a shiver of fear. "Do you think we should just stay away from the house altogether?"

He let out a breath almost like a sigh, but shorter and sharper. She wasn't sure what to call it. "No," he said, and she could tell giving that answer did not make him happy. "Your home at least has wards to offer a degree of protection, though you will strengthen those as soon as we return. You also keep your materials there, and you may need them to defend yourself. I will protect you to the best of my ability, but if we are outnumbered or separated by our enemies, you will need to be prepared. I presume you have studied at least some combative magics."

This time, she sighed, and made a face to top it off. "Not my strong suit, but yes. I'm better at protection, so I can do a few things to give me some magical shields of a sort, and I'm good with protective charms, like the goofer dust and drive away salt. I'll make sure I have plenty of both on hand."

"Those will help, but against the stronger forces, offensive spells work best. All Wardens study them as part of their training."

"Yeah, well, I'm not a real Warden, remember?"

"We will consult with your uncle. He is unable to cast

such spells himself, but he could teach you a few important ones to have on hand. It is best to be prepared."

Wynn swallowed down her reflexive bitterness and focused on the matter at hand. It didn't matter anymore that the Guild had rejected her. She had to live in the moment, and this moment called for learning the skills of a Warden. "Strive for peace, prepare for war, huh?"

"There will be no peace until the Seven have been contained once more and the Order has been driven into exile."

And didn't that put a happy little cake topper of optimism on the day?

She had no idea what to say after that, so she just stared straight ahead for several minutes while Knox continued to drive them south and west, away from Chicago. They cleared the city easily before rush-hour traffic hit, and by the time she started to see signs for Bloomington, she had managed to pry her numb fingers off the roof strap and regain her sense of equilibrium. Being shot at could apparently throw a girl completely off her stride.

The incident did manage to get the two of them talking again, Wynn realized with a hint of wry humor. Sure, all they had spoken of was protecting their butts and preparing for more attacks on said backsides, but considering last night and earlier today, she called that progress. Plus, the grumpy Guardian had actually thrown himself between her and a bullet. Maybe it counted as scraping the bottom of the barrel for blessings worth counting, but the fact that he wanted to keep her alive gave her at least a spark of hope for the future.

Go ahead, call her a cockeyed optimist.

Of course, the impromptu truce still felt too fragile to test, so Wynn settled back in her seat and tried to decide what to do next.

"I'm still confused," she admitted after several more miles of silence. "What would prompt Coleman to show his hand like that?"

He slid her a glance. "What do you mean?"

"I mean, he had me completely fooled. I was convinced he was a dead end, that he had nothing to do with the Order. I mean, I didn't like him at all, and something about him definitely rubbed me the wrong way, but he fooled my detection spell, and he gave me all the right answers to my questions to throw me off the scent. After accomplishing all that, why would he stage an attack so closely timed that we had to think it was him? What would it get him?"

"It could have gotten you out of his way permanently," Knox growled, and she saw the way his hands clenched around the steering wheel, the color in his knuckles bleeding to white.

"Yeah, but I just don't see that I really pose that big a threat to him, especially when he gave me nothing I can use as evidence against him."

"You alone he might very well dismiss as unimportant, but you with a Guardian at your side? That poses a threat to anyone in the Order."

She frowned at him. "But I specifically didn't bring you with me. You waited downstairs. He couldn't have known we were together, even if he had somehow known you were a Guardian."

He snorted and merged onto another route that would begin a looping course back to the city. "Do you really think that if a man as powerful as you tell me this Ronald Coleman is were connected to the Order, he would not have spies everywhere? You think he would take a meeting with someone who popped up out of thin air, no matter what story she spun him, and not have minions watching her every move from the moment she entered his territory? Do not be naive, little witch. Coleman's men saw us enter together, they saw you leave me, and they saw you return to me. Any of them with a modicum of talent could easily have seen through my disguise and recognized me for what I am, even if they had not already been looking out for one of my kind."

Wynn swore. The only reason she didn't smack him upside the head was because his driving already had her in fear for her life. "If you knew it was likely to happen that way, why the hell did you come with me? Why didn't you just stay back at the house and wait for me? If you hadn't been there, they would have had no reason to doubt my story."

He bared his teeth at her. "Again, do not be naive. He had enough power to hide from you, he could have easily seen through your story, your protections, and your spells. He merely enjoyed playing with you, and waiting until you left to order his men to kill you just prevented the employees of his mundane business from witnessing the attempt on your life."

That silenced her, at least for a minute or two. She tried to follow the train of logic, but it looked more like a roller coaster, all sudden dips and sharp turns and upside-down loop-de-loops. Still, there had to be a nugget of something worth digging up in there. Somewhere.

"I really feel like we're out of options now," she said

after a few minutes of chasing that crazy train. "We've
got to find Bran. At this point, he feels like our only link
to the Order and what they're planning. He had to have
been looking into it. It would explain why he's disappeared, why Coleman wouldn't be led to even mention
his name, and what he might have needed a box at a bank
to hide."

Wynn's mind turned back to the moments before the
gunfire, before everything went haywire and they got too
distracted by running for their lives to discuss what
they'd learned. The epiphany hit like Newton's apple, and
she sat up straight. "The bank."

Knox grunted and lifted an eyebrow.

"Before someone shot at us, we were talking about
noticing the bank in the lobby of the tower," she reminded
him. "At the time I thought it was a long shot, but now
that we think there's an actual connection between
Coleman and the Order, it makes a weird kind of sense.
If Coleman is *nocturnis,* and that list of Bran's means
he was watching the guy and trying to find out for sure,
then why wouldn't he have rented a safe-deposit box at
that bank? It would have given him an excuse to visit there
regularly. Plus, I know Bran, and he would have thought
it was funny to operate right under Coleman's nose
like that. He always did have a kind of twisted sense of
humor."

"But you also said that it would be difficult to discover from the bank if the box exists."

She pursed her lips. "Legally, it would be. Unless Bran
put my name on the access list for the box, the bank
won't confirm they even have it, and without me knowing the number, even if I produced a key they won't just

take me to 'Bran Powe's box.' And we're going to ignore the key thing for a minute, because just finding the
box is a big enough problem. Luckily, I know someone
who finds things like laws more flexible than most
people. And even better, she's a friend of Bran's."

Knox opened his mouth, probably to ask more questions, but Wynn had already dug her phone out of her
bag and pulled up her contact list. She scrolled down to
the correct name and hit DIAL.

Her foot tapped against the carpeted well of the passenger seat while the phone rang in her ear. A quick
glance at the dashboard reminded her it was late afternoon, so at least she didn't need to worry about waking
anyone up. Probably.

"Acme Industries, how may I direct your call?"

The female voice on the other end of the connection
sounded breezy but sincere, and Wynn found herself
grinning. After last night and this afternoon, it felt good.

"Kylie E. Woyote. It's good to hear your voice. How
are you?" she asked.

"Well raise my rent, it's Wynnie-the-Pooh. I am
awesome, given this unexpected pleasure. What's up,
sistah?"

Kylie E. Woyote was the alter ego and one of the many
online presences of a young woman whose real name
appeared on legal documents as Kylie T. Kramer. Wynn
had been trying for years to find out what the *T* stood
for, but her friend refused to divulge.

The two women had met several years ago on the East
Coast, while Bran Powe had pursued his undergraduate
degree at Boston University. It had been Bran's chance to
flee the nest and have his first taste of independence that

had him choosing a school so far from home when several midwestern schools also offered the program he wanted to study.

In the end, he had enjoyed his time in New England, but Wynn couldn't let him get away with running so far without consequences, so she had visited him often. During his freshman year, he had briefly dated an IT and computer science student named Kylie, and while the romance had quickly fizzled the friendship had endured. Since Wynn had adored Kylie right from the start, she had been delighted to maintain contact with the brilliant and charming young woman, and their own friendship had developed from there.

"Wow," Wynn blew out a breath. "I didn't even realize how much I've been missing you until I heard your voice. I guess I should have called sooner."

"You certainly should have. You're a very bad girl and should be punished accordingly." Kylie's voice paused, then turned serious. "Um, any word on the Bran flake?"

"No, but that's kind of what I'm calling about. Ky, I need your help."

"Why you wasting time asking, Pooh Bear? Just tell me what you need."

Wynn glanced at Knox and saw him frowning into the windshield. "First, I have to warn you. Not only could you get into trouble for this, but you could get into *trouble* for this, Ky. I can't tell you much, but there's weird stuff happening around here, and I'm not happy about getting anyone else involved."

Kylie scoffed. "Now you're just teasing me. Stop. I'm already seduced. This sounds like fun. Besides, you always wanted to know what my *T* stood for, right? Well, Trouble, my friend, is my middle name."

"You know, I wouldn't actually be surprised."

And Wynn wouldn't. Kylie had dropped out of Boston University after her sophomore year, when a certain social networking site discovered she had written a program that retooled their algorithms to display the information she wanted to see, not what their advertisers wanted to show her. They had offered her a choice between working for them, and going to prison. Kylie had chosen the job.

She'd only kept it for a year, though. After that, she wrote another program that established a different social media platform that allowed users to customize an interactive experience especially for themselves— complete individualization. She'd parlayed that idea into her own company, which Wynn had heard was sold nine months ago for somewhere in the tens of millions of dollars.

Basically, Kylie qualified as a genius among computer geniuses. Even though she never had to work another day in her life, she still bled bits and bites. You see, at heart, Kylie still considered herself a hacker, and those were the skills Wynn needed at the moment.

"Okay, so here's the thing," Wynn began. "We recently found something of Bran's that made us think he might have rented a safe-deposit box before he disappeared. For all we know, it's got a copy of his manifesto and the GPS coordinates for his Unabomber shack inside, but we can't find any back records that say where it is."

"And you want me to find it."

"Can you?"

"Absolutely. Although, unless you can narrow it down to a couple dozen banks, it might be a year or two before I manage it. That's a lot of data to wade through."

"I know, but I just have a feeling that I might know what bank to look at," Wynn said. "Start looking at First Illinois Fidelity, the CG Towers branch. If you don't find anything there, let me know, and I'll rack my brain for another short list."

"Easy peasy," Kylie chirped. "Banks are never half as secure as they think they are, but it will still take some time. Give me forty-eight hours?"

The thought of more waiting grated on Wynn's nerves like a nutmeg rasp, but she knew they had no choice. "I'm going to owe you one for this."

"For this? Pfft." Kylie made a rude noise. "I consider this an early birthday present. I'm gonna have me some fun."

"You're the best."

"Better than all the rest," the woman agreed. "But if you want to reward me, I'd love to see your pretty face. Come for a visit? I'll even buy the ticket."

Wynn laughed. Oh, but didn't a vacation sound like just what she needed at the moment? Too bad this saving-the-world gig was taking up so much of her time. "Rain check? I really am in the middle of something right now."

"You're serious." The laughter fled from Kylie's voice, and Wynn could picture her dainty features drawn up in a frown. "Are you in danger, Wynn? Because if someone is messing with you, I will kick their asses. And if they're too big for me to kick their asses, I will hire people to kick their asses, and then hold them down while I kick 'em some more."

The image flashed in Wynn's head, a handful of burly, mercenary-for-hire bodyguard types pinning Ronald Coleman and his *nocturnis* buddies to the floor while tiny, pixieish Kyle Kramer went all medieval on their asses. It gave her a sudden craving for popcorn.

"I know, Koyote, but I've got it covered, I promise. I have someone big and bad looking out for me. I'm safe."

"Pinkie swear?"

"Pinkie swear."

"Good." Wynn could practically hear her friend's decisive nod. "Forty-eight hours, Pooh Bear. I'll call you. In the meantime, I'm gonna go hunt me some wabbit."

Wynn ended the call still smiling. Trust the irrepressible and irreverent self-proclaimed hacker goddess to make her feel halfway normal in the middle of the apocalypse. Someone should bottle that girl, so Wynn could dose herself at regular intervals.

"Your friend will help us."

Knox's rumbling bass cut through the silence and jerked Wynn back to reality. She nodded. "Sorry, I forgot to put the phone on speaker. That was an old friend of Bran's from college. Well, my friend, too. She's a genius with computers. She's going to access the bank records and tell us if we're right about Bran's safe-deposit box."

"I heard. The speaker function was unnecessary. Guardians have excellent hearing."

Of course they did. As the universe's watchdogs, that just made sense. Wynn just hadn't bothered to think about it before. "Anyway, we should know in a couple of days about the box."

"We should contact the other Guardians and their Wardens and tell them what we have learned."

"You're right. And after that, we can really get to work."

"Get to work?"

"Finding the box won't be very helpful if we can't get to what's in it. We need to find that key."

Chapter Thirteen

Night fell as Knox finally steered the car into Wynn's narrow driveway. She thought more than four hours on the road might verge on an overabundance of caution, but she kept her mouth shut. A tentative peace had developed between them during the drive, and she hadn't wanted to risk destroying that. She liked it much better, she realized, when the Guardian didn't hate her.

The quiet time had also given her a chance to think. A dangerous activity, thinking, but almost inevitable after someone tried to kill you, or so it seemed to Wynn. And she found she had a lot to think about.

The last two months, going all the way back to Montreal, could best be categorized, she decided, under the heading of Life-Changing Events. How else could she describe the way she'd tumbled headfirst into the sort of situation she'd only heard about as a child? Sure, in most families the stories they told around the fire featured more in the way of ghosts and ancestral westward journeys, but in Wynn's family, they spoke of the eternal struggle between good and evil.

She'd grown up hearing about epic battles between Guardians and demons, of legendary Wardens and their brave fight to keep the *nocturnis* at bay. To her, it all had the air of fairy tales, history through the lens of the Brothers Grimm. She listened to the tales the same way she listened to *Beowulf,* and had the same expectation of ever featuring in one of those famous battles as of facing Grendel's mother in a Scandinavian swamp.

Yet here she was, not just fighting the forces of evil but somehow tied to her very own Guardian, acting for all intents and purposes like the Warden she had once dreamed of becoming. And not only that, but the Guardian she currently served had proclaimed her to be his mate. It all felt so unreal, she spent a few minutes contemplating the steps required to legally change her name to Princess Leia. Lightsaber fights with stormtroopers sounded like a tropical vacation compared with what she faced.

And somehow, the threat posed by the *nocturnis* scared her not even half so much as Knox.

The immense, powerful warrior made her knees wobble, and not because he could swat her like a mosquito with just about as much effort. No, he terrified her by turning her entire view of herself and her place in the world upside down.

Before the Guardian came along, Wynn thought she had a pretty good handle on herself. She had molded herself into a strong, independent woman, the sort who could run her own business and manage her own life with one hand tied behind her back. She had good friends

and a family that loved her. She had power at her fingertips, and a conscience that guided her decisions to
use it. True, she had no romantic partner, but she didn't
need one. She dated when she felt like it, but she was
content with her own company, complete whether or not
she had a partner to share her life with. Things had been
good.

The one fly in her ointment had been her brother's disappearance. She had missed Bran like an amputated
limb, but she truly believed he was alive out there somewhere, and that when he felt able and ready he would
come home. *That* Wynn had faith.

This new Wynn felt like a stranger, a version of herself as reflected in a fun-house mirror. She felt bigger
and smaller at the same time. She wasn't just a witch
and an herbalist, a friend and a daughter anymore. Suddenly she was a Warden, the very thing that years of disappointment and bitterness had taught her to disdain. She
had a Guardian at her side, protecting her with his immortal life.

And she kept finding herself in situations where she
needed protecting! That was a new one for her. Instead
of hearing stories about fighting the forces of evil, she
had—involuntarily—joined the fight; and wow, the evil
turned out to be even more forceful than she had imagined. People honestly wanted her dead, in a way entirely
different from the take-the-last-cookie-and-I'll-kill-you
sort of way she was used to.

She felt as if fate had lost its damned mind, and she
was caught up in the results of its bad LSD trip. It kept
throwing things at her that should have no part in her
life, and the biggest one had slammed right into her chest,

knocked the wind out of her, and changed everything. Forever.

Because the truth was, she loved Knox.

Admitting that, even to herself, made her teeth chatter with an adrenaline rush of fear. It felt stupid, so stupid, to let herself go there, to give her heart to someone who wasn't even human, who had never lived a life or been in love, or seen the world. Sure, intellectually, she knew he had sprung to life knowing more about the world and the things in it than Wynn ever would. Heck, he had access to knowledge that had died with the cultures that developed it. He probably remembered the Big Bang, if he thought about it hard enough. But he was still something different, something entirely out of her realm of experience, and her feelings for him made her want to throw up.

Okay, that didn't sound very romantic, but it was the truth. She had fallen in love with a creature who wasn't human, who could take on the shape of a massive stone gargoyle, who could fly and stop bullets with his skin and hear a mouse burp about a mile away. He had been not born but summoned from some sort of pool of endless potential that she didn't even understand, and unless something really drastic happened, he could theoretically live forever.

Scarier than all of that, though, was the idea that he wanted to give almost all of that up. For her.

If Knox truly wanted to take Wynn for his mate, it meant he would change forever right alongside her. According to the stories, when the Guardians found their mates among the women of power, they gave up their immortality. After they won the battle against the Seven, they demanded to be released from their obligations to the Guild. In doing so, they surrendered most of the powers they had been summoned with. They became mortal, living normal human life spans beside their mates. They gave up the ability to shift into the Guardian shape, bound forever to their human forms, which meant no more flying, no claws or fangs or skin like stone, nearly impervious to knives and bullets. Their senses became more human—still acute, but nothing like the vision and hearing they had once enjoyed. All they retained was a tiny bit of magic, something like the Wardens commanded, but since they could not use magic as Guardians, most of them had no skill to wield it.

Wynn had always wondered what happened after the stories ended. After the Guardians took their mates and became human in order to stay with them, did any of them regret it? She couldn't imagine they hadn't. After all, to have known all that power, to have it at one's fingertips for a heartbeat or a millennium, how did someone experience that and then give it up? Did they grow to resent their human mates and the bargain they had struck?

If Knox ever grew to resent her, Wynn knew more than her heart would break. She imagined shattering into a thousand bloody pieces and knew no magic in the universe would be able to put her back together again.

In the end, she found herself left with the question: Was the reward worth the risk?

Wynn followed Knox to the back door of the house, her eyes on her feet while she thought her deep thoughts. It wasn't until she heard the click of the door opening and he stepped inside to check for intruders before waving her in that she looked up and caught her first look at his back.

Two dark stains marred the cotton of his Henley-style shirt. The gray fabric just above and just below his shoulder blade had turned red with blood.

"Oh, my gods, Knox," she choked out, her eyes wide and stinging as she reached for him. "I thought bullets couldn't penetrate your Guardian skin. How bad is it? Do we need a hospital? Are the bullets still in there?"

He made an impatient sound and reached out to drag her into the quiet house. He locked the door before he bothered to answer her. "I told you, I am fine. The bullets did no real damage, but because they caught me just as I shifted, they chipped a bit of stone from my skin. They are just scrapes. You do not need to worry yourself."

"I get to decide when I worry." She narrowed her eyes at him and planted her hands on her hips. Sure, she was angry he hadn't mentioned his injuries, but really she assumed the aggressive pose so he wouldn't see how badly her hands were shaking. "Take off your shirt. Now."

He gave a sigh so put-upon, Wynn almost cracked a smile, but until she saw for herself how badly he was hurt, she didn't think her lips could physically bend that way. Not at the moment.

The look he cast her gave nothing away, dark and inscrutable, but she thought she might have seen a quick spark in the black depths of his eyes. A stray tendril of hope took root in the pit of her stomach, and she quickly kicked it beneath another layer of soil. Too soon, too fragile, too much else to worry about. Right now, she needed to see his wounds.

"Sit at the table so I can see your back."

He obeyed without protest, and Wynn felt a surge of fear that maybe he didn't argue because he had been hurt more seriously than he had indicated. After all, in the time she'd known him, she'd never known the Guardian to take orders.

She watched uneasily as he crossed to the tiny table in the corner and turned one of the two straight-backed chairs around to straddle the seat. Pausing to draw in a bracing lungful of air, she reached out, flipped on the kitchen light, and prepared for disaster.

She didn't find it. Instead, she saw two small circles of raw, red flesh, each about the size of a nickel. One had hit the meat of his shoulder, above the bone of his shoulder blade about halfway between his spine and his biceps. The other marked him lower and to the outside, toward the center of his rib cage about two inches from his side.

Stepping forward, she raised a hand to his back, taking care not to touch her fingers against the sore spots. Had either bullet impacted human flesh, she imagined the damage would have been extensive; in fact, she wasn't entirely certain Knox would still be alive. The lower bullet looked like it might have punctured the bottom lobe of a lung, and the other would certainly have rendered his one arm entirely useless.

But Knox wasn't human, not even remotely. The wounds looked just as he had described, as if someone had chipped away a layer of flesh about a quarter of an inch deep with a sharp round chisel. From each depression, blood and fluid welled sluggishly, but she saw no serious damage and no reason for concern. A good cleaning, some antibiotic cream, a couple of gauze bandages, and the Guardian would be right as rain.

So why did Wynn still feel like weeping?

Hard muscles rippled beneath her fingers. Knox turned his head to look at her, his dark brows drawn close together. "Why do you cry? I told you I was unharmed. You have seen for yourself. What troubles you?"

She shook her head, suddenly unable to speak. The trembling that had begun in her hands while they were still in the car began to spread, first up her arms, then down her torso until within seconds she shook so hard, she felt as if she might rattle herself into a million pieces. She probably looked like she balanced a precarious half step away from hypothermia, which—given the comfortable ambient temperature of her kitchen—made no sense at all. But none of that mattered. She didn't know why it had started, but she couldn't stop it any more than she could stop the tears from rolling down her cheeks.

At first, Knox eyed her warily, as if she played some sort of trick on him, luring him in so she could once again push him away. She didn't blame him. Fear had ruled her actions for most of their time together, fear of what his appearance in her life meant, then fear of being hurt, of having her heart broken. To keep from being hurt, she had hurt him first, and there had been nothing fair in that. Yet now, when she had finally realized that holding herself away from him would hurt just as much as anything he could do to her, he held back.

Goddess, she'd turned herself into some lonely-hearts version of the boy who cried wolf.

The hardest thing she ever did in her life happened right then. Weak and shaking and crying and more exhausted than she had ever even imagined, she reached a hand out to her mate and waited to see if he would take it.

Knox did not consider himself a forgiving creature. His mate's rejection of the previous evening had sliced deep. Truth be told, it had gutted him. He had not understood, still did not understand, how she could deny the connection between them, much less why she would want to. He had assumed, foolishly it turned out, that she understood what it meant for them to be mates. He had assumed she would find the possibility as wondrous and exciting as he did. How could she not?

At first, her denial of their mating simply baffled him. He let himself ignore her protests because they made no sense to him, and he had been too focused on the pleasure of having her. Her small, female body enchanted him. When he held her in his arms, touched her, kissed her, made love to her, she responded eagerly, her passion a match for the fire that burned in his soul. She accepted him so eagerly into her body, he had not bothered to wonder at his place in her heart.

A misstep he would not repeat. Her rejection had stung on many levels, wounding his pride as much as his heart. He had made a vow to himself as he stormed out of her room that when he realized the depth of their bond, she would have to come to him to repair it. He would not throw himself again at her dainty feet only to leave with her shoe prints on his spine.

But that was before she stared at him with wet, glittering, shattered eyes and held out a shaking hand. For that, for the way she stared at him, filled with hope and vulnerability, he could meet her halfway.

He did not break his vow by going to her, but he turned in his chair to leave no barrier between them. Then he reached out to grasp her hand and pulled her steadily to him. She came, if not eagerly then openly. Hesitant, but he couldn't blame her for that. They had enough reasons between them for caution.

He spread his legs and drew her in, caging her lightly with his knees. She quivered but offered no protest. The dainty, delicate fingers of her free hand lifted, still trembling, and pressed gently against his chest. Just a simple touch, but he felt the bond between them snap back into place, proving to him, at least, that the connection could never be severed. What the Light had wrought was not fragile, but eternal. It could bend or stretch, rebound or recoil, but it would endure, and nothing could change that, not him, not the Order, not the Seven themselves, and certainly not a single, infuriating little witch with a head as thick as stone.

Knox kept his gaze on hers. Releasing her hand, he shifted his grip, holding her lightly with one hand at her hip while the other reached up toward her face. He cupped her soft cheek in his palm and used the pad of his thumb to smooth away a fall of tears.

"Why do you cry?" he asked again, his voice barely above a whisper in the stillness of the room.

The question only brought more tears, and Wynn

shook her head. He saw her struggling to speak and waited. When he held her close, he found he could wait forever. Just having her in his embrace soothed something inside him, made his beast settle its head onto its paws and purr like a great cat.

She opened her mouth once, then again, but nothing emerged other than a watery hiccup and a half-stifled sob. He imagined she experienced some form of shock after the recent events and the culmination in this afternoon's attempt on her life. He could feel the chill in her flesh, see the pallor in her always fair skin, and he pulled her closer, letting her share in the heat of his body.

Fascinated, he watched the way she grabbed hold of herself. He could almost see the internal war she waged with her emotions, struggling for control in the face of being overwhelmed. She had such strength hidden away within her small, human body, not in her muscles, but in her soul. She possessed such a will to fight against any foe, a determination he gazed on in wonder while she marshaled it to her and subdued her rioting emotions enough to allow her to speak.

She drew in a deep breath that shook and shivered into her lungs, then another that slid in on little more than a tremor. By the third, she swallowed the air smoothly and opened her eyes to face him in truth.

"I cry because I'm an idiot," she told him, her voice soft and tired and full of regret. "I'm crying because I got so confused and so afraid and so angry about being confused and afraid that I kept trying to push you away. And I'm crying because the last time I pushed so hard you almost went."

He frowned at her, but something within him felt

unbearably light, like a bud had begun to unfurl and inside it contained pure, glowing happiness. "I am right here, little witch. Sitting right in front of you, and I have gone nowhere."

She shuddered and threw herself against him, pressing her face to his chest as another sob managed to break free. "I almost lost you."

Knox shook his head and closed his arms around her, cradling her close. She felt so good aligned curves-to-planes against him, and she fit so perfectly in his arms. He bent his head to hers and pressed his cheek against her tumble of silky waves. "You cannot lose me, little witch, not when you are a part of me. The best part. We are bound together now. You cannot lose what has become a part of you."

"But you got shot," she sniffled "You could have been killed."

He kissed the top of her head. "Guardians are immortal, sweeting. Did no one ever tell you that?"

She lifted her head to glare at him through the tears. "Immortal means you'll never die of natural causes. It doesn't mean you're invulnerable and can never be killed."

"Is this really the time to dwell on technicalities?"

And there it was, the tiniest glint of humor in her soulful brown eyes. "I guess maybe it's not," she admitted grudgingly.

So he pounced.

He used his hand at her cheek to guide her face up to his and laid his mouth across her sweet, wet lips. She tasted salty and tangy, like tears and worry, and he licked the worst of it away. He felt her soften against him, and his beast roared in satisfaction. He deepened the kiss, dove into her and pulled her under the wave of desire.

She returned his embrace with an openness he hadn't experienced before, and the power of her surrender went through him like a lightning strike. He moved his hands so he could grasp her closer, lifting her from the floor to press her fully against him. She came willingly, spreading her legs to straddle him and the chair he sat on.

"Make love to me," she whispered, and he marveled that she thought he could do anything else.

He removed her clothing with tender care, unwrapping her like the precious gift she was. As soon as the fabric of her sweater left her skin, it lost all meaning and he dropped it carelessly to the cold kitchen floor. The struggle to remove her trousers had her giggling and him cursing as he tried to yank them off her without allowing her to leave his lap.

Of course, he failed. He knew he could have used his strength to tear the cloth from her body, but it seemed somehow wrong to use even that much violence on such a fragile, beautiful creature. In the end, he pushed her to stand only as long as it took to yank the trousers down to her feet, and when she stepped out of them, he lifted her immediately back into his lap.

The feel of all her smooth, naked skin made him come undone. All his thoughts of the gentle, tender loving she deserved, the care he would use to show her how he valued and cherished her went right out of his head. He crushed his mouth down on hers like a barbarian and exulted in her soft cry of surprised pleasure.

He drank her down in great, greedy gulps, taking her in more important than air. If he had to do without air and water, he thought he might manage it, as long as he could breathe her scent and swim in her sweet green energy.

His little witch couldn't content herself with simply giving; she had to take something of her own. Releasing her grip on his shoulders, her hands darted down between them, clever fingers unfastening his jeans and reaching inside to close around his painful erection. He thought already that he couldn't want her more, but her firm grasp and teasing caresses sent his need rocketing from desperate to frantic. He needed to be inside her, to reclaim her as his own and make them as close to one single entity as he could hope to achieve.

It took only one eternal and frustrating moment to adjust their positions, to lift his hips and shove his jeans down his thighs and out of the way. His fingers tightened on her hips and he lifted her to bring her down over him.

Her sheath closed around him, a hot, wet welcome that tore a groan from deep within his core. Her head dropped backward, her hair cascading down behind her and tickling the bare skin of his thighs. He wanted to let gravity settle her on him, but he was too greedy and too impatient. Holding her steady, he thrust up, taking him to the hilt inside her, and he heard her wordless cry of delight. Her body tightened around him and immediately her hips began to shimmy, as if she couldn't wait to chase the erotic sensations into the storm of waiting pleasure.

For Knox, all the world fell away. His new reality condensed, leaving nothing within it but him and his mate and the sharp whip of need and ecstasy. Lowering his chin so he could watch the expressions sliding over her beautiful features, he titled his pelvis and began a strong, hard rhythm that made him want to howl at the intensity of the connection.

Above him, Wynn writhed and wriggled, circling her hips above him, then rocking back into his thrusts. He could feel her focus on their joining and knew she was with him all the way. It made everything feel so much more amazing that he wondered how he didn't just shatter into a million tiny pieces of stone. If he did, he thought they might turn out to be lava rock, with bits of obsidian, all sharp edges and dangerous shine, mixed in.

Need clawed at him, need not just for the climax he could feel bearing down on him with the force of a hurricane, but need for the moment, for the pure, incandescent joy of giving himself to his mate and knowing she gave herself in return.

Like all perfect moments, it could not last. The greedy claws of desire dug in deeper, squeezed tighter, and he found himself moving under his witch with barely restrained ferocity. For her part, she seemed to revel in his lack of control. Her fingers gripped hard at his sides, nails digging into the flesh above his ribs and leaving marks he knew he would see there for hours. It felt so good, so perfectly right that she should leave her mark on his hide as surely as she had left it on his heart.

Her breathing turned into a series of high-pitched whimpers. Faster and harder she rolled her hips against him, her body stroking him in a vise of hot, wet silk. He felt the moment her climax hit. Her nails bit deeper, her pussy clenched around his cock, and she began to shake, trembling like a leaf above him. It was all he needed.

With a roar he loosed his death grip on his control and let the tsunami wave drag him out to sea. He poured himself inside for long, endless minutes, and when he had emptied out his soul, she snuck inside him and filled him again, with love, with peace, with contentment.

One by one he pried his fingers from her hips and snaked his arms around her to pull her against him, relishing the warm weight of her draped in exhaustion against his chest. He blinked into the empty room and realized everything in his universe had settled into a new alignment, its center now a small, witchy female with power like spring and a will like steel.

It felt just perfect.

Chapter Fourteen

Wynn couldn't even think about that scene in the kitchen. The moment she did, her face lit up like a neon sign. Red, of course, because that's the color her cheeks turned at the memory. Afterward, she hadn't been capable of speech, much less movement, and even Knox had barely managed to carry the pair of them into the bedroom to collapse into a deep, dreamless sleep.

All of that meant that the next morning, the first item on her agenda was warding. Now that they knew the threat from the Order was real and immediate—and that it had already been directed against her—the wards around her house needed to be shored up and improved where possible. For that, she needed the help of someone with a bit more experience defending against the forces of the Darkness.

A phone call to Uncle Griffin managed to find the man awake and alert even at the ungoddessly hour of five AM. He listened to her story with alarm and concern and agreed to head her way immediately. "I'll bring a few things you might find helpful," he said. "Just because I can't work a spell these days doesn't mean I can't teach one."

Now the clock read a little after six thirty, and Wynn stood waiting for the cavalry at her back kitchen window, a coffee cup cradled between her palms. The steam rose in gentle swirls from the creamy liquid, but she had her eyes fixed on something even tastier.

Outside her window, her backyard stretched half in shadow. The sun had just begun to rise, and hadn't yet cleared the trees on the horizon, but she didn't need the light to watch the magnificent sight before her. A half-naked man, stripped to the waist and clad in nothing but loose, black cotton trousers stood with his feet planted firmly on the earth. Ropes of powerful muscles flexed and stretched in a sinuous dance as he swung a multi-bladed weapon in controlled arcs around his body.

Not being an expert in weaponry, swords, battle, or, you know, anything remotely related to those subjects, she couldn't give his sword-staff-thing a name. To her, it looked like two slim curved blades attached to either end of a short staff. He twirled the thing around like a baton, with the same ease and casualness, but the way the edges glinted in the brief rays of dawning light assured her the thing was wickedly sharp and monstrously dangerous. No wonder he'd said he needed to practice this morning to keep in fighting form. That was not a weapon she'd want to get rusty at wielding.

She heard a footstep outside the kitchen door and tore her gaze away from the mouthwatering vision before her to see her uncle mounting the back steps. Bringing her coffee with her, she unlocked the door and waved him in, her hormones dragging her immediately back to the window. Seriously, the exercise was beginning to raise a sheen of perspiration on his skin. It was all she could do not to run out there and lick it off. Playing voyeur seemed like a reasonable compromise.

"There's coffee on the stove, Uncle Griff. Help yourself."

She sipped from her own cup, mostly to give herself something to swallow other than her own drool. She heard her uncle puttering around behind her, setting a small cardboard box on the kitchen table, opening the cabinet for a cup, the drawer for a spoon. She heard the coffee pour and the tinkle of metal against porcelain as he stirred in his two teaspoons of sugar. Then she felt him step up beside her and join her in her window gazing.

"They look so normal in their human forms," he mused after a moment of comfortable silence. "Sometimes it's easy to forget they're still warriors underneath all that."

Wynn smiled into her coffee. "That right there is a pretty good reminder."

Griffin chuckled. "He does look pretty comfortable with a weapon in his hands."

"He's a Guardian."

"He's your Guardian now. Isn't he?" He slanted her a sidelong glance.

Wynn braced herself for the moment of panic to overwhelm her. She waited. And waited. Then she smiled. "Yeah, I guess he is. Ain't that a kick in the pants, hm?" She chuckled. "When I was really little, I was so convinced I'd be a Warden one day. And not just a Warden but a personal Warden to one of the seven Guardians on earth. Then when I understood that the Guild wasn't going to take me, I got so angry that I spent the rest of my life resenting the heck out of the very idea of the whole system. And now, here I am—a personal Warden after all. Only without any training or preparation or an oath to swear by. Who'd've thunk it?"

"We all should have."

The quiet words caught her attention, and Wynn turned her head to see her uncle watching her with grave brown eyes several shades lighter than her own. Her shade, she had always thought, looked like the soil she grew her herbs in, dark and peaty, and sometimes full of shit; but her uncle's shade looked like well-brewed tea, clear and rich, full of golden flecks and amber lights. Right now they looked steeped in regret.

"We all should have thought about everything a lot harder," he told her, cupping his mug to his chest as it if could warm him. "For so many generations, the Guild just didn't accept women for training. Or if they did, it was only because they had powerful connections that went all the way to the top, and even then they had to have powers someone needed for a specific purpose to make the cut. No one said why things worked that way, and I never even bothered to ask. No one asked, and we should have. It was wrong of us not to."

Hearing someone say it, hearing someone articulate her own thoughts and admit to the very thing she had craved so long to have acknowledged, should have given her a sense of triumph. Instead it felt a little hollow, not because she didn't value the words, but because they weren't important anymore. She knew that her life events, all of them, even the ones that had left her bitter and scared, had come together to lead her to this moment. At this moment, she stood exactly where she wanted to be, so everything else had faded into the background, and Wynn felt content to leave it there.

She smiled at her uncle, a genuine smile, and shook her head. "You know, it's okay. I mean, you're right; it was wrong. It was stupid, quite frankly, but so what? Water under the bridge." She thought for another second, and felt her mouth curve in a different sort of smile. Just as real, but a lot toothier. "Of course, once we get things back under control and we can start to rebuild the Guild again, I can guarantee that at least three women are going to have quite a few things to say about how the system should work in the future."

Her uncle chuckled and reached out to squeeze her arm with warm affection. "You go ahead and breathe fire on them, my little dragon. I'll be proud to stand and watch."

Impulsively, she set aside her mug and hugged him. In the new light of day, everything really did seem better than before.

Griffin hugged her back briefly, then cleared his throat and patted her shoulder uncomfortably. "Well, yes. Well," he said, coughing into his fist. "Now that we've both had some caffeine, I think maybe it's time to get to work on those wards. What do you say?"

Grinning, Wynn picked up her coffee and drained it. "I say release the hounds, old boy!"

He spoke through his laugh. "Okay, then. Let's start by taking a look at what you've got."

The front door seemed the logical place to start. She'd

laid the strongest of her wards there when she'd first moved into the bungalow, reasoning that the best defense should go to the most common point of entry. While the wards she'd placed were permanent, she took care to recharge them regularly, so when she reached out and laid her hand against the woodwork of the door frame, light flared and her handiwork glowed visibly to the naked eye. Her uncle ran his gaze around the entire opening from floor to ceiling and around both sides before nodding.

"Not too shabby," he admitted. "It's definitely a general-purpose barrier, but I think it would do well, even against a moderate demonic spirit."

Wynn felt a rush of pride. "Thanks, Uncle Griff."

"Are they all like that?"

"No, unfortunately. This was the big display of fireworks. Most of the rest of it is a little more basic."

He hummed and nodded. "Okay, then. We'll take a look and make adjustments as needed." He smiled and reached out to flick a finger against the bundle of keys tied to the doorknob with a length of red string. "I see you took your mother's advice and went with the traditional touch, as well."

Wynn shrugged and smiled ruefully. "Hey, maybe the keys only keep out the dumb bad energies that can't figure out how a modern lock really works, but a little bit of folk magic never hurt anyone."

"No, it didn't. You're right. Every layer of protection is worthwhile, from the simplest all the way up to the most complex. They build on one another, and that's always a good thing. Keys tied to all the doors?"

"Yes. And sachets of salt on all the windows."

"Okay. So, let's see the rest of it."

She led him through the small house, room by room, giving him time to study the magical protections she had erected at each door or window. In the living room, he examined the fireplace chimney as well, and in the small laundry off the kitchen, he pointed out that she had left the dryer vent unprotected. "It only takes the smallest opening for a demon to slip through in the form of smoke or mist."

Wynn hadn't thought of that, but the idea made her shiver. Yeah, that was something she would definitely be fixing.

When they finished the tour, her uncle turned to her and nodded. "Not bad, Wynn-dixie. You did a nice job with what you had to work with, but I brought a few spells I think will make you even more secure. I'm hoping you have the materials we may need here, but I can run home to fetch anything you can't put your hands on right away."

"Great. In that case, let's raid my supplies and get to work."

Griffin stopped by the kitchen to fetch his box, which turned out to contain three battered books and a couple of yellow scrolls containing spells from the Guild's vast store of knowledge. That he was willing to share the information with her touched her and made her actually *feel* like a Warden for the first time in her life. Even having Knox for a giant, stony shadow hadn't accomplished that. She found herself actually looking forward to the day's work.

Stepping up to the worktable in Wynn's ritual room, Griffin set down his box while Wynn mentally ran

through the list of items he had said he would need. Salt
and charcoal were no problem, of course, and she felt
confident she had enough frankincense and cedar to
get through anything short of a demonic nuclear attack,
but the dragon's blood had her wondering. She knew
she had plenty of the *Daemonorops* variety of the resin,
but for magic like this, she'd really prefer the *Dracaena*
type. Most people these days didn't distinguish, but
she'd always found the latter had a stronger banishment
energy.

Peering into the back of a cupboard, she moved bottles and jars around looking for the correct label. If she
also muttered a little to herself, that was nobody's business, now was it?

"You still have it."

Her uncle's words pulled her from her search, and she
turned to see what he was talking about. He stood in
front of her table with a wide smile on his face and her
mirror box in his hands.

"I remember helping you make this when you were
ten," he mused, turning the small wooden container in
his fingers as he examined the rough edges and faded
color of the wood. "Your mom wouldn't let you use the
saw, so you needed help cutting the wood to size."

Wynn remembered that afternoon well, but she had
trouble focusing on the memories because all she could
think was that she'd completely forgotten. "I can't believe it slipped my mind."

Griffin shrugged. "Well, it was a long time ago, a—"

"No, sorry, Uncle Griff. I remember building the box
with you, but I forgot I've been waiting on a spell in it.
I should have checked on it days ago." Shaking her head

at her own stupidity, she took the box back from him and stared in confusion at the clear glass knob on top. "It's still not showing it's finished."

"What do you mean?"

Briefly, Wynn explained the spell she'd put into the mirror box the night the detective had broken in and attacked her. "I was trying to get the spell to bounce back on the caster so we could trace it back to him, but after the first week of waiting, things got so crazy, I just totally forgot to keep checking on it. I've never had a spell take this long in my life."

"Hm, well you know that the more powerful the caster, the longer it would take for the spell to dissipate."

"Sure, but my record is currently six days, and that spell had an entire coven behind it. It's been almost three weeks for this one." She shook her head. "It's just too weird."

"That is an awfully long time for the box not to have finished working." Griffin frowned, looking from her to the box and back. "Maybe you should open it and see what's going on."

"I don't see what else I can do."

Brows furrowed, Wynn set the box back on the table surface and carefully grasped the clear knob. She felt nothing unusual, the transparent glass cool and hard between her fingers. Cautiously, she tugged just hard enough to break the seal between the lid and the box and paused. Nothing. Deeply curious now, she lifted the lid free and peered into the depth of the wooden container. What the . . . ?

When she said nothing, just continued to stare into the box, Griffin shifted to peer over her shoulder. She heard him give a disappointed huff. "It's empty. There's nothing in there."

"I know. Which is really weird, because Knox and I put that scrap of cloth in there together. Admittedly it wasn't very big, but I know the two of us didn't hallucinate it."

"Which means it has to have gone somewhere," Griffin agreed. "Could the spell have run too hot and burned it up?"

She held the box up and tilted it so they could both look inside. "No scorch marks, and no ash."

Her uncle paused for a moment in thought. "What if there were two spells on the fabric? One to trace you, and the other to sort of self-destruct when it had done its job?"

"Mission Impossible: *Nocturnis* Protocol?" She shook her head. "I can't think of a better explanation. Damn it, though, I was hoping that would get us a location. I mean, we think we know who's involved now, but we don't know where they're operating, and we still don't know what they're trying to accomplish."

"Yes, you do. They're trying to take over the world."

Wynn rolled her eyes at her uncle's deadpan teasing. "Okay, we know what they're trying to accomplish, but we don't know what step they're on. Feel better, Mr. Exact-o?"

Griffin flashed her a smile, his skin creasing in easy, familiar lines. "Eh. What will really make me feel better is getting this place secured. You find what we need?"

She nodded, and grabbed the jar of dragon's blood, which had been right under her nose all along, on the shelf beside her table. She tucked it into her uncle's box along with the other items she'd gathered. "Let's do this."

"Good girl. Let's go show those *nocturnis* how we do things in the real world."

The warding took all day and into the evening, mostly because the spells Griffin showed her were just so new to her. Since he remained unable to cast reliably himself, he had to teach Wynn how to cast each one, talk her through step by step, and show her how to correct any mistakes.

The first few times proved the most challenging. For the first time, she was dealing with a flavor of magic she felt entirely unused to. It was like someone had slipped a ribbon of caramel into her mocha chip ice cream. She didn't dislike the taste, but she hadn't been expecting it, so it took her a while to get used to it.

When Knox finished his exercises outside, he came in during one of their breaks to check on their progress. Wynn filled him in on the mirror box spell, but he seemed neither terribly disappointed, nor particularly surprised. He simply nodded, kissed her, and went to take a shower.

She ignored her uncle's knowing look, bowed her head, and waited for her blush to subside. Then she got back to work. By the end of the day, she was ready to collapse, wrung out and almost physically aching, like she'd overused muscles she hadn't exercised in a long time. Incapable of facing the idea of cooking, she suggested ordering pizza for dinner. Knox, easy to please when it came to food—hot and abundant seemed to be his only criteria—agreed readily, but her uncle shook his head and gathered up his things.

"If I sit down right now, I won't get up till morning," he told her. "I'm that exhausted, and I'm sure you feel the same. I'm going to head home, grab a quick bite, and turn in. You keep me updated, young lady. Understand?"

Wynn nodded weakly and waved him off from the end of the sofa where she had already collapsed. Her conscience niggled at her, telling her she should have at least stood up and hugged him before he left, but honestly, if she used up that energy, she didn't think she'd have enough to place the phone call to the pizza place. She just hoped Griff would understand.

Her eyes scanned the room and spotted her cell phone lying on the coffee table at least three whole feet away from her hands. She groaned. This was when she didn't want to be a witch, she wanted to be a Jedi, so she could use the Force to make her phone fly right into her hand.

What the hell, right? Lifting one arm she reached out an open hand toward the small electronic device. *Use the Force, Wynn,* she thought and had to stifle a slightly punch-drunkg iggle.

From his seat in the oversized chair, Knox eyed her strangely. After a moment, she gave up and dropped her hand to her side, rolling her head along the sofa cushions to meet her mate's gaze. "What were you just doing?" he asked warily.

"Using the Force."

He looked from her to the table and back again. "Did you do this successfully?"

She shook her head and grinned. "The Force is weak with this one. I'll never be a Jedi Master." Which only served to make the Guardian look more confused. "Remind me to rent *Star Wars* for you one day. It will make everything clear. In the meantime, could you do me a favor?"

She flashed him such a flirtatious and ingenuous smile that his gaze immediately sharpened, and she saw flames flare behind his eyes. When he spoke, his voice came out as a rough purr. "What do you require, little witch?"

Maybe she really was drunk off too much magic used too quickly, or maybe the feeling of sitting here in quiet intimacy inside a secure private space with her mate had gone to her head, but suddenly pizza sounded a lot less appetizing to her than taking a bite out of Knox.

She let her interest show in her face and licked her lips to tease him. "I don't know," she said, deliberately lowering her voice to a playful, husky register. "I think it's going to take a big, strong warrior to get me what I need. Do you think you're up for the challenge?"

He sprang at her, a blur of motion and mass, leaping from his chair and landing over her to press her back into the sofa's soft cushions. "Are you implying I might not be, little witch? Must I show you once again how well I can handle you?"

The tightening in her groin had Wynn panting, as desire flared from a tingle of casual interest to full-blown need in the space of half a second. "Mm," she murmured, rubbing against him like a cat in heat. "I think maybe I forgot. Would you like to remind me?"

The flames shot higher in his dark gaze, almost singeing her with their heat. As he lowered his head to hers, she could swear their light reflected against her skin. "Perhaps I should."

His lips had just touched hers when her phone chimed a cacophony of church bells. The sound startled Wynn so that she jerked up and banged her forehead against Knox's, whose skull appeared infinitely harder than hers. In a literal sense, anyway. The Guardian cursed and slumped back into the sofa, glowering in the direction of the coffee table.

Shooting him a look of apology, Wynn leaned forward to take the call. "Hello?"

"I am making it rain up in here, baby girl," a voice crowed into her ear. "Who said I couldn't work miracles, huh? Give me the names. I'll take 'em on in one big group, I swear it."

Wynn sighed. "Hi, Kylie. What's up?"

"What's up is that I rock, sistah, didn't you hear me?" The young woman bubbled, as effervescent as soda pop. "I told you forty-eight hours, and here I am clocking in at just over twenty-six, thank you very much. No applause, please; the accolades just slow me down."

It took a second, but Wynn's mind cut through the chatter and latched on to the thread of actual meaning buried beneath it. She looked at Knox and widened her eyes. "Did you find it?"

"First Illinois Fidelity, CG Towers branch, Box Seven One Eight Three. You ask, and I deliver," Kylie said with dramatic flair. "I gotta admit, though, you called it, Wynnie-the-Pooh. The box was exactly where you said it would be. He rented it under an assumed name, though—Gwion Bach. How's that for weird monikers."

She was so excited over Kylie's discovery, Wynn even managed not to wince at the mispronunciation of the old Welsh name. "Gwee-on Bach," she corrected. "*Ch*, like in a Scottish *loch*. It's the name of a character in Welsh mythology. That's definitely Bran."

"I know, right? Weirdo. Anyway, there you go. You need anything else from my magical fingertips?"

Wynn choked back a laugh. Kylie had no idea what the joke would be. "That's it, Koyote, and trust me when I say, I owe you big."

"I'll settle for a visit and a chance to kick Bran in the shins when you find him."

"Done."

"Awesome. Catch ya later, Pooh Bear."

Wynn ended the call and felt the renewed energy of excitement race through her. "Did you hear that? Kylie found the box."

"I did hear," Knox rumbled. "It is good news. But do you—"

Her phone rang again, and Wynn assumed it was Kylie again, so she didn't bother to check the caller ID. "What did you forget?"

There was a startled pause and then her uncle laughed. "I didn't think you had the power to read minds, Wynn-dixie. How did you know I was calling because I forgot something?"

Wynn blinked in surprise. "Sorry, Uncle Griffin. I just got off a call with somebody else, and I thought you were her calling back. What's up? Did you actually forget and leave one of your books here?"

"No, I just forgot to tell you something," he said. "I noticed it while we were setting our first wards, but I forgot when Knox came in from the backyard. Now, it may be nothing, and I remember how your mother always liked to keep at least a couple of keys on each red string charm, but you know that's not necessary, right? Even one key will work."

"I know, Uncle Griff," she said, surprised by this line of conversation. "But I like the jingling, too. Is there a problem?"

"No a problem, and maybe I'm just old-fashioned, but I noticed the charm on the kitchen door has a modern key mixed in with the old skeleton keys we usually use. I just thought maybe it wasn't a good idea to mix up the energies like that."

Wynn frowned. All the keys she used in her red string door charms were antiques. She combed flea markets and garage sales specifically looking for them every summer. She never used modern keys. She had no idea what her uncle was talking about.

"Now, it's completely up to you," Griffin continued, "but I just thought I'd mention it since you did say you wanted to be extra careful about the details at the moment."

She pushed off the sofa and padded into the kitchen, barely noticing when Knox rose to join follow her. Maybe she had just gotten so used to him shadowing her, but honestly, her mind was busy trying to puzzle out the meaning of her uncle's warning.

"No, I appreciate the call, Uncle Griff. I'll double-check it right now."

"Good girl," he said, sounding relieved. "Well, I'm bushed. I'm going to call it a night. Be safe, sweetheart."

"I will."

Wynn ended the call with one hand and flipped the kitchen light on with the other. Standing in front of the door, she stared down at the charm as if seeing it for the first time She'd hung them the day she moved in, and over time she'd grown so used to the cheerful little noises they made and the sight of them against her door that she'd stopped noticing them altogether.

"Do you believe your uncle is correct and that mixing old and new keys is dangerous?" Knox asked, his voice curious.

Absently, Wynn shook her head, her gaze still focused on the charm. "No, I think he's an old worrywart."

"Then why do you look so unsettled?" he demanded, reaching out to wrap one arm around her shoulders. He tugged her against his side, but Wynn barely felt it.

She reached out and lifted the charm, staring at the four keys tied to the bright red string. Wynn always used pairs or sets of three keys, never four. But there, nestled amid the three dark, clunky old skeleton keys, hung a bright, shining golden key, the kind that might fit the small lock on a portable safe.

Or on a safe-deposit box.

"That jerk," she muttered, finally snapping out of her trance to begin untying the extra knot that had been added to hold the gold key in place. "He hid the damned thing in plain sight, knowing I'd never notice. And I'll bet he laughed his ass off while he did it. The little shit."

Knox shifted to look down, realization hitting him. "Your brother left the key to his secret safe box in your house, not his own?"

"He totally did, which makes me wonder if he knew he might have to disappear at some point." She glanced up at Knox, frowning in concern. "Bran would have known that the minute we realized he was missing, the family would go through all his stuff looking for clues. A safe-deposit key with no record of a box would have confused the hell out of us. I suppose he thought he was sparing us that."

"But it also indicates he did not want the contents of the box found," Knox pointed out, and Wynn felt a tightness in her chest she couldn't identify. Was it fear for her brother's safety? Or hurt that he had a secret so private, he hadn't wanted anyone in his family to know about it?

"I know," she muttered, finally tugging the key free and letting the rest of the charm fall back into place. "Trust me, I've thought of that."

Gently, Knox grasped her shoulders and turned her to face him. "We have known all along that there was a chance your brother could be in danger. He is a missing Warden at a time when being a Warden has become a dangerous occupation."

Wynn blinked back tears. "Yeah, but I'm trying not to think about that. I've always said I would know if Bran was dead. I mean, I know we're not twins or anything, and I'm not a psychic, even if I'm a witch, so I can't prove it. But I know he's still alive. I know it inside." She closed her hand around the key and tapped her fist against her chest. "Whatever he was hiding, the only thing I care about is that it leads up to him. Because he might be in danger, but he's *not* dead. He's not."

Her mate drew her close and pressed her head against his broad, warm shoulder. He made shushing noises and rocked her gently. "All right, little witch," he murmured. "Tomorrow we will go to the bank, and we will open this box. And then we will use the information inside to find your brother and ensure that the Order cannot touch him. Then, we will use it to bring the *nocturnis* down."

"Right," Wynn agreed, wrapping her arms around Knox and hanging on to his comforting strength. "Then I'm going to punch him in the gut and hold him down while Kylie and my mom take turns kicking him."

She felt his shoulders shake with laughter. "Whatever you need, mate, I will see it done."

Taking a deep breath, Wynn let it out and forced herself to calm down. It was after eight o'clock at night. The banks were closed, she was exhausted, and there was nothing they could do until morning. On the bright side, when morning arrived, they had an actual plan for what to do next. They knew the location and number of Bran's hidden deposit box, and now they had the key to open it. They might actually be getting close to both finding her missing brother, and discovering what the Chicago Order had been up to that had been so bad, a Guardian had been summoned to stop them.

Okay, so maybe she was putting too much faith that this one box would hold the clue tying everything together and breaking their investigation wide open, but something told her they were close, and she couldn't shake the feeling.

But for now, it was still late, she was still tired, and oh yeah, she'd just remembered she was also still starving.

Tilting her head back, she looked up at Knox and managed a weak smile. "Whatever I need?" she repeated.

"Anything," he rumbled.

"Perfect." Stepping back, she handed him her cell

phone and turned toward the fridge. "In that case, you order the pizza. I need a drink."

Behind her, the Guardian grumbled, which brought an actual smile to her lips. If she had to conduct herself in patience until tomorrow, she could at least keep herself entertained. Right?

Chapter Fifteen

Her brother could not have chosen a more perfect institution from which to rent his safe-deposit box. First Illinois Fidelity, Inc. (or FIFI, as Wynn preferred to call it in the privacy of her own mind, just for shits and giggles), turned out to be an old-fashioned sort of bank, the kind of place where the wood was dark, the colors subdued, and no one paid any attention to anyone else. In fact, all of the employees seemed to give off the slightly aggrieved impression that really this would all be so much more pleasant if the customers would just go away and leave them alone with the lovely money.

After having done a little bit of online research, she knew that access to the safe-deposit box was a beautifully Swiss affair of discretion and as little human contact as possible. While Knox hovered beside her, looking like a badass bodyguard—which she thought added nicely to the impression that she was an incognito heiress withdrawing the funds for a spur-of-the-moment elopement to Argentina—she filled out a small slip of paper with the number of the box, her brother's Social Security number, and a forged version of his signature. She'd committed both those last bits to memory as a teenager, because hey, she was nosy and she liked to mess with him.

An employee beleaguered by the whole experience of having to withstand human contact compared the information with the box's control file, then led her through a security counter into a vault full of locked boxes. He found number 7183, removed it from the stacks, and placed it on the bare table in the center of the room. Then he appeared to brace himself before he had to endure the trauma of speaking to her.

"When you are quite finished, lock the box, leave it on the table, and summon an employee with the call button by the door."

Apparently emotionally wrung out and bitter at the experience, he turned on the heel of his shiny polished shoe and stalked out.

"Oh, goodie," Wynn murmured, pressing a hand to her stomach as if she could quiet the rioting butterflies in there. "I think we just made a new friend."

Knox grunted, but his eyes glinted with humor. He jerked his chin toward the box. "Shall we?"

"We shall," she said, and gripped the key she had already shown to the employee as part of the authorization process.

Before she could fit it in the lock, Knox reached out and gripped her wrist. "Remember," he said. "Coming back to Coleman's territory was a risk we had to take, but we must limit our exposure. Whatever is in the box, it goes in your bag immediately, and we leave. Immediately. We will have time to look through it later, when we are safely away from the Order's reach."

They had gone over all this last night, and again this morning, but Wynn didn't resent the reminder. She knew the temptation would be strong to look at what they found, because she wanted so badly for it to lead them to her brother. But Knox was right. As long as they remained in Coleman's building, they would be in danger. Better to get in, get out, and sort through whatever they found once they were safe at home.

She nodded her agreement. "I remember."

He withdrew his hand, and she opened the lock. Opening the lid of the long, rectangular metal box felt like opening the fictional door and not knowing if she would find the lady or the tiger. Or maybe the lady *was* a tiger, and either way, Wynn would end up with her throat ripped out and an unpleasant end to an unpleasant story.

She didn't know what she had expected to find in there, but nothing jumped out and tried to eat her face; no beam of light or flurry of ghostly spirits escaped. Nothing happened at all, so Wynn had to look down to see a battered, theme-style notebook that refused to close properly due to all the additional bits of paper, photos, and other items that had been stuffed inside.

Sensing Knox's impatience, she grabbed the book and stuffed it into her canvas messenger bag, then stuck her hand into the box and felt around to see if she'd missed anything. Other than the book, the box appeared to be empty.

"Is that it?" Knox growled.

"It looks like."

She felt her face settle into a mask of worry as she locked the box once more and slipped the key into her jean pocket. Her fingers itched to flip through that book, but she knew they had to stick to their plan. Knowing that didn't make it any easier.

Knox reached out and took her hand before he drew her to the door and pressed the call button. While they waited, he twined their fingers together and squeezed reassuringly. She hadn't realized how cold her fingers had gotten until she felt the warmth of his skin seeping into hers. She glanced up and forced her expression into a tense smile.

The same employee who had guided them into the vault reappeared, returned the locked box to its place along the wall, and ushered them back into the lobby. The moment they passed through the security gate again, he whirled and disappeared without a word.

"You are correct," Knox murmured as he tugged her gently through the lobby toward the entrance of the bank. "He clearly likes us."

The giggle that escaped her owed more to a release of tension than her sense of humor, but it still felt good. Her Guardian could be surprisingly witty at times, especially when he played off the juxtaposition between his jokes and his harsh, deadpan facial features.

Wynn followed him obediently through the lobby and out of the bank into the tower atrium. He pushed them relentlessly but inconspicuously through the crowd and out into the street. This time, instead of parking in a similar location to their last trip, they had left her car on the edge of the downtown area and taken the "L" to their destination.

At the time, she'd understood his caution and had agreed with his plan. Now she wanted to scream, since getting back to a spot where she could take out the notebook and begin searching for answers would have to wait. First they needed to walk to the train station, catch the red line, walk to the car, get in the car, and drive through the eastern half of the city just to get back home. She would never make it. Some poor schmoe would find her body slumped over her seat at the back of a train car because her heart would explode long before they reached their destination.

Knox held on to her hand while they traveled, his dark eyes narrow and alert as he constantly scanned the area around them for threats. Wynn, by contrast, stared straight ahead, her eyes fixed on nothing, all her attention focused on the notebook nestled in her canvas messenger bag.

She wore the strap crossed over her chest and kept her free hand pressed against the bag and probably looked like a zombie. Or an idiot. Or an idiot zombie, but she couldn't bring herself to care. She felt like if she so much as blinked, she would lose control, tear into their prize, and bring the entire Order down on their heads in broad daylight. As improbable as she knew that was, she couldn't shake the twin feelings of impatience and impending doom.

Were they having fun yet?

Hopping off the train a stop before their destination, Knox led her on a circuitous path back to the car. He looked like a perfectly normal guy out for a walk with his (zombie) girlfriend, but Wynn noticed the way he remained hyperalert. He never turned to look over his shoulder, but she saw him using reflections in their surroundings to make sure they weren't being followed. His vigilance only served to once again underline the big fat "no" next to CIA in Wynn's career prospects list. She simply let herself get swept along in his wake.

Even when they made it to the car and began the drive back home, Knox reached over the center console to grip Wynn's hand. She squeezed back briefly, because she understood that now he maintained the hold to offer comfort, but she couldn't see being comforted right now. Not until they knew what they were dealing with.

She barely remembered the car ride afterward. She passed through most of it in a daze, emerging with an aching jaw and head from gritting her teeth, and crescent-shaped divots in her palms from clenching her fists until her nails dug into her own skin. Still, only Knox's hovering, protective presence kept her from throwing herself through the door and ripping the notebook out of her bag so she could start pawing through it immediately.

The Guardian watched her like a hawk, insisting that she stay in the car until he could walk around and open her door for her. She would have liked to chalk the order up to his archaic sense of chivalry, because then she could have ignored him and done just as she pleased, but she knew very well he wanted her right by his side for safety's sake. If more bullets came shooting toward them, he wanted to step in front of those as well.

He also insisted that he unlock and enter her home before her, which was trickier to maneuver than it sounded. The new wards her uncle had helped her install on the front and kitchen doors required passwords to get through, even for her, so Wynn and Knox had to work in tandem. He led the way and released the physical locks before letting Wynn step forward. She used the password to put the wards in stasis, then stepped back so Knox could enter first before ushering her inside to reset the wards. It seemed almost ridiculous, a stupid cha-cha of paranoia, except this time she wanted to be double-secret-probation sure that they were safe, because the notebook in her bag might be the key that unlocked everything.

And now that they were home, safe behind locked doors and powerful wards, Wynn sank into a chair at her kitchen table, laid her bag out in front of her, and had second thoughts about even wanting to look. Goddess, what was up with her? All of a sudden she had late-onset bipolar disorder, or something. She wished her mind would just make up its damned mind.

She sat there for a few minutes, frozen in the same sort of tense immobility she'd suffered for the entire trip home. The reasons might have changed, but the effect hadn't. A wild thought flew through her head, darting around crazily like a bat trapped in a glass box—what if she just stayed like this forever, unable to move either forward or backward, just stuck in suspended animation eternally?

Then Knox broke through. Without a word, he double-checked the locks, then drew the second chair around the table so it nestled close beside hers. Taking his seat, he reached out and laid a hand over one of hers, his heat beginning to melt the ice that held her trapped.

Like someone waking from a trance—and wasn't that what she was?—she drew a deep, shuddering breath and blinked until the haze resolved from her vision. She straightened her spine, flipped her hand over to squeeze Knox's, and nodded. "Let's see what we found."

She released the comfort of the Guardian's skin against hers and flipped open the front flap of her messenger bag. Hesitantly, she reached in to withdraw the black-and-white-covered notebook. It looked battered, as if it had been carried for years, repeatedly opening and closing, being dropped and dragged, having glasses set down on it and small repairs made to it. In fact, Wynn could see the dark, ring-shaped stain that looked like it came from a cup of carelessly handled coffee, and in two places metallic gray duct tape had been applied to reinforce the outer binding. Bran had never been easy on his things.

She continued to examine the outside of the book, mentally preparing herself for what she might find inside. The edges of the pages had begun to wave, the way paper did sometimes when the hand that wrote on it pressed heavily and the ink bit deeply into the pages. It contributed to the way the book refused to fall completely closed, the front cover raised as if issuing an invitation to peek inside.

Of course, it didn't help that some of the pages appeared to have things inserted between. She could see the edges of what looked like newspaper clippings, other pieces of folded-up paper, even the glossy edge of a photo here and there. The notebook held any number of secrets.

"Together," Knox rumbled, the rasping gravel of his voice a comfort. "I am with you, little witch, and we need your brother's help."

"I know." Another deep breath, and she ran her hand over the cover, feeling her fingertips tingle at the contact. Her brow creased in a frown. "He's protected it."

Knox muttered something unpleasant. "How?"

"Some kind of ward. I'm not quite certain." She probed at the energy. "Damn it. I'm just not familiar enough with Warden magic, and I can tell that's what it is. It feels a little like what Uncle Griffin had me working with yesterday, but I don't think it's any of those spells." She ran her fingers along the perimeter of the cover, feeling the edges of the pages. A quick jolt zapped her skin, like a snap of static electricity, and she swore again.

"Can you get past it?" Knox asked, his jaw set.

"I don't know," she admitted. "I'm afraid at what might happen if I try. Since I can't identify the spell, I can't predict what it will do. If it was specifically put on to protect the information inside, there's a chance that trying to unlock it improperly would set off a trap. It could rebound on us, or it could cause some sort of self-destruct jinx and set the book on fire."

"Call Griffin," he ordered.

Wynn sighed and nodded. "I can't think of what else we can do. I'll call right now."

Luckily, Griffin answered on the third ring. She cut through his greetings with rude abruptness. She'd feel guilty about it later, but for now she needed to stick to business.

"Uncle Griff, I'm sorry, but I need your help again. Knox and I found something of Bran's. It's warded somehow, and we think it's important. I need to know if you can come and help me get through the wards."

There was a moment of silence while Griffin absorbed

the information; then he spoke calmly and decisively. "I'll be there in fifteen minutes."

She couldn't ask for much more. Hanging up the phone, she pushed back her chair and stood to pace the confines of the small kitchen. Here came the bipolar train again, because now that she knew they couldn't get into the book before Griffin arrived, she wanted to with the same anxious impatience she had felt on the trip here. Maybe when this thing was over with, she should get her damned head examined. Just in case.

Knox watched her with dark eyes and a brooding expression, all narrowed eyes and tense lips. If she was driving herself crazy, she knew she must be getting to him, too, but he never said a word. He just kept his eyes on her face and waited.

The waiting lasted for days. At least that's what it felt like. By the time Griffin arrived to knock on the kitchen door, she'd wound herself so tight, she imagined one wrong move would send her into a suicidal death spin, like a top gone out of control.

She froze the wards to let her uncle through, while Knox once again unlocked and relocked the physical for him. He entered the kitchen with a frown, his gaze immediately going from Wynn to the notebook on the kitchen table.

Griffin's eyes widened, and he made a startled sound. "Oh, my. Yes, I certainly see the problem, my dear. Goodness."

"You can see the wards?"

"Well, they're not wards precisely, but yes, they're quite visible. I believe that you're dealing with here is a series of locking spells, laid one atop another. At least three, maybe four. It does get a little hard to tell at the bottom layers." He shook his head and looked at Wynn. "Whatever is in that notebook, your brother wanted very much to keep anyone else from seeing it."

Knox nodded once and crossed his arms over his chest. "That is why we need to see it. As soon as possible."

"Of course, I'll help in any way that I can, but I won't be able to remove the spells myself. Wynn will have to do that."

"Can I?" Wynn asked.

"If you want to get inside there, you have to. I'll walk you through it, but it will be complicated, and time consuming. When would you like to start?"

Wynn set her mouth into a thin, straight line and raised her chin. "Now. We'll start right now."

She had known her uncle was an honest man, but she hadn't realized exactly what he'd meant by "time consuming." She'd thought he meant an hour or two. No such luck. He meant the rest of today and into the night.

Wynn wasn't sure they had that long. She noticed within the first hour that the longer the book sat in front of her, the more a feeling began to build inside her. It felt separate from her own impatience—more like a sense of approaching danger, of impending doom. At first, she felt ridiculous for even entertaining the notion, so she kept it to herself. She sat quietly while her uncle examined the notebook, trying to pin down exactly which locking spells Bran had used, and in what order he'd laid them. Then he asked for a pen and paper so he could write them down before they attempted anything directly on them.

The first spell, of course, was the weakest, the easiest to dismantle. It also contained a thread of deception that attempted to fool the unwary into believing it was the only protection, and once it fell the notebook would be free for the taking. Griffin warned her about that, though, so Wynn paid little attention to the whispers in her mind that urged her to flip open the cover the minute she unraveled the last bit of the first lock.

It fell with a quick burst of power, the way a lightbulb sometimes flashed just as it burned out. Her uncle gave a small hiss of triumph, but Wynn got hit with a wave of something so profoundly unsettling, it rocked her back in her chair.

Immediately Knox appeared beside her. He gripped the back of her chair with one hand, blocking the side of her closest to the notebook, and rested the other hand on her leg. His eyes searched her face. "Are you all right?" he demanded, watching her intently. "Were you harmed?"

"No, I'm fine." She glanced at her uncle, who frowned at her. She returned the expression. "Did you feel that?

"The release of the spell's energy? Of course. I was expecting it. Weren't you?"

"No. I mean, yes." She shook her head to clear it. "I expected something from the spell, sure, but that's not what I meant. Don't you feel anything else? There's something in the air now that wasn't here before. Like a heaviness, a sense of dread." She looked between the two men. "Neither of you feels that?"

Knox frowned and answered in the negative. Griffin looked almost bewildered. "Nothing."

Maybe she really was going crazy. "Okay," she said, trying to sweep the reaction aside. "Let's keep going, then."

The second spell felt considerably stronger, and when Wynn read through the information Griffin had jotted down, she understood why. This one had been cast with bindweed and bloodroot, to seal the lock and make it almost a part of the book itself. Conversely, the very fact that herbs had gone into the spell gave Wynn an advantage. Anything that had once been a living and growing plant responded quickly to her energies, allowing her to manipulate and dissipate the power it gave to the spell. Once that was done, she could uncast it according to Griffin's instructions.

It struggled hard against her, and the unfamiliar feeling of combining her own inner magic with the Light-powered magic used in all Warden spells forced her to concentrate until she feared her head might explode. When this was over, she thought she might need an ibuprofen the size of Milwaukee.

The second barrier fell with another flash of light, this one nearly enough to blind her. As it was, she blinked several times to clear her vision and glanced around. Griffin wore an expression of guilt and Knox looked ready to chew through steel. "What's wrong?"

"It took you almost four hours to break that lock," the Guardian growled, anger vibrating in his voice. "I feared you might collapse before you finished. You swayed toward the end, as if you would fall off your chair onto the hard floor."

"It did seem to take more out of you than I expected," Griffin admitted, his brow knitted with worry. "Maybe you should take a break before you try the third one."

That was when the wave hit her, another rush of dread, this one almost strong enough to send her into a panic. She whipped her gaze around the room, half expecting to see something big, dark, and ugly lurking in one of the corners. Of course, nothing was there. The room appeared perfectly normal, if a bit dimmer than it had the last time she'd looked around. Hours really had flown by while she worked, and she could tell that sunset was almost upon them. Part of her wanted to agree with her uncle, and her stomach backed that up emphatically. She hadn't eaten in hours. She felt like she'd just run a marathon, all damp skin and burning muscles, but the oppressive sense of doom that hung around them made her shake her head.

"No, I have to do this."

Knox made a sound that threatened to out-threaten whatever it was hanging over all of their heads. Wynn knew it was serious, so why couldn't anyone else seem to feel it?

The guardian shifted from his position leaning against the wall beside the kitchen table. He'd placed himself there, she was sure, so he could catch her if she fell, or jump in to save her from any threat that appeared, but she saw no way he could protect her from a feeling.

"I forbid you from continuing," Knox snarled, reaching down to haul her from her chair. "Not until you have rested and eaten something nourishing. This task has visibly weakened you, and I will not allow another session until you have regained your strength."

The fact that her knees buckled the minute Knox stood her up and she tried to put weight on them did not support her position. Wynn knew that for sure. But she also knew that she had to keep going. The negative energy only she could feel demanded that she continue. It hung like a black cloud over her head, and she knew the only way to get rid of it was to confront it, by finishing her task and facing whatever the notebook contained head-on.

Now she just had to convince her overprotective mate that she knew of what she spoke.

She circled her fingers around his forearms above where he grasped her waist. The warmth of his skin comforted her and gave her strength. Which was good, because if he made her fight him on this, she'd need all of that she could get.

She tilted her head back to look up at him, letting her determination show in her steady brown gaze. "I am exhausted. And I'm hungry. And I'm sick to death of being worried and frightened and completely in the dark. This is important. We need to finish this, and get a look at what's in the book. I'm strong enough for that. I know I am. Let me do it, then I swear I'll rest. I promise, but we *need* to *know*."

War waged across the Guardian's face. She could almost hear the ring of swords clashing and smell the sharp tang of cannon fire. Honestly, maybe he wouldn't be so good at poker after all. His sense of honor and need to perform the duties he'd been summoned for must be going toe-to-toe with his feelings for her, his need to protect and defend her stronger than any other impulse. If she was his mate, it had to be, and she had stopped doubting the mate thing. What was the point? She'd fallen in love with the giant warrior, so any fighting she did now would only hurt her. And there were plenty of other things out there more than happy to hurt her instead.

After several minutes of Knox's tension nearly blocking out the atmosphere of dread, he threw back his head and gave a brief, frustrated roar. When he locked eyes with her again, he had his Guardian's eyes, black and shining, and they burned with livid flames.

"One word, just one hint that you might be in trouble, and I will end this, little witch. Do you understand?" His fingertips bit into her waist, but she didn't flinch. She could feel his worry like a living entity and hated to be the cause. "I will do whatever is necessary to keep you safe, even if it means the cursed notebook goes up in flames and the Order succeeds in whatever it has planned. Is that clear?"

Wynn nodded, her gaze steady and serious. "Perfectly."

Knox snarled, human lips curling to reveal inhuman fangs, clear evidence of how close he sat to a total loss of control. She could feel his reluctance to let her go even as he forced his hands to release her, one unwilling finger at a time. Also, this time he didn't step back against the wall. Instead, he took up a position directly behind her chair, ready at any moment to snatch her up and put an end to her risky spell work.

He looked to Griffin. "If she must do this, show her how to do it quickly. As quickly as possible. I want this done and over."

"Don't we all," Griffin muttered under a vigorous nod.

He looked no more pleased than Knox by Wynn's decision to proceed, but he visibly gathered himself together and went over the instructions for removing the third spell. "I think this is the last one, so it's going to be hard to break. In this case, Knox is right. Quicker really is better. A fast dispellment gives the magic less time to build a backlash against you. Work carefully, but as fast as you can."

Wynn nodded, her attention already focused on the notebook. She felt like a prizefighter perched on his corner stool between rounds, his coach and trainer trying to pump him up for the next three minutes of battle. She hoped she made it out of the ring under her own power, and not passed out cold on a stretcher.

Hovering her hand over the cover of the book, Wynn felt for the third spell. She didn't have to look hard. It lurked right there on the surface, like a coiled cobra waiting to strike. Or a rattlesnake, because she swore she could hear a thrumming sound in the air, a low uncomfortable sound of warning. She pressed carefully against it and gasped, then snatched her hand back on a wave of panicked nausea.

"What is wrong?" Knox demanded. "Are you harmed?"

"No, what's wrong is that spell." Wynn continued to stare at the book, but her expression now had turned to straight-out fear, tinged with revulsion. "That spell was cast with blood magic." She looked helplessly at her uncle. "Why would Bran ever used blood magic?"

Blood magic, no matter what the intention behind it, always tripped straight over the lines between magic. Very little of magic qualified as truly white, because power had its own agenda, and even the noblest of goals could have unintended consequences. Gray magic encompassed most energy work, whether the worker was witch, Warden, or whatever. Gray magic intended no direct ill, but it acknowledged the possibility that its outcome could either harm or help, depending on the situation. But black magic was another thing entirely.

Black magic either sought to harm or resulted from harm. Hexes made up an obvious example, their intention simply and clearly being to cause the object of the hex harm or strife. Living sacrifice sat on the extreme end of the spectrum, the blackest art in practice because it cost a life in its casting, either animal or, even more disturbingly, human. Clearly, the Order's magic ran to inky black, but Bran's never had. Until now.

Blood magic always counted as black magic, because it required harm by its very definition. Not even the smallest amount of blood could be drawn from even a willing victim without the infliction of harm. Even a caster who used a single drop of blood willingly given from his own hand had to injure that hand to collect it.

Wynn had known one or two magic users in her time who might dabble in blood magic when their need for power became extreme. They tended to do what she had just described, prick themselves with a needle or create a shallow cut, then use the drop or two of blood that welled up to fuel the spell. They weren't really evil people, at least not the ones she knew; they just believed that blood would create a shortcut to their end goal. Wynn didn't believe any goal was worth that.

Blood was the essence of life, because without it, no animate creature could survive. This truth gave it enormous power, power greater than any other sub-stance on earth, be it earth, water, fire, or air. Magic cast with blood drew on that power to boost its energy into the stratosphere. The principle of it made sense to Wynn; the idea of her brother using it did not.

Beside her, Griffin uttered something that sounded halfway between a curse and a prayer. Wynn didn't blame him. If she'd been a Christian, she'd be crossing herself right now.

"He must have been desperate," her uncle whispered. "To take that route, the contents of the book must be in-credibly important."

Wynn chewed on her lower lip and rubbed her hands across her face. "I've never touched blood magic before. I don't know if I can do this."

She felt Knox's hands settle on her shoulders and squeeze. "You do not have to. I meant what I said. The book can burn for all I care. We can defeat the Order without its secrets."

Temptation whispered in her ear. Oh, how she wanted to believe that. It would be so much easier, so much neater and less disturbing if she could just toss the note-book into her fireplace and strike a match. She might even do a little dance while it burned, freed from the burden of its weight.

But would that change anything? Bran would still be gone, the Order would still be rising, the world would still be in danger, and Wynn would have to live with the knowledge that she might have been able to stop it, if she'd just pulled up her big girl panties and gone to work.

Reaching up, she patted Knox's hand. "No, I can do this. I said I could, and I meant it then. This doesn't change anything, really. In fact, it just makes it more important."

Griffin patted her knee. "Remember, too, Wynn, that Bran's blood is your blood as well. You're brother and sister, born to the same mother and father, connected by genetics and a lifetime of togetherness. That gives you an advantage. In fact, it means you're probably the only one who can lift the spell. Maybe Bran used the blood for a reason."

Wynn couldn't think why she should find that reassuring, but somehow she did. Not because Bran might have planned this somehow, all those months ago before he disappeared, but because it reminded her that this was her brother, and any risk was worth it, because if they found the Order, maybe they could find Bran as well.

"Okay." She raised her hands again, sent a quick prayer winging to the Goddess, and carefully centered herself. "Let's try this again."

This time she steeled herself against the crawling sensation the blood magic caused against her skin. It slithered under the throbbing warning vibe, somehow oily and unclean. Black, not by its intent, but by its nature.

The whole spell actually felt like a spiderweb, now that she examined it more closely. It brushed against her skin the same way, simultaneously insubstantial and disconcertingly strong. It stuck to her just as quickly, and she felt just the same impulse to brush it away with a girlie shriek and a quick stamp of her feet. Instead, she concentrated on tracing the threads from the perimeter all the way to the center, studying its construction.

Just like a web, the spell appeared to have been built

in concentric rings tied together by radiating spokes. They wrapped around the edges of the book, sealing it shut. Experimentally, she used the Light magic her uncle had taught her to access and watched the web clamp down in reaction. Clearly, it did not want to be messed with. Out of curiosity, Wynn refocused, reached out with her own energy, and tugged a radial string. It vibrated as if she'd just strummed a guitar. Now, that was interesting.

With careful deliberation, Wynn moved to another spoke and tugged again. Again, the web vibrated, this time at an even higher frequency. She wished vaguely that she were a musician with the ability to identify the sounds that thrummed through her, but this probably wasn't the time to try to play chopsticks, anyway. A third spoke, a third pluck, and this time Wynn watched carefully as the vibration traveled down the string to the center of the web. For a brief moment, something there appeared illuminated, and in an instant she could see the end of the woven pattern.

Excitement rushed through her. Working quickly but cautiously, she strummed one more sting, her inner gaze never straying from the center of the web. There. She snatched up the glowing thread before the note could fade and slowly, very, very slowly, began to unravel the web.

It gave reluctantly, each thread sticking to the others it crossed, as if clinging to them for support. The process demanded patience, concentration, and painstaking attention to detail. Sometimes the central thread she tugged lay on top of the radial spokes, sometimes it darted under, forcing her to take extra care to untangle it. She could feel time ticking away, but to her it felt like a million years, and half a second, and she had no idea which estimate might hit closer to reality.

When she finally reached the end of the concentric circles, she paused to look down at what she had revealed in the framework of spoke threads. Those twined together as well, the entire pattern apparently built on one unbroken thread. She could admire the intricacy of it, but now she could feel exhaustion pressing in on her, and she just wanted the whole thing over with.

With one last, firm tug, she watched the remnants of the spell unravel and the filaments of magic release their grip on the pages of the book. Just as the last one snapped, she heard an enormous sound, like a clap of thunder directly overhead, and then she felt herself falling.

Into what, she hadn't the faintest idea.

Chapter Sixteen

Knox acknowledged his existence so far had been a short one, but with the knowledge of the ages at his disposal, at times he felt very old indeed. Many of those times, he had begun to notice, resulted directly from the much-too-familiar sight of his mate throwing herself wantonly into the path of danger.

It went against every instinct he possessed as both a Guardian and a male to allow the woman he had claimed for his own to risk herself for the sake of others. Despite the fact that they had met due to one of those very risks—when her commitment to assist the other Wardens and their Guardians in locating more of his kind had resulted in the attempt on her life and his summoning into the world—the very thought of Wynn in danger sent every one of Knox's nerves on edge. Allowing her to meet with Ronald Coleman without Knox present had nearly cost him his sanity, but watching her attempt to dispel a blood magic warding cast by her own brother almost cost him his life.

It flashed before his eyes in an instant of explosive radiance and concussive power. He had watched her sitting at the table, seemingly in a trance, silent and motionless for the past three solid hours while she worked at dismantling the last magical lock on the old notebook, wondering if its contents could ever be worth what she had already done trying to access them. Unable to do anything else, he had hovered behind her chair, waiting to grab her and haul her out of danger if her attempt backfired. But he'd been more afraid that he would have to catch her when exhaustion overwhelmed her and she fell over sideways because she no longer possessed the strength to hold herself upright in a seated position. His muscles ached from being tensed to handle either scenario.

He hadn't expected the world to explode.

That's what it felt like. One minute he stood and watched his mate work herself to the point of weakness to protect the world from the Order; the next, he felt himself being hurled backward, away from a supernova of light and pressure that detonated over the kitchen table.

Instinct was all that saved them, because instinct was what had his arms closing around his witch from behind the instant his body sensed the change in atmospheric pressure that heralded the magical explosion. Had he failed to carry his mate with him away from the center of the impact, they all would have died, because his grief at losing her would have seen him on a murderous rampage that ended in his own self-destruction.

Clutching Wynn to his chest, Knox slid across the slick vinyl of the kitchen floor until his head slammed into the bottom of the stainless-steel refrigerator, halting his momentum. He heard an almost simultaneous thud, and expected that Griffin had also landed somewhere nearby. He hoped the older man remained unhurt, but his first thought went immediately to his mate.

She lay still and unmoving atop him, her chair still separating her body from his. It must have gotten trapped between them when he wrapped his arms around her. He couldn't smell any blood, but all kinds of injuries might be present without it. Cursing violently, he rolled gently to the side to free himself from beneath her, laying her carefully onto the floor.

The chair, he tossed aside without a thought, not caring where it landed. When he heard no scream, he felt content he had at least missed her uncle's head. Crouching over her still form, he patted his fingers softly against one pale cheek and spoke her name.

"Wynn," he called through an unfamiliar tightness in his throat. "Little witch, wake up. Come. Open your eyes and look at me."

A groan sounded in response, but it didn't come from Wynn, so he ignored it. He cared not if the world had ended, so long as his mate lived.

"Wynn, wake up," he ordered more strongly. "You must wake now and speak to me."

A heavy shuffling noise came from nearby, then he saw Griffin's shaggy head pop into view near his shoulder. The man had apparently crawled across the floor to get to them, and he still appeared dazed from the explosion. His glasses sat askew across his face, and he looked almost as pale as his niece. "How is she?"

"Unconscious," Knox growled over the fury in his chest.

"Here." Balancing on one hand, the former Warden reached into his pocket and withdrew a tiny vial. "Hartshorn," he explained with a bashful shrug. "Sometimes when the magic goes awry, I get dizzy, so I've gotten used to carrying it with me."

Uncapping the vial, Griffin held it close to Wynn's face and waved the fumes beneath her nose. Almost instantly she coughed and jerked, her eyelids flying open.

"Goddess, what happened?" she asked weakly, coughing again. Griffin withdrew the smelling salt, and she attempted to sit up.

Knox's hands on her shoulders pressed her straight back down. "You tell us," he bit out, his voice as deep as thunder. "You worked on that spell for three hours, and then just before I thought you might collapse from the exhaustion, something exploded."

Wynn lifted a hand to press her fingers to her forehead. "Yeah, I remember that much. It felt like getting caught in the middle of a sonic boom. Was anything destroyed?"

"You mean other than you?" Knox snarled.

Griffin pushed himself to his feet and looked around. "No, everything looks completely normal. No broken glass, no sign of flame." He shook his head, clearly baffled. "Even the notebook looks untouched. The explosion must have been a release of pure magical energy."

"Good."

Knox looked down at the sound of Wynn's relieved sigh. "Good?" he repeated, incredulous and furious. "You once again put yourself at risk, and once again you could have been killed. This is unacceptable, witch. I will not allow such behavior to continue!"

He knew he had worked himself into an uproar. Wynn watched him warily from her position on the floor, and her uncle had backed away, shoulders hunched, face grimacing at the sight of a Guardian in a full-on fury. Knox didn't care. All he cared about was Wynn. He steeled himself for her to argue. The exchange of heated words between them had become something of a tradition.

Instead of speaking, Wynn braced her hands behind her and attempted to push herself into a seated position. Unable to watch her struggle, even at something so small as this, he helped her pull herself erect and prop her back against the refrigerator door.

"I know this must have scared you," she told him quietly. "Heck, I scared myself. Trust me, I get no enjoyment out of being flung across the room, and I especially don't like it when it's my own brother's spell that does the flinging. No matter how many times we wrestled growing up, that did not bring back fond memories."

Surprised and a bit deflated at her lack of stubborn insistence on her right to choose to take insane risks if she wanted to, Knox frowned down at her. "So you agree with me that this behavior must stop." He couldn't keep the note of uncertainty entirely hidden.

Wynn tilted her head and pursed her lips. "I agree that I can't take stupid risks. None of us can. There are too few of us out there as it is. So far, it's just the six of us against the Seven and the entire Order."

Beside them, Griffin cleared his throat, and Wynn's lips curved in a small smile.

"Seven," she corrected. "Only seven of us, and that's

just not enough. We can't afford to lose anyone, so no one can take silly chances. But when it's something vital? Something that could help us put these bastards down once and for all? That's not a silly chance; that's a calculated risk. Sometimes those, you have to take. If you're asking me to stop doing that . . . well, that I can't agree with at all."

Knox bowed his head, frustration like a boulder on his back, weighing him down. Hell, boulder? He felt as if he had the entire mountain bearing down on him. The thought of losing his mate was simply too much for him to deal with.

"I cannot stand back and allow you to endanger yourself," he ground out, not looking at her, knowing if he did, he would drown in the dark pools of her eyes. "How can you ask me to do this?"

Wynn laid a hand against his cheek. "I'm not asking you to stand back. I'm asking you to stand beside me. You have strengths I can't even imagine, *strength* I can't even imagine. I'm the one who can work magic, who can cast and uncast spells. You know as well as I do that if we're going to win this war the Order has started, it's going to take every single Guardian and Warden we can muster. We each have our strengths, and we have to trust one another to play to them. That's what I'm asking you to do, Knox. Just trust me."

Already, he had trusted this small, stubborn female with his heart and his life. What more did he have to give her? He did not know, but he felt more rise up within him. For her, it seemed the well was infinite.

"You will be the death of me," he sighed, pressing his

forehead against hers and cupping her face between his hands. "One way or another, little witch. I swear it."

Her lips twitched into a mischievous grin, and that more than anything reassured him of her well-being. At least for the moment. "Hey," she teased, "don't blame me because you decided to give up immortality, big guy. That one's on you."

Knox chuckled and pushed to his feet, reaching down to pull Wynn up after him. "You might have had a little bit to do with that, witch."

He took a moment to embrace her, needing to feel her in his arms, to feel her heart beat against his chest, to feel the warmth of her skin and the gentle weight of her arms around his waist. Of course, he couldn't stop himself from running his hands over whatever he could reach, making certain he felt no injuries or broken bones. "You are certain you are well?"

"Still feel like I could sleep for a week, but no new damage," she assured him. "So, let's hurry up and take a look at this book before I fall asleep on my feet."

Knox took in the pallor of her skin, the signs of strain at the corners of her mouth, the dark bruises beneath her eyes, and hesitated. "Perhaps we should wait until morning. Deciphering information always comes easier after rest."

She glared at him. "Not a chance. I don't care how tired I am, I'm never going to sleep if I have to lie there wondering exactly what was locked up behind those spells. We look now. At least try to get an overview."

Her wave brought Griffin to the table, where he settled into his chair. Knox picked up the chair he had thrown after rolling Wynn out of it and checked it for damage before replacing it at the table. Before Wynn could take a seat, he claimed it himself and tugged his mate down into his lap.

When she raised a brow at him, he shrugged. "There are only two chairs. Besides, last time I stood as close as I could behind you, and I still barely reached you in time. It is much more efficient if I simply hang on to you from the beginning."

Griffin snickered, then tried to disguise the sound of amusement behind a weak cough. Knox ignored the noise, but Wynn shot her uncle a glare.

"Uh, right," the man said, clearing his throat and offering a completely serious expression as he gently pushed the notebook toward the others. "Would you care to do the honors, my dear?"

Knox felt his little witch's ribs expand as she took a fortifying breath. He tensed as she reached out, ready to snatch her away if it became necessary, but her breathing didn't change as she carefully flipped back the cover.

All three of them stared down at a page filled with minuscule script, densely packed so that two written lines occupied one measured line on the paper.

"Wow," Wynn said. "This might take us a while to go through."

"Is it all like that?" Griffin asked.

Wynn laid her thumb against the cut edges of the pages and fanned rapidly through them. "It looks like it, if you mean, 'did he pack that much onto every page,' but it looks like there's other stuff in here, too. Clippings, photos, even some drawings."

The Warden sighed and pushed his glasses back along

the bridge of his nose. "Maybe we should get some sleep before we tackle this. I'm not sure I'd be able to stay awake reading something that heavy."

Knox felt his female's shoulders slump with disappointment. "Maybe you're right." She flipped through the notebook once again, a little slower this time, exposing more of each page as they rifled by. "I mean I was already exhausted. This might tip me over the edge."

Having nestled Wynn comfortably in his lap, Knox had no trouble seeing over her shoulder to the notebook on the table. She was such a tiny thing compared with him that she impeded his view not at all. Which was why when something caught his eye on a lined page of white paper, he knew he hadn't mistaken the image.

His hand shot out, almost too quick to see, and he stopped the pages in mid-flip. He slapped his palm onto the paper, holding the notebook open to a very particular page. Then he felt a touch of the dread his mate had described earlier.

"May the Light save us."

He heard the benediction over the buzzing in his ears and looked up to see that Griffin had gone even paler than his niece, the man's gaze fixed on the same drawing that had caught Knox's attention. The Warden looked almost as horrified as the Guardian felt.

Wynn stirred in his lap. "What is it?" she asked, looking from him to her uncle in quick little jerks of her head. "What's the matter with you two? Knox, you could have damaged something, and Uncle Griff, you look like you just saw a ghost. What's going on?"

Griffin just shook his head, staring dazedly at the notebook. Knox had to grit his teeth to make himself give voice to his suspicion. Only he knew it wasn't a suspicion. He recognized the item Bran Powe had sketched, and it made his belly tighten in uneasy fury.

"It's the Eye," he spit out, his arms tightening unconsciously around his mate. "The Eye of Uhlthor. Your uncle recognized it, too."

Still unable to speak, the man only nodded, his Adam's apple bobbing as he swallowed hard.

"What does that mean? What is the Eye?" Wynn must have sensed the tangle of emotions in his voice, because she stiffened and took a closer look at the page in the notebook.

Finally, Griffin blinked and tore his gaze from the drawing. He pushed away from the table as if trying to escape from the reach of the evil thing, and Knox couldn't blame him.

"Do you have any coffee, Wynn-ding?" The man muttered nervously. "I'll make coffee. Trust me, we'll be needing it."

Wynn turned to face her Guardian and frowned. "Okay, tell me what's going on. You guys are starting to scare me."

"Good," Griffin said under his breath, and Knox shot him a warning glare.

"The item your brother sketched in his book is called the Eye of Uhlthor," he explained, after focusing his attention back on Wynn. "It is an ancient artifact of power that I had thought long destroyed. According to my memories, the last time anyone saw it, the Guild had possession and were supposed to destroy it."

"I thought it had been," Griffin insisted. He had found the small tin of coffee Wynn said she kept for guests and emergencies and was measuring grounds into a small device his female called a French press. "Everyone thought it had been destroyed. The Guild masters at the time recorded that it had been done."

"And when was this?" Wynn asked.

"In the year 847."

"Wow, that's a long time ago." Wyn frowned and turned back to the book. He saw her tilt her head to study the drawing from a new angle. A moment later she stiffened and made a sound as if someone had just struck her in the stomach, like the wind had been knocked out of her.

"What is it?" he demanded, arms tightening around her.

"Oh, my Goddess, I saw that," she breathed, her gaze fixed on the notebook, her form trembling. "Recently. I saw that recently. At least, I think I did. It was in pretty rough shape, but I'm fairly certain it was this."

Griffin spun around, spraying coffee grounds onto the floor. "Where? Where did you see it?"

Wynn lifted her head and met Knox's burning gaze. "In Ronald Coleman's office. He said it was one of the artifacts found at the dig at the CG Towers site. It was the only one he kept."

Wynn's head spun like a merry-go-round. She felt off balance and vaguely queasy, and her heart had begun to race the moment she'd recognized the item in the drawing. She just couldn't figure out how any of this made sense.

"I'm having trouble processing this," she said. "I mean, I dropped the aura detection spell I cast before

Coleman showed me his collection, but artifacts aren't like people. People can have deceptive energy, but objects are either magical or they aren't. I looked right at this thing, so why didn't I pick up that it had power?"

"Describe for us what you saw."

"Coleman had it mixed in with a lot of other items, stuff from all over the world. This was just sitting in the middle of it all. I mean, it doesn't look exactly like this anymore."

She brought up the memory of the round metal disk she had seen in the case in Coleman's office. "It's obviously deteriorated. There are a couple of places where the metal's worn completely through, and I think there were a couple of chips taken off the edge. Plus, the surface is so weathered, you can't read any of the decoration that's drawn here. I didn't even realize some of it was supposed to be letters. You can sort of see that something was there at one time, but you'd never be able to read off it, like you can here."

Griffin clutched the countertop and stared at her. "But you're certain what you saw is what Bran drew there."

"Yes. I mean, Bran even got the dimensions right. That's about the size that I remember. But like I said, I didn't feel any magic from it. I'm having a hard time matching up what I saw with the reaction you two are having."

Knox appeared thoughtful. "How close were you to the object? Did you try to touch it?"

She thought back. "I'm sure I was no more than two feet in front of it. Maybe less, because I leaned forward to look at a couple of things in the case with it."

He made a humming noise. "Then it was contained somehow."

"Just with glass. He displays this things in a glass-fronted cabinet in his office. It's pretty fancy, electronic locks, built-in feature lighting, the works. So, no, I didn't try to touch it. I'm pretty sure the whole setup is alarmed, and I doubt Coleman would have let me, anyway."

Knox nodded. "I would guess that the entire cabinet must be dampened somehow, built to contain the magical energy of the object or objects inside. A bit like your mirror box."

"But that would make the cabinet itself magical, so I should have felt something coming off that."

Griffin shook his head. "Not necessarily. There are blocking spells out there that don't leave a trace, because why bother blocking something if the block itself gives away the secret."

Wynn did not like the sound of that. She turned back to Knox. "So what is this thing anyway? Why was it supposed to be destroyed?"

The Guardian shifted beneath her, and she could tell from his expression that he did not relish what he was about to tell her. "The Eye of Uhlthor is an artifact created by Uhlthor itself, forged during its first time on earth. It is a disk of silver and copper, engraved with the demon's image and inscribed with a very particular spell."

"Wait, maybe I'm wrong then. The disk I saw looked black, like wrought iron, not silver or copper, no matter how tarnished it might be."

"You are not wrong. The Defiler forged the disk of

those two metals, but when the creature gazed upon it, the metal changed, becoming blackened and discolored, because nothing can remain pure in its presence."

Wynn winced. "Lovely."

Knox grunted his agreement. "The Eye has one purpose. It exists to focus the Defiler's power. Whatever strength the evil has is multiplied when it wields the Eye. At full strength, the Eye assisted Uhlthor in tearing a gash in the fabric of the planes, allowing him to move freely between them."

The impact of his words almost knocked her off his lap. "So theoretically, he could use it to rip open the prisons that the other six demons are housed in and let them out to play."

"Yes."

"Okay. Okay, give me minute here." Feeling her head spin, Wynn quickly bent down until her forehead pressed against her kneecap. She thought briefly about asking for a paper bag to breathe into, but she didn't think she was actually hyperventilating. She couldn't breathe at all, let alone too rapidly.

"I do not think that is our immediate concern," she heard Knox say from somewhere way far above her still-light head. "You said yourself that the Defiler is not at full strength, and he would need to be to accomplish such a task as that."

"I said, we don't *think* he's at full strength," Wynn spit out, her vehemence a bit muffled by her position and the denim of her jeans. "It's a theory, Knox. We have no way of knowing for sure. What if we're wrong? The Order has that thing, so clearly it's only a matter of time before Uhlthor gets his hands on it. What do we do then?"

"Don't panic," Griffin said, grimacing when Wynn turned her head just enough to shoot him an upside-down look of disbelief. "I know, do as I say, not as I do." He drew in a deep breath. "There could be other ways the Order would intend to use the Eye."

"Oh, really? I suppose they're going to use it to deliver presents to all the good little boys and girls in the land, huh?"

Her uncle was used to her sarcasm and didn't even flinch. "The Guardian said himself, the Eye concentrates whatever power the Defiler possesses. Well, if he's weak the way you and Ella and Fil theorize, using the Eye makes even more sense. You're smart girls. I see no reason to doubt your theory, especially given the evidence you've told me about. A weakened Defiler has even more need of the Eye to increase his abilities."

Carefully, Wynn pulled herself erect and scowled. "Somehow, I'm not feeling terribly comforted by that prospect."

"What should comfort you is that you saw the artifact with your own eyes, little witch," Knox pointed out. "While it rests in Coleman's cabinet, it is not in the hands of the Defiler."

Wynn hadn't thought of that, but now that Knox made her, she found it odd. "That's true, but why isn't it?"

"Why isn't what?"

"Why isn't the Eye in the Defiler's hands? Can anyone other than Uhlthor use it? Because if not, then it really is just an interesting artifact in someone's collection."

She could see Knox's brow knit as he considered that. "I am not certain. I have heard of no being but Uhlthor itself who has wielded it. I do not believe it concentrates the power of any other."

"A priest," Griffin said. "There was speculation among the Guild masters that a priest within the Order might be able to use it on the Defiler's behalf, to feed souls to him in his prison in order to make him strong enough to break free. That was one of the reasons everyone agreed it had to be destroyed."

"And yet it was not."

Her uncle winced at the condemnation in Knox's words. Wynn just shook her head. "Maybe you were right about the Guild, too, but if they deliberately failed to destroy the Eye when they had the chance, then the corruption would go back centuries."

Griffin jerked away from the counter and stared at the two of them. "Corruption? Are you saying you think the Guild of Wardens is corrupt? That's impossible."

"Is it?" Knox asked. "You and your niece have both related stories of actions by the Guild that do not sit well with either myself or my brother Guardians. Add this to the destruction of the Guild hall in Paris—a building guarded by some of the most talented magic users in the world, might I add—and it raises questions in my mind, as well as the minds of the other risen Guardians. We will be looking into it, you may be certain."

Wynn cut off her uncle's protests. "We can talk about that later. Right now, we have more important things to worry about. Uncle Griff, if you're right about a priest of the Order being able to use the Eye to channel power to Uhlthor, that might explain what they plan to do with it. I imagine that if he is still weak, it would help him regain his strength a lot faster than he would otherwise manage."

"It could even allow him to regain his physical form," Griffin hypothesized. "That would take an enormous amount of power, but bringing him to full strength would be the first step."

"And we do not want it to reach full strength, especially not with the Eye at its disposal."

She had noticed before that Knox always used *it* to refer to the demon, rather than *he* or *him*. It just underlined his bone-deep loathing of the malevolent creature. He made a good point, though. They definitely did not want Uhlthor reaching full strength.

Yet something still bothered her. "About that. The one thing that I'm confused about is why they wouldn't have already used the damned thing. I mean, why sit around twiddling your thumbs when you have the means to strengthen your greatest weapon sitting around on a shelf?"

Griff reached out and pulled down the calendar Wynn had hung on the wall near the kitchen door. He joined them at the table and laid the calendar down next to Bran's journal. "Look at that," he said, pointing a finger at the box for the following Friday.

Wynn glanced down, but saw nothing unusual. She had made no notes in that box. It was blank except for the number that indicated the date, and the small black circle printed beside it. Her shoulders had half lifted in a shrug, and she was about to look away to ask her uncle what he meant when her gaze flew to another box at the beginning of the month. Twenty-eight days before the one he pointed at.

He must have seen her expression, because he nodded and tapped the glossy paper for emphasis. "This month we have two new moons, Wynn-dixie."

"A black moon." Wynn considered the possibilities, and shuddered. Oh, this was so not good.

Knox shifted beneath her. "Explain the significance. Why is this detail important to you both?"

"It's likely to be important to the Order, too," Griffin said sourly.

"Since you don't use magic the way Wardens or witches or crazy cultists do, it probably doesn't mean anything to you. You *are* magic, but you don't use it," Wynn explained. "But to those of us who do use magic, a black moon is kind of a big deal, the same way a blue moon, or a second full moon in a month is. They only happen about every two or three years, and they mark times when magical power is especially concentrated. Witches love blue moons, because the full moon is the absolute best time for spell work. Power just brims up during the full, and during a blue moon it can increase tenfold. It's almost dizzying. But most of us won't cast spells during a new moon. As far as I know, even magic users are wary of them."

"Better to say we're selective of them," Griffin qualified. "The energy of a new moon is very different from the full moon. It's much darker. Anyone not practicing black magic will only perform certain spells during the new moon. Bindings, breaking hexes, that sort of thing. The energy just isn't suitable for positive works."

"And a black moon is ten times that," Wynn added.

"Ten times the negative energy. Not only won't witches cast during that time, they practically tie their own hands together and hide under the bed. Usually I lock my workroom door and take a long hot bath in a tub full of Epsom salts. But . . ."

"But?" Knox prompted impatiently.

"But, if I were a crazy evil cultist intent on feeding negative power to a crazy evil demon? That's the night I'd want to do it."

Chapter Seventeen

Their discovery necessitated a full-on mustering of the troops, a powwow of international proportions. Literally. The next evening brought a conference call using a VOIP service with everyone attending, Canadians and Americans alike. Wynn felt almost like the International Olympic Committee, only the last she'd heard, fighting demons had not yet been named an Olympic event. So much for her dreams of a gold medal.

In the hours leading up to the call, she and Griffin and Knox spent all day poring over the rest of Bran's journal. It was slow going, as his research into the Order activity in the area went back at least three or four years. Also, trained academic that he was, he had felt compelled to support his conclusions with evidence, including footnotes, photos, articles, citations of both ancient and modern texts, and the occasional hand-drawn illustration. Within half an hour of starting, Wynn had already given thanks for Knox's insistence the night before that she not tackle the project without some sleep.

If she had tried, she felt pretty sure her head would have exploded.

Fortunately, the notebook yielded a lot of information, including one particular tidbit that had Wynn cursing like a sailor, then blushing and apologizing profusely to her shocked uncle. "I can't believe it," she said once she'd calmed down a bit. "I was right there and I had no idea. Someone in this damned cult is the best magic user I've ever seen when it comes to obscuring spells. The bastard."

That curse she hadn't apologized for. Because according to her brother's meticulous and thorough research, the Chicago-area cell of the Order of Eternal Darkness currently operated out of the abandoned Van Oswalt estate in Lake Forest. The very one where Wynn had first gone looking for a Guardian and nearly gotten her throat slashed by a minion in a security guard's uniform.

Son of a bitch.

The Canadian crew had a similar reaction when she explained it to them.

"Well, no wonder they blew up the other Guardian," Fil said. "Can't be resurrecting demons and throwing around black magic with a Guardian looking over your shoulder, can you?"

"It was probably the first thing they did when they took over the place," Ella agreed, her pretty face drawn into a frown. "I wonder why a new Guardian didn't appear right then, though. I thought when one of you guys gets destroyed, another always takes his place."

"We do, but first we must be summoned," Kees reminded her.

"Put another nail into the coffin of the Guild," Fil said.

"Did they screw up there, too? Did they know about the statue being smashed and not bother to summon a replacement?"

"We can't know that," Griffin frowned. Despite the way the Guild had treated him, Wynn's uncle still bristled at the idea of his fellow Wardens being corrupted. "We know the Order has focused on eliminating Wardens and weakening the Guild for a while now. If they killed the Warden before they destroyed the Guardian statue, the Guild might very well never have been made aware of what had happened."

"Either way," Wynn said, hoping to head off an unproductive argument, "Bran seemed certain that that's where they're operating, which means that's probably where they would conduct a ritual to give Uhlthor a big boost of adrenaline."

Ella's voice gentled as she asked, "Do you think they might be holding your brother there?"

Like she hadn't asked herself that question a million times already. Pressing her lips together, she shrugged. "No idea. We still don't know for sure what happened to him. Did they kidnap him and are still holding him hostage? Did they kill him and dump his body where no one has found it? Did he get sucked into some other dimension like Fil's friend Ricky? There's no way to tell."

"Oh, Wynn, I'm so sorry," Ella murmured, and Fil added her own note of sympathy.

"Thanks, but that's not what we need to focus on right now. I'll find my brother eventually, but for now we need to stay on task." She used the side of her palm to brush away a fall of tears, while Knox reached out and squeezed her leg in silent comfort. "We need to come up with a plan that covers as many eventualities as possible. That's why we called you guys, and that's our immediate goal, so let's get to work."

Kees nodded, the gesture sharp even over the Internet video connection. "In that case, let us assess our choices. Have we considered simply retrieving the Eye from this man who holds it, thus averting the entire problem?"

"I don't see how we could manage it," Wynn said, though the idea of avoiding everything did have a certain appeal. "We'd have to break into a very public and from what I could tell well-secured building, then get into Coleman's office, steal the Eye, and get out again without being seen. Or, you know, killed. And that's assuming he hasn't moved the Eye somewhere else. After all, he flaunted it right under my nose. Even though I didn't know what it was, leaving it in the same place after I saw it wouldn't be the wisest strategy."

"Also, to make so obvious a strike against the Order without simultaneously reducing their numbers and crippling their capabilities in this area would only rally them into a counterattack," Knox added. "We have no way of knowing what they are able to do with or without the Eye. I believe the risk is too great."

Spar cut through to the point. "What would you prefer that we do, Knox? You are the one at the center of this, and you know more than we do about what is necessary, as well as what is possible."

Knox grimaced. "Although not much more, unfortunately. I would like to see us wipe out this cell of the Order. If we are correct about a coming war on our doorstep, then we must take every advantage to whittle down the enemy's troops. Also, it is clear that the Eye must be retrieved and destroyed, properly this time. We cannot risk it falling again into *nocturnis* hands."

"Sounds to me like we need to get all those suckers into one room and swat 'em down like flies." Trust Fil to sum the situation up in a few pithy words. "So how do we make that happen?"

Wynn and Knox exchanged a glance, then Wynn turned back toward her laptop and gazed into the camera. "We think they're going to gather soon. We can pin down a date when they're most likely to try to use the Eye. In fact, I think they've been saving it for this special occasion. On Friday night, we're going to have a black moon."

Quickly she outlined the magical significance of the month's second new moon and the fact that a similar event had not occurred in the last three years, not since before the Eye was uncovered during the dig at the foundation of Coleman's tower.

"That means Friday is their big chance," she said. "With the black moon in the sky, they'll have the greatest concentration of dark power they're likely to see in the next two to three years. They have to take advantage of it. If I were trying to accomplish what we think they're trying to accomplish, I would gather every *nocturnis* at my disposal, round up as many sacrifices as I could get my hands on, and throw one hell of a party."

"Sacrifices." Spar spat the word like the foul thing it was. "It seems that some things about the filthy cult never change."

"Blood is magic," Wynn said, shrugging. Not that she didn't care about the idea of lives lost, but the idea made her so incredibly sad and weary that it was the biggest show she could manage. "Specifically, blood is black magic, and that's what the black moon is all about. Blood sacrifice during a black moon will raise an enormous amount of power. Twisted, perverted, evil, and malicious power, but power nonetheless. And with the Eye at their disposal, the Order will be able to concentrate that power and funnel it straight to Uhlthor. Like I said, they *have* to take advantage of this."

Knox picked up the thread. "Which means they will all gather in one place to perform the magical acts. Turning it into a ritual will also lend them more power, so they will need a secure place where they are unlikely to be disturbed. If we follow them there, we will have the best opportunity to both foil their attempt to strengthen the Defiler and dismantle the cell in one blow."

"But how will we find out where they're meeting?" Ella asked, clearly concerned. "Friday is only a few days away. Do we have time to ferret out their secret clubhouse before then?"

Wynn nodded. "Bran gave us that information as well. According to his notes, they've been using an abandoned estate up in Lake Forest, just north of the city. In fact, it's the same place you sent me to look for the Guardian they destroyed, El."

The other woman made a face. "Yeah, I think I could have lived without the irony."

"Good." Kees's deep voice boomed over the Internet

connection, drawing everyone's attention. "If we know when and we know where, then all that is left is for us to plan our attack. Who will be going in?"

Knox bared a fang. He had taken this meeting in his natural form, which seemed to suit the nature of the conference call. "I will."

"We will," Wynn corrected, shooting him a warning glare. They had had this argument several times already. He made it clear he wanted her nowhere near the field of battle, while she dug her heels in and made it equally clear he would not chance facing a demon, Coleman, and an unknown number of cultists all on his own. "Knox, myself, and my uncle Griffin."

"That is all?" Kees scowled fiercely. "You need greater numbers than that to deal with the entire cell."

"The existence of a large cell is merely speculation," Knox growled. "We could just as easily face no more than a weakened Defiler and a single *nocturnis,* the one who holds the Eye."

"So Knox deals with the demon, and Uncle Griff and I have his back," Wynn said, tamping back a stirring of unease.

"Foolishness." Spar glared at them, his gaze cutting even over the Internet. "You have already acknowledged the likelihood that every *nocturnis* in the area will gather for this event. Knox, would you really set your mate against an unknown number of *nocturnis* while you will be fully engaged by one of the Seven itself? I have the greatest respect for Wynn's power, but as a Warden she remains untrained, and her uncle has lost his ability to use magic reliably. The danger to them is much too high. You need greater numbers."

"Ella and I will come," Kees declared, his tone brooking no argument. "Already Ella has used her magic in battle against the *nocturnis,* and I can deal with a number of the scum unaided. With us at your side, the odds shift greatly in our favor."

Spar made a noise of obvious frustration, and they saw Fil squeeze his shoulder with her good hand. Her other arm still rested in a dark-blue sling. "We would be there, too, but I'm just not up for the trip right now, let alone the battle. I'm so sorry."

"And I will not leave my mate unprotected."

"Don't apologize," Wynn hastened to reassure them. "There's no way we want anyone risking their own safety just to help us out. We couldn't impose like that." All eyes turned to Wynn, five gazes expressing a shared incredulity. She shifted uncomfortably. "What did I say?"

"We are all Guardians and Wardens here," Kees said, sounding as if he were explaining something to a toddler. "We work together to defeat the Darkness. Always, in whatever manner is necessary. There is no imposition, only duty and the sincere desire to perform it well." He paused for a moment after that—maybe waiting for it to sink in?—then continued, "Ella and I will make arrangement to arrive in Chicago before Friday. In the meantime, any information on the *nocturnis* meeting place that you can gather could prove useful, especially maps or drawings of the land and the buildings it contains. Once we arrive, we will strategize together our plan of attack."

Ella nodded enthusiastically. "Right. And once we get this sorted out, Wynn is going to take me into the city.

I've always wanted to stroll down the Magnificent Mile. You and I can have a girls' day. It'll be awesome."

Okay, then. Wynn supposed that meant they had a plan.

She just hoped they'd live to enjoy the after-party.

Chapter Eighteen

This whole experience might be a lot more fun if only she were a ninja. That way, Wynn theorized, she would have enough skill at sneaking around in the dark, blending into shadows, and engaging in hand-to-hand combat that she might actually feel prepared for what was about to happen.

Instead, she crouched down in the midst of an all-too-familiar copse of trees along with her mate and her uncle, and waited. Whether for something to happen or her heart to give out, she hadn't quite decided.

They had arrived at the Van Oswalt estate a little less than an hour after nightfall. Wynn had calculated that the best time for the cult's ritual would be during the hour between midnight and one in the morning, when the black moon would reach its highest point in the sky. It was a guess, really, but it made the most sense from a power perspective. She just really hoped she was right, because they had based their entire mission on that schedule.

She, Knox, and Griffin had taken up a position in front of the mansion with a view of the driveway in the hope of spotting some of the cultists arriving for the night's events. Meanwhile, Kees and Ella had flown toward the back of the property to approach the house from the rear. Kees and Knox would keep in touch via a telepathic connection the Guardians shared, which apparently emerged whenever they operated together. Handy, that. Wynn wished she could listen in, just because being out of the loop sucked, but she knew she could trust Knox to let her know what she needed to stay safe.

The first stage of their plan involved surveillance, keeping watch for *nocturnis*. Once cultists had arrived and entered the house, Wynn and Griffin would watch for lights to estimate where in the building they had gathered, and Knox would relay the information to Kees. They would then wait for the hour to approach midnight before they began stage two, which was a much simpler plan—bust in, take the Eye, and kick some evil asses. Oh, Knox and Kees had gussied it up with details, and talk about flanks and pincer maneuvers, and a whole bunch of other words and phrases that Wynn didn't really understand, but it all boiled down to the same thing.

Crouching in the cold damp of the woods turned out to be an experience she could have lived without, and she came to that realization fairly quickly. Not only did she not have thigh muscles like King Kong like some other people she could mention—coughKNOXcough—but the position had started to put strain on her ankle that she really couldn't afford. Of all the nights in her life that she wanted to be able to run if she had to, this was the one. In the interest of preserving her own mobility, she used a hand on the Guardian's broad back to help lever herself to her feet.

The change in position sent blood flowing back through constricted vessels, and she had to strangle the urge to stamp her feet to get the circulation in those appendages going again. To distract herself from the pins-and-needles sensations, she scanned her gaze along the drive one more time, but it was movement in the trees beyond the stretch of gravel that caught her attention. She narrowed her eyes to peer more intently in that direction.

A moment later, she silently poked Knox in the ribs to get his attention. When he threw her an irritated look, she returned it with one of insistence and pointed in the direction of what she had seen. She knew the exact moment when Knox saw it, too. His huge gray body stiffened, and his wings shifted restlessly but soundlessly against his back. In the trees on the other side of the estate's wide drive, shadowed figures in what looked to be long, hooded cloaks moved through the natural cover toward the edge of the bluff.

Wynn and Griffin had managed to dig up a few helpful items during the days leading up to that night. The City of Lake Forest had conveniently possessed copies of the building plans for the Van Oswalt mansion, as well as a plot map of the estate grounds. That, along with photos dug up from the Internet, had confirmed that Wynn's first impression of the property had been right. The Van Oswalt family owned the entire bluff, including the cliff face and the tiny strip of rocky beach that ran along the bottom. In a family filled with generations of avid sailors, it had only made sense for them to install a long, zigzagging stairway along the cliff face down to a floating dock, complete with a boathouse for mooring an appropriate sort of sailing vessel.

From what Wynn had memorized of the maps, the cultists tonight had no intention of entering the deserted and shuttered Van Oswalt mansion. The path they walked on the other side of the woods led them directly toward that stairway along the cliff.

Beside her, Knox glided to his feet and signaled for her and Griffin to wait. Then he eased through the trees to a spot where the night sky glittered through a clearing in the canopy and launched himself into the air.

Watching a Guardian in flight was a sight Wynn knew she would never forget. Looking at one of the gargoyle-like creatures on the ground, it was easy to get distracted by their huge muscled bulk, the threatening, nearly demonic features, the long fangs, and the heavy, razor-sharp talons. A person could look at the gray skin the color and texture of weathered stone and consign the Guardians to the earth, but at its essence, a Guardian was just as much a creature of the air.

In the darkness of the starlit night, Wynn lost sight of him quickly, but she could picture clearly the brutal grace of his body arrowing into the sky, huge wings battering against the pull of gravity. It amazed her that a creature so huge and heavy on the ground could appear so light and fluid in the air, as quick and graceful as an eagle as he cut through the night toward where the edge of the bluff dropped off into the shore of Lake Michigan.

She waited, practically holding her breath for what

felt like hours but in reality was only a little more than five minutes, for his return. As he dropped lightly to the ground in the same place where he had taken off, Wynn found herself unable to keep from rushing to him, and Griffin followed closely behind her.

"We were right about the estate, but wrong about the house," he confirmed, leaning down toward the humans and speaking in a toneless whisper that didn't carry far through the dark stillness. "The *nocturnis* do not gather in the building. I saw others already on the stairway leading down the cliff face."

"They're going to do this ritual in a boathouse?" Griffin sounded skeptical. "It doesn't seem practical. Even if there were room, the power of water might reflect and amplify magic, but a natural body of water as large as Lake Michigan has elemental powers of its own, and I doubt it would welcome or cooperate with magic as dark as what the Order has planned."

"I saw them on the stairway, but they do not reach the dock at the bottom. There appears to be an entrance into the cliff face about halfway down. It angles just after the entrance, so while I could see torchlight, I could not see into the cavern itself."

Wynn bit back a groan, not because she didn't feel like whining, but because she feared the sound might carry and alert the *nocturnis* to their presence. "Great. So not only do we have to go into a cave, which, just gross, but we have no prior knowledge of what it might look like on the inside or if there might be more than one entrance and therefore more than one exit."

Knox nodded grimly, and Griffin sighed. "I suppose that brings an end to the plan where Kees and Ella enter from a point at the rear so we can catch them in a scissor move."

"It does. I have already alerted my brother to what I saw. He and his mate have altered their course to bring them out along the cliff face a bit north from the top of the stairway."

Wynn clamped her lips together while she struggled for calm. When she found it, she managed to ask a simple question. "Okay, so what do we do now?"

"Materially, the plan has changed little. The location of the ritual means that we will not be able to flank the enemy, but our basic strategy remains in place. We enter the cave together. Kees and I will take the lead. If we lose the element of surprise for any reason, he and I are the most impervious to damage. The *nocturnis* spells have little effect on us, and our hides are tough enough to weather physical attacks. You two and Ella will stay behind us."

Wynn had no problem with that plan. She liked not being shot at or having offensive dark magic hurled at her head.

"Once the confrontation begins, I will handle the demon. It is what I exist to do. Kess will need to make a judgment call. I suspect that Coleman is the cell's most powerful priest, and if that is true, Kees will deal with him. If another emerges as a greater threat, my brother will shift his focus to the newcomer. You three Wardens will be responsible for any remaining cultists."

He turned to focus solely on Wynn. "I want you to allow Kees's mate to take the lead. He is correct that his mate has already done battle with the Order and has spent as much time as she is able in studying the spells useful in combat. I respect your power, little witch, but you have had only a few days of instruction at your uncle's hands. Do what you are able, but above all, keep yourself safe. Do you understand?"

She understood perfectly. Her competitive spirit might not like to acknowledge someone else as the more skilled magic user, but she wasn't stupid, and she had no intention of dying in that cave. She would take no unnecessary risks. She nodded emphatically, and Knox looked to Griffin.

"You are to stay at Wynn's side and assist her," the Guardian instructed. "Coach her so that she can use the spells you have been teaching her as effectively as possible. Also, Kees will be working to seize the Eye from Coleman or whoever else might wield it. Once he does, he will find a way to get it to you. You will keep it secure. Allow no *nocturnis* to lay hands on it. Once we have defeated the enemy, we will see to its proper destruction." He drew a breath and surveyed both of their reactions. "Are we all agreed?"

"Yes," Griffin replied, his voice trembling slightly, even as Wynn spoke simultaneously. "Agreed."

"Good. We wait for the half hour before midnight, then we move. Go as quietly as you can and do not speak except in the most dire of circumstances. Above all, stay close."

And then they hunkered down to wait some more. Shortly after eleven, Wynn noticed that no more stragglers appeared in the woods moving toward the cliff. Within a few minutes of her realization, Knox gestured to them to wait while he flew across the drive once more.

He reappeared after a quick survey of the area to wave them across behind him.

For the first time, Wynn actually felt a touch of gratitude for the darkness. Dressed, as they all were, in black clothing, the utter lack of moonlight made her feel much less exposed as she and Griffin made the mad dash from concealing tree to concealing tree. After a brief gesture reminding them to remain silent, the Guardian led the way stealthily through the trees toward the cliff stairs.

A landing enclosed by a wooden railing and flanked by an unlit lamppost marked the top of the long staircase. Knox stopped them just as the landmark came into view through the trees and once again signaled them to wait. Wynn gritted her teeth and wished she could pull out her smartphone to check the time. She wasn't nearly stupid enough to do so, because she knew the illuminated face would immediately give away their position to any enemies left behind on sentry duty, if the cult's paranoia ran that way, but the urge niggled at her like an itch she couldn't scratch. Knox had said he would track the time during their operation, but since there wasn't a watchband in the world big enough to circle the monstrous wrist of his Guardian form, she had no idea how he was doing it. It was the uncertainty that drove her crazy.

The wait dragged on interminably, but eventually the time must have crawled by to eleven thirty. Just before Wynn forced herself to shift again to stave off her right foot falling asleep, Knox rose and waved them forward. He led the way toward the stairs, moving slowly and cautiously, scanning the area around them for possible *noc-*

turnis guards. Wynn, of course, saw no one, but she knew a Guardian saw more keenly in the dark than a cat, so if they were out there, he would spot them. Unimpeded, they reached the lamppost in minutes.

The night was so dark that it wasn't until the couple were nearly upon them that Wynn saw Kees and Ella approach from the opposite direction. The Guardians nodded briskly to each other, but Wynn didn't dare speak, not now that everything suddenly became very real and her body began to tremble with the mixture of cold and adrenaline. She felt a rush of gratitude, though, when Ella stepped up beside her and squeezed her hand. Instinctively, Wynn returned the gesture and reached out her other hand to repeat it with her uncle. Griffin's smile flashed briefly in the darkness, a little weak and unsteady, but game nonetheless.

With another simple hand gesture reminding the Wardens to stay close, the party began to descend the long, winding staircase along the cliff's face. The Guardians walked in front, Knox leading with Kees following close behind. Griffin went next, because he had the most Warden experience and therefore the best chance of detecting any magical traps or wards they might encounter on the way to the cave. Wynn followed behind with Ella in the rear, her magical experience affording her the privilege of guarding their backs.

Wynn stepped as lightly as possible, but her footsteps still sounded like drumbeats in her own ears. She could hear the soft falls of Griffin's and Ella's as well, but she marveled at the absolute silence with which the Guardians glided forward. They were both so huge, they should have made the staircase shake like a pair of elephants, but they passed across the surface like shadows, insubstantial and undetectable.

It didn't take long for Wynn to realize that the key to making it down to the cave was *not* to look over the railing. In the moonless night, the starlight that reflected off the surface of the lake looked to be a long, long way down. A bout of vertigo appeared nowhere on her to-do list for the night, so she kept her eyes on her feet and took one step at a time.

The stairs turned twice before Knox reached a third landing and drew the party to a halt. Somehow, Wynn had expected that the landing would simply widen at the mouth of the cave, allowing them to step from the wooden platform directly onto the floor of the cavern. Oh, if only. She nearly lost her mind when she saw what really awaited her.

Wynn didn't consider herself to have a particular fear of heights. She could look out windows in tall buildings without a problem, ladders bothered her not at all, and she'd spent a good portion of her childhood climbing the tallest trees she could find, even falling out of a few. Still, when she saw the narrow ledge carved into the face of the cliff and winding at least twenty-five feet from the stairway landing to the cave entrance she nearly turned around, tucked her ball under her arm, and went home to play by herself.

Dear, sweet Lord of the Wild Hunt, were they supposed to sidle along that trail like mountain goats to get into the cavern? Sure, that might be all well and good to the members of their merry band who had *wings* and wouldn't *die* if they *plummeted* off the edge, but Wynn felt distinctly human, especially human, in that moment, and she did not want to take that stroll. Nuh-uh. No way. No how.

In the darkness, Knox's eyes blazed at her as if he could read her thoughts. Beckoning her toward him, he bent his head until his lips brushed her ear before he whispered, "Do not be afraid, little witch. When you cross I will be right behind you. I will catch you if you fall. I would never let you touch the water, let alone the rocks below. Do you trust me?"

Wynn swallowed a shuddering laugh and tilted back her head. She was crazy, felt thoroughly, certifiably insane, even as she looked into his flaming gaze and gave him the only answer she could. "With my life." Then she shook her head and added, "Apparently," mostly under her breath.

Knox nodded and motioned for the others to move into formation. As planned, a Guardian went first, which meant Kees got the privilege of being the first to step out onto the dark, narrow ledge. He did so without hesitation, crossing the distance in long strides. When he reached the entrance to the cave, he stepped just inside and leaned against the stony surface of the rough walls, his gray skin blending almost perfectly into the background. Talk about natural camouflage. He nearly disappeared from sight, like a chameleon.

After seeing someone of Kees's size clear the path in minutes, Wynn told herself she had nothing to worry about. After all, the Guardian was easily twice her size and took up proportionally more room on the path, so if it was wide enough for him, it was probably wide enough for her. But she still held her breath the entire way across.

True to his word, Knox walked close behind her, and somewhere in the back of her mind she was vaguely aware of Griffin and Ella following along. Still, her mind raced with dire possibilities until she reached the wide opening of the cavern and could slump against the wall beside Kees. He gave her a nod of approval while Knox and Griffin also stepped off the path, and Knox reached out to pull his mate close beside him.

Once they were all assembled at the mouth of the cave, the Guardians looked to Griffin with expectant expressions. Her uncle frowned in concentration as he moved slowly around the small area, scanning walls, floor, and ceiling for signs of magical defenses. Finally, he finished and faced the others. Shaking his head, he turned his hands palms-up and gave an exaggerated shrug. They all caught his meaning. He had found nothing here at the cave's entrance, but he could make no guarantees about the tunnel that led deeper into the cliff face. They would simply have to take their chances.

Their small group reordered itself in their agreed-upon formation and followed the faint glow of firelight shining around the curve of the tunnel. Wynn's heartbeat finally managed to drown out the sound of her own footsteps, but she didn't count that as much of an improvement. The solidity of the tunnel's stone floor felt more secure than the wooden steps that had vibrated with every step downward, but something else seemed to vibrate in the air around them. It felt like power and it tasted like magic and it stank of the Darkness.

Ella was following closely behind, so Wynn noticed when the other woman's shoulders stiffened and looked around to see what had caught her attention. Then she heard it, the distant hum of chanting voices.

Sure, chanting cultists might sound like something out of a cheesy horror movie, but only because the general public had no concept of how to raise and concentrate power. The image that made it into B-movies actually contained a kernel of truth. Magical energy operated on similar principles to light energy or sound energy. It traveled on waves and was composed of molecules all vibrating at a tuned frequency. Therefore, tuned sounds like rhythmic chanting could help to align the particles or even influence the particles to vibrate at a slower or faster frequency, thus lowering or raising the levels of power. This chant raised not just the levels of energy, but all the hairs on the back of Wynn's neck.

She stilled, just a split second before Knox's fist shot up, signaling them all to freeze. She watched him inch forward along a curve in the tunnel and knew he must have spotted the end of it somewhere up ahead of them. He would try to get a look into the area up ahead without being seen, and then it would be showtime.

A minute to center herself might not be a bad idea at that moment, Wynn decided, and she drew a deep breath in preparation for a moment of down-and-dirty meditation. A quick few seconds spent focusing inward to be sure her energy lay ready and aligned for the confrontation to come might make the difference in a sticky situation, so she needed to work fast. Now or never, right?

Apparently, the universe voted never, because within a hairbreadth of time chaos erupted, flowing over her like lava from a volcano. One minute she stood frozen in the dim cavern tunnel waiting for Knox to scout ahead and the next she heard the faint chanting shatter into many discordant voices while the battle cry of an enraged Guardian shook the very earth and stone around them.

Kees launched himself forward before Knox's roar even passed the first note. He was weaponless, but his talons flashed sharper than ten honed stilettos as he flew the length of the tunnel and into the mysterious space beyond. Ella didn't even spare Wynn and Griffin a glance. She merely shouted, "Go! Go! Go!" as she took off after her mate.

Heart in her throat, Wynn followed with her uncle close at her heels.

So much for the element of surprise.

The thought skittered through her brain as she took the curve of the tunnel at a dead run and found herself disgorged into a large, open cavern nearly eighty feet long and more than a hundred feet wide. Roughly oval in shape, the space appeared to be a natural formation, with rough walls and ceiling carved by time. The floor felt like packed sand over dirt, likely the result of the nearby lake flooding and receding through the centuries. Torches in metal sconces dotted the walls near the center of the open space, lighting what had just become a field of battle.

Ahead of her, she could see Kees closing in on Ronald Coleman while the man cast ball after ball of rusty-red magic at the Guardian's impervious hide. He clutched the Eye firmly in his off hand, attempting to protect it from the monster that stalked him. Created from magic, Guardians could neither wield the energy nor generally be harmed by it. Coleman was wasting his time and his power, but Wynn had no intention of telling him so. In fact, she hoped Kees made him eat one of his own dark fireballs.

At least six other figures in dark, hooded robes occupied the large chamber, and Ella had already engaged with them. Wynn could see a giant shimmering ball of energy surrounding one, clearly trapping him in place. Another time she might have laughed at the sight, because he looked like a little medieval monk in a plastic hamster ball. Now, though, amusement had been trumped by fear.

Her gaze scanned the room for a glimpse of Knox. At first, she couldn't see him because of the shadows that pooled wherever the torchlight didn't reach, and she felt a wave of panic. Then a movement at the corner of her eye caught her attention and she turned toward an area of the cavern where the floor sloped upward, forming a sort of natural platform, like a dais against the far wall. On the dais sat a stone table, and the eerie similarities to another stone table on an island in the St. Lawrence River made her shudder. Then Wynn blinked and shuddered again as her brain finally made sense of what her eyes were seeing.

In front of the table, a little off to the side, Knox loomed, his huge hands clenched into fists, his wings rustling in impotent rage behind him. He faced the table, so Wynn couldn't see his expression, but she could see exactly what he was looking at.

Sitting on top of the table, lower legs kicking like a child's, a lone figure perched. Dressed in dark clothing but unencumbered by a bulky robe, her brother Bran looked over at Wynn and smiled.

Chapter Nineteen

Wynn felt like the bullets that had missed her the week before, deflected by Knox's thick hide, had suddenly struck their mark. She staggered backward, one hand flying up to cover her mouth as reality cracked and splintered around her. Her brother. Here. In the den of the Order. Free and unfettered and looking completely healthy, as well as unfazed by the battle raging around him.

What in the name of the Goddess was going on?

As she stared, unable to move, she saw the smile on her brother's face widen, and when his lips moved, she heard his voice as if he stood right beside her. "I know you," he said. "Sister. Wynn. Witch. Sister-witch. How very, very interesting. Come here, sister, and greet a brother properly."

And then her heart shattered, because whatever wore her brother's face was not her brother, merely an occupant in Bran Powe's body. She could feel it in the way her soul recoiled even while her brain shouted in relief and joy and urged her to *run to him, embrace your brother! He is alive and well!* But inside she recognized the black taint of evil, the writhing mass of powerful dark magic, and her soul sobbed, telling her, *Yes, run! Run away! Flee from the demon before he devours you!*

Broken and helpless, Wynn fell to her knees and nearly choked on her own sob.

It all happened in an instant, the sight, the recognition, the repulsion, but beside her, she became aware of her uncle crying out, his voice hoarse and thick with joy and relief.

"Bran!" Griffin shouted. "Wynnie, it's Bran! Here's here and he's alive. Come on!"

He grabbed her arm and tried to lift her, tried to drag her forward, but Wynn fought him and sobbed harder. "Uncle Griff, no! No, it's not Bran. That's not Bran. That's Uhlthor. Griff, I know it looks like him, but it's not. That's the demon."

Griffin jerked in surprise. His gaze flew to his nephew's familiar shape, then back to Wynn. He frowned. "Don't be ridiculous, Wynn. That's your brother. Look, I'll show you."

She grabbed at him, tried to stop him, but her uncle shrugged her off and began to walk toward the stone table. "Bran," he called out. "By the Light, boy, we've missed you. Where have you been all these months?"

Wynn watched while her uncle strode forward, and she saw the moment when the thing in Bran's body first noticed the old Warden. It turned its head and tilted it slightly, gazing at the approaching human with an unblinking, reptilian stare.

"You are familiar," the demon mused, "but you do

not interest me. Your power is useless. Go away." It flicked Bran's fingers, and their uncle went flying backward through the air, slamming against the cavern wall to crumple in a heap on the ground.

Wynn screamed. She couldn't stop herself. The sound welled up from somewhere deep inside her and clawed its way from her throat to spill out into the night. She stared at Griffin's unmoving form trying to detect if he still breathed. Then another cry echoed around her, but this one came from Ella.

"Wynn, behind you!"

Her movement restricted by her kneeling position, all Wynn could do was twist to the side and throw her weight backward, hopefully out of the path of whatever danger her friend tried to warn her about. She mostly made it. Whatever spell the *nocturnis* had tried to cast on her hit the sand beside her instead. Another bolt of energy, this one a pale, crystalline blue, flew overhead, and the *nocturnis* who had attacked Wynn fell to the ground.

Ella raced up beside her and tried to haul Wynn to her feet. "What is wrong with you?" the other woman shouted at her, grabbing her by the shoulders and shaking her hard. "What the hell, Wynn? Snap out of it. We need your help."

"My brother," she managed to choke out. "It's got Bran, El. It's got him."

The Warden cursed and let go, one hand darting right back to steady Wynn when the witch swayed on her feet. "Okay, that sucks, but if you have even the slightest hope that we can save him, you need to pull yourself together and fight! Come on!"

Wynn stumbled, then caught herself as her friend dragged her away from the bodies of her uncle and the fallen *nocturnis* and back into the fray. She looked around for the first time since setting eyes on her brother and tried to make sense of what was going on.

Two more *nocturnis* lay unmoving on the sandy cavern floor, while the hamster ball cultist remained imprisoned with a companion now floating in a second energy ball beside him. The final robed member of the cell had joined Coleman in his battle against Kees, fighting back-to-back with the businessman to prevent Kees from getting a clear opening of attack.

On the other side of the chamber, not-Bran continued to watch the action with an expression of polite interest and cold snake's eyes. Knox had not moved, standing like a statue before the demonic creature.

"Why isn't Knox moving?" Ella demanded as soon as she sent a spell winging toward the two remaining cultists. "He's supposed to take care of the demon."

"I don't know," Wynn answered, distracted by the sight of the item in Coleman's left hand. The Eye of Uhlthor, which had appeared cold and black when they had entered the cavern, now appeared equally black, but it had begun to radiate a noxious glow. Or what would have been a glow had it not consisted entirely of dark energy. "But I think we need to focus on that."

Coleman appeared to have stopped throwing useless spells at Kees and now concentrated on maintaining an energy shield around himself. He and his partner began to back toward the table where their demonic master waited, looking handsome and harmless in Bran's familiar skin.

"Shit, what is that?" Ella demanded, trailing Kees as he stalked the cultists' every movement. "Did they manage to charge that thing before we got here?"

"Maybe. Some. I doubt it's anything like what they had hoped for, but there's definitely energy there. We can't let them feed it to Uhlthor."

"But I'm so hungry," the demon whined, in the same tone Bran always used to convince their mother to make his favorite treats. "And it looks so very satisfying."

The remaining anonymous cultist reached the edge of the natural dais and stumbled. Before anyone else could react, Coleman shoved the man until he crashed against the table, then used a small dagger to slit his exposed throat. Blood splashed against the stone just inches from where not-Bran sat, and the demon threw back his head and sucked a breath in through his teeth.

"Yesssssss," the thing inside Bran hissed, ending on an almost sexual groan. "Oh, so tasty." Its eyes glinted nastily as it reached out toward its priest with imperious fingers. "Now give us our Eye, servant, and let us behold the beginning of the end."

As the demon spoke, Knox's head whipped around, his gaze locking on Wynn. "I'm sorry," he growled, just before be beat his wings and descended on not-Bran with the fury of an avenging angel.

And she knew. With those two words, Wynn had the answer to Ella's question and all the proof she needed that Knox loved her not because she could keep him awake for the rest of his life, but because he did. Period. End of sentence. He loved her. His love was what had stopped him from attacking the demon. Once he had seen Uhlthor wearing her brother's skin, his love for her had rendered him unable to kill the body that looked like Bran. It made him loving and noble and the biggest idiot she had ever met. Wynn loved her brother, but the thing in this cave was not her brother. It held her brother hostage.

Bran's voice screamed as Knox landed the first blow, and Wynn had to fight back an echoing cry at the sound. *Not Bran. Not Bran,* she chanted in her head over and over. *Not my brother.*

But oh, the familiar sight and sound of him felt like daggers in her heart.

She forced her eyes open as soon as she realized she had unknowingly squeezed them shut. Calling herself ten kinds of idiot, she forced herself to take stock of the situation as dispassionately as possible. She would not be the crying, fainting, useless idiot who cowered in a corner when the bad guy threatened. Already, her friends had risked their lives for her. She could do no less.

Everything in the universe at that moment seemed to be happening on and around that huge, stone table. The body of the last cultist hung bonelessly from one end, torso sprawled out and legs dangling while blood continued to flow out onto the stone. Some even ran off the side and dripped onto the sandy ground. He, obviously, posed no further threat.

Meanwhile, Kees and Coleman struggled nearby. Or rather, Kees repeatedly threw his entire body weight against the dark energy shield the *nocturnis* priest had erected around himself. The cultist himself seemed preoccupied with finding a way to pass the Eye to Uhlthor without compromising his own safety.

Ella muttered to herself as she held her hands stiffly

at her sides and began to speak a spell, no doubt one to attempt to penetrate Coleman's defenses.

At the other end of the dais, Knox held not-Bran over his head, claws piercing the thing's sides as it howled and writhed in its attempts to get free.

Wynn took one look at what had been her brother's face, saw it twisted and perverted by the evil behind it, and she did the one thing she had always known how to do. No Warden spells, no special training, nothing but the power of her own magical soul. She threw a banishment.

All her drive away salt and goofer dust, all her bits and baubles, all of the talents she had always felt flowing beneath her skin: They all came back to this. The pure, new green of her energy reflected her connection to the earth and the power of new buds to spring forth and prosper. Because nothing could prosper in despoiled ground, Wynn's energy was the cleanser, the thing that swept aside the Darkness and let Light shine down.

She didn't plan to do it, didn't think about it, didn't strategize, and didn't hesitate. She simply drew back her arm like in her old days on the softball team and let the magic fly at her brother's much-loved face.

It split open and peeled back, and if she hadn't already felt numbed and blank from grief and trauma, she might have vomited at the sight. Her brother's head split down the middle, as if an invisible zipper had suddenly opened, and the thing inside shed his body like an ill-fitting costume, leaving it to fall broken and bloody to the chamber floor.

The demon rose into the air, a form without form. Without the structure of Bran's body to hold it, it expanded and drifted, unable to make itself solid, but taking shape like clouds against a summer sky. Wynn got the impression of huge, thick horns, curving back from the base like a ram's. She saw a face like a goat, long and triangular, and eyes like a snake, the same eyes she had seen look at her from behind her brother's face. Broad shoulders and heavy muscles tapered to arms of unnatural length, arms that ended in four clawed fingers, positioned like the talons of a raptor and equally sharp. Below the chest, though, even the insubstantial form evaporated, swirling into mist like a cartoon djinni.

As if from a distance, she heard an excited cry, and she turned just in time to see Coleman raise the Eye above his head to direct the sinister black glow toward his master. She gathered herself to throw her body at the priest, anything to stop him from fulfilling his intention, but Ella beat her to it. Or rather, her shout halted Wynn in her track.

"Oh, fuck no!" the sweet, innocent-looking Warden screamed as she circled her arms once above her head and shot a bolt of magic at Coleman so strong, Wynn felt the heat of it against her skin nearly ten feet away. It hit the *nocturnis*'s shield like a lightning bolt, slicing through the energy so that the protection shattered into a billion tiny particles of energy that dissipated immediately into the air. Before their lights had even winked out, Kees was on the cultist, claws slashing through skin and severing the arteries in the man's neck just as he had done to his fellow servant of the Darkness.

An inhuman bellow of rage made the ground shake as if an earthquake had struck the Chicagoland area. Taken off guard, Wynn rocked to one side, then fell to the ground, once again making the kind of hard contact with the earth that she really could have lived without. Dazed, she rolled to her side and pushed herself up enough to see the swirl of Darkness that was Uhlthor the Defiler contract into a sphere the size of a bowling ball, then explode outward like an atomic bomb.

Blinking, Wynn looked up to search for the mushroom cloud, but all she saw was the rough-hewn ceiling of the cavern and the reflected light of the flickering torches. And all she heard was her own heartbeat, pounding hard and fast in her own ears.

"What was that?" Ella demanded, also pushing up from the ground. Apparently the quake had knocked her down as well. "What just happened? Was that Uhlthor? Where did he go? Did you send him back to prison?"

"No," Knox snarled, rising up from his crouch. Being stronger than a frickin' mountain apparently gave one the ability to keep one's feet when the entire world shook like a wet dog. "He escaped."

"But we have the Eye," Kees said, also standing, one clawed hand clenched around a small circle of rusty, pitted metal. "We won that, at least. And the Defiler remains in its incorporeal state."

Ella grunted and let her mate pull her to her feet. "So there is a bright side after all."

Wynn ignored them. She ignored everything, even the man she loved. She had only one thought, only one goal. Shaking too hard to walk, she half crawled, half dragged herself across the floor of the cavern to the place where her brother's body had fallen, and curled up next to the mangled remains. A small detached voice in her head recoiled at the grisly scene, but she ignored it. This was her baby brother, her Bran-flake, and she had killed him.

Pressing her cheek to the cool sand, she reached out to touch his silky dark hair and wept.

"No, little witch, you did not kill him."

The voice spoke in her ear, but she didn't hear it right away. It had to repeat itself over and over in the same deep, tender, gravel-coated whisper before it penetrated her cocoon of grief.

Gradually she became aware that the voice sounded so close because it was. Her Guardian had joined her on the floor next to her brother's body, lying down in the rough sand so he could curl protectively around her body. He had wrapped his arms around her and rocked her slowly while she poured out the pieces of her broken heart.

"I did," she sobbed, choking on her own guilt and sorrow. "I killed him."

"No," Knox insisted, his voice deep and strong and very, very certain. "The Defiler killed Bran, the moment it consumed his soul. You did not harm your brother, sweet witch. You freed him."

And then Wynn wept harder.

She snatched her hand away from her brother's cold remains and grabbed frantically at her mate's arms, clutching him to her as she fell to pieces, knowing he would gather them all up. Then, someday, he would help her put them back together again.

She didn't know how long she cried, but it felt like lifetimes. The tears poured out of her soul, from a bottomless well that bore Bran's name.

At one point she heard Knox's name and vaguely recognized the voice as belonging to Kees.

"The old Warden still lives," the Guardian murmured to his brother warrior, "but he is badly injured. He needs medical attention. My mate and I will fly him out and get him to the nearest hospital. You remain and care for your female."

She didn't hear Knox's reply, and she didn't care. Oh, she cared about her uncle, and she wanted Griffin to make a swift and full recovery, but she didn't care who helped him to the hospital or what happened to her. She didn't care if she ever left that cave.

Her mate let her wallow in her misery for a few more minutes. She heard the distant sounds of Kees and Ella collecting the Eye and scooping Griffin up for the trip out of the cave. Eventually, her sobs subsided into ragged breathing, and her tears dried up, leaving sticky trails of salt across her skin. Knox held her awhile longer in silence, then he eased her around until she faced him and frowned at her.

"I will not tolerate you shouldering the blame for your brother's death, my Wynn. His end was not your doing, and I do not believe the man you described to me, the man who left you the clues to stop the demon, would have wanted you to think that, either."

"He wouldn't." Her answer came on a hoarse, nearly unrecognizable noise, half whisper, half croak. Her throat still felt swollen and achy, and her body and soul felt waterlogged and wrung out. "He wouldn't have wanted his body to keep functioning like that, with something so evil inside of it. If he could have, he would have asked me to set him free." Fresh tears welled, even though she didn't think she had any more in her. "And he would have done the same for me."

"Then we must do all we can to honor his memory," Knox said gently, his huge hand coming up, one clawed finger brushing a strand of hair back with exquisite gentleness. "What would he wish us to do?"

Wynn released a shuddering breath. "He'd want us to get him out of here first. This place has got to be contaminated if the Order has been using it. Then he'd want us to take him home. To my mom. He would know how important that will be for her. He'd want her to have that."

Goddess, she would have to tell her mother what had happened. For a crazy, reckless moment, Wynn considered taking it all back, letting her brother's remains stay here so that her mother could continue to hope that her boy would come home eventually. The idea of being the one to kill that hope made Wynn feel physically ill.

But the thought faded almost as soon as it appeared. She couldn't do that to either of them. Bran deserved better than to rot alone in some gods-forsaken cave above the lake, and Mona deserved better than a lie. She would grieve for what had happened to her son, but she would go on. They had all known what was possible when he had gone missing, especially as the weeks and months dragged on.

While her mind raced, Knox drew her to her feet. She swayed there for a moment, searching for balance. Then his hands settled around her hips and she found it. Knox was her balance, the thing that kept her steady on her feet, and he would continue to be for the rest of their lives.

Leaning into his warm, hard strength, Wynn let

herself bask, just for a moment, in his presence. Then she pulled back and tilted her head to meet his tender gaze.

"Let's take my brother home," she said softly. "We both know the war's not over, but this battle is. It's time to pick up the pieces and move forward."

He hummed in agreement. "It is time to bury our fallen, and mourn for their loss. And then we will give thanks for what we still have."

"Like each other," she whispered.

"Always."